ABOUT THE AUTHOR

Jack Daniel lives in Bath, England with his wife, Elizabeth and two small longhaired dachshunds. He has two sons.

He is a naval constructor, now retired.

He saw sea service with the British Navy in World War 11 and was assigned to the US Manhattan Project for the Bikini atomic tests.

He subsequently designed several classes of warships for the Royal Navy, notably frigates and nuclear attack and ballistic missile submarines, reflecting his lifetime association with submarines that began in the war.

He was Head of the Royal Corps of Naval Constructors when he resigned and joined the Board of British Shipbuilders.

His memoirs, the End of an Era, were published in 2003.

Nemesis is the nineteenth of twenty books featuring the Hawkridge family and their friends in pursuit of the ungodly.

For Liz and the two boys

Who make everything enjoyable.

Chapter One

SAM HAWKINS put down his breakfast coffee cup and gazed at the letter that he'd taken from the envelope that he had just slit open. He'd had abusive and plain stupid letters before and one or two threatening ones during his playing career but this one was different, to start with it had been sent to his home; usually they went to the club. Sometimes they were laboriously put together from letters cut from a newspaper or magazine or sometimes printed in block capitals, presumably in the belief that block capitals don't have characteristics that might identify the writer, but this one was typed, the same as the address on the envelope. It looked like the letters that came out of his wife, Stella's, printer. He read the letter again, there were no preliminaries,

Most of your players are rubbish. Your chance of getting back into the big money of the Premiership depends on young Bruce Somers. It would be worth a lot to you to make sure that he doesn't have an unfortunate accident, wouldn't it? I'll let you know how much in my next letter.

"What's up Sam?" asked his wife from across the table, "you've been sitting looking at that letter for nearly five minutes."

He handed it across the table. She read it and passed it back, remarking,

"Some crank, I expect. I wouldn't give it another thought."

"But whoever he is, he's right pet, I'm building the side around young Bruce."

"Where did it come from, I mean, what's the postmark?"

He looked again at the envelope. The post-mark was smudged but he thought that he discerned London and what might have been NW something.

"It looks local but it's difficult to tell. The Post Office seem determined not to tell you where and when letters are posted these days."

Stella took the envelope and manoeuvred it in the light to see if she could make more of it than her husband had. He found himself reflecting on the changes that the Post Office had introduced since he was a boy in County Durham. In those days the stamps were small and unchanging and featured only the profile of the monarch and the price. From his stamp collection he had come to realise that the smaller and less prosperous a nation was, the more often it brought out new issues, usually colourful new issues. Now it was the UK who's new issues were so frequent that no two letters that popped through the letterbox seemed to bear the same stamp. And the stamps were more colourful, too.

Then there was the matter of showing the time of posting, it doesn't appear these days. He reckoned that the people who ran the Post Office thought that might show too much. He reminded himself that it was some time since he checked up on whether Sam junior was adding to her collection the stamps that he brought home from the office. Now that she was an undergraduate she seemed to have so many other things that took up her time. Most girls didn't collect stamps (he wondered why not?) but his Samantha had taken to it when quite small and now had a collection that incorporated his and must be quite valuable. He hoped that she was keeping it up.

His wife's voice brought him back to the present.

"I think that you're right, it looks like London to me. What do you intend to do about it?"

Sam was surprised that she should ask what seemed to him to be a silly question

"Why, nothing of course."

"You won't tell Bruce?"

"Good Lord no. One, I don't want to worry him and two, I don't want him getting a swollen head."

"He's a nice sensible boy, a cut above the other players. Will you tell the police?"

"There's not much point, is there? They can't do anything and there would be the risk that the press would get to hear of it."

"Surely not," said Stella, "how would the press get to hear of it?"

"The Chief Inspector who was in charge of the police at one Saturday match was chatting to me and remarked that there is always someone in the nick who passes-on juicy tit-bits to the local press."

"I thought that they signed some sort of Official Secrets Act?"

"Yes, I suppose that they do," said Sam, "but they probably think that leaking things like the news that some solicitor's been bashed by his wife when she caught him in bed with his secretary is hardly likely to threaten national security."

"Away with you, solicitors don't do that sort of thing," said Stella.

"What about the one in yesterday's paper, caught red-handed," said Sam.

Stella giggled and said,

"More like caught with his trousers down. In Bath, wasn't it? I didn't know that they did that sort of thing in Bath."

"It happens everywhere. The thing that stuck in my mind was that his office is in Gay Street."

"That's enough of that," said Stella, grinning, "so you intend to keep it to yourself?"

"I don't think that we've any alternative, pet. Gosh, look at the time, I must be on my way."

Stella watched him drive away. After twenty-three years of marriage she knew her Sam better than he knew himself and she knew that he was more worried by that anonymous letter than he had admitted. She turned back into the house just as their daughter came down the stairs.

"Morning Mummy, sorry that I'm a bit late, I saw Daddy driving off. Now I'll have to go by bus."

"You shouldn't get in so late at night," smiled her mother. "I'll drive you down to the bus stop. Have you got an early lecture?"

"No, not 'till after lunch."

"At the Waterfront Campus?"

"No, Mummy, at Highfield."

"I meant, you're not going off in a boat or something?"

"No," said Samantha, coping with the young person's problem of welcoming her mother's interest in her university studies yet wanting to be left alone, "as I told you the other day, I'm reading Economics and Management Systems and the fact that we may make the occasional visit to the Waterfront Campus where the National Oceanography Centre is, doesn't mean that I have to spend a lot of time in boats."

"I thought that was why you picked that course, all those pictures in the prospectus of handsome bronzed young men and bikini clad girls messing about in boats and on coral reefs," said her mother.

"Well, that's different but there aren't any of those sort of coral reefs in Southampton Water and I don't exactly enjoy being in a boat in England, even in the summer.. Anyway, when I graduate, if I graduate, I intend to specialise on the business side."

"You've got it all worked out, haven't you?" said her mother, smiling, "say that your future husband doesn't approve?"

"Look Mummy, I don't intend to get married until I've established myself and that means that I'll be at least thirty and at that time my future husband will have to lump it, won't he? I'm not going to move from one dismal football-town to the next one like you did."

"Football was Daddy's job, I knew it when I married him and we've never gone short, have we?"

Samantha moved across the kitchen and put her arms round her mother.

"No, Mummy, you're the best parents a girl could ever have."

Stella said, "Come on love, sit down and have your breakfast."

While she was making the toast and some fresh coffee, she made conversation,

"Where did you go last night?"

Here we go again, thought Samantha, "Out."

"With the people in your class?"

"No Mummy, if you must know, I was with Bruce."

Coming so soon after the breakfast conversation with her husband, Stella said,

"Not Daddy's footballer?"

"Yes, I've seen him once or twice lately and I'm seeing him next Sunday. He's nice."

"I agree that he seems to be a nice boy," said her mother, "but you mustn't let it interfere with your studies."

"Don't be such a fuss pot, Mummy, I know what I'm doing and anyway, he isn't a boy. He got a degree in Economics and Sports Management from Bath University and played in the Team Bath that did so well in the FA Cup. He's a man."

"Your father would say that's even worse."

"Daddy's got to realise that I'm grown up now."

Stella looked at her, she really was attractive, enough to turn any man's head. Who would have thought that she and Sam would have such a girl?

Samantha took up her toast and indicated that, as far as she was concerned, that was the end of the discussion, on that subject at least.

Stella was in a dilemma. If there was any substance in the threats in the letter, there could be an attempt to injure or abduct Bruce Somers and if Samantha was with him, she, too, might be hurt. Her instinct was to tell her daughter that he had been named in a threatening letter but Sam had warned her not to tell anyone. She said,

"You will be careful darling, won't you."

Samantha looked up, surprised and said, "I told you Mummy, he's a nice person."

"No, dear, I didn't mean *that*, I meant that the world seems to be such a dangerous place these days, you hear of people attacking total strangers for no reason at all. It's dangerous to be out late in the dark."

"Don't fuss, Mummy, I can look after myself."

"Well, keep your eyes open and don't go to lonely places."

"Next Sunday we're going to a country pub that one of the other players told Bruce about in a place called Tolbrite in Dorset. That should be safe enough unless some country bumpkin runs amok with a pitchfork, shouldn't it?"

"You may think it funny, my girl, but just you keep your eyes open, for my sake."

"Oh, Mummy, of course I'll be careful, in *all* ways, please don't worry."

"Come on then, it's time you were off, I'll get the car out."

Samuel Charles Hawkins, christened Samuel after his father, a Newcastle United supporter, and Charles after his mother's father, a Sunderland supporter, was driving automatically, his mind still on the letter in the breast pocket of his jacket. Sam was of the old school, he always wore a business suit to work and changed into a track-suit and shorts for training sessions when he got to the ground.

The writer of the letter had mentioned the two things that seemed to govern British football these days, the Premiership and Money. He wondered if these were two things or only one because, in the end, it all boiled down to money. He stopped automatically at a traffic light that was showing red and found his thoughts wandering over the changes that had taken place in the post-war years in the game that he loved.

The biggest changes, he thought, were the television coverage given to the game and the massive income that this brought and the fact that the players had organised themselves into a union and demanded their fair share of this money. Some would say considerably more than their fair share of the money.

The fact that the pendulum had swung too far in the player's favour was acknowledged by everyone who thought deeply about the game and especially by people like himself, the manager of a first-division club, who's players had received ridiculously high salaries last season when Southampton had been a Premier league club and still expected to receive them following relegation to the lower division, notwithstanding the fact that the club's share of the TV and other sponsorship monies was a now small percentage of what it had been.

The players argument was that if the board expected them to win promotion back into the Premiership at the end of the new season, they'd have to pay them what they individually thought that they were worth. Privately, none of them considered that he, personally, had contributed in any way to the club's poor performance last season; it was all down to the manager, the other members of the team and bad luck.

Even the titles given to the leagues stuck in Sam's craw. In his father's time there had been four divisions, first, second and third north and south. The latter to avoid impoverished clubs travelling the length of England for fixtures. After the war this became first, second, third and fourth divisions. Then the big clubs, the greedy clubs, had decided that they were more powerful than the Football League or the Football Association and threatened to go-it-alone and form a super-league if they weren't given more privileges and the major part of the money that came from television coverage of their games. They formed the Premiership and were persuaded that they should permit promotion to their ranks from the league below and by the same token, relegation from their august ranks to that league. . Consequent upon this, fairly obscure second division clubs now found themselves restyled as first division clubs and so on down the divisions.

A beep on a horn from the car behind reminded him that the traffic light was now green. He increased the pressure on the accelerator and moved ahead. He thought what a boon an automatic gearbox was. When Stella had suggested it, he'd resisted the idea of getting an automatic car as a way to ease the pain in his left knee but she'd gone ahead and bought one anyway. As usual, she was right and he found driving much easier. His painful knee was the result of the injury that had ended his playing career. He'd been talent spotted as a school-boy by Newcastle United and had played for them for three seasons before they sold him to Manchester United for what in those days was a fortune. Much against her father's advice, Stella had become Mrs Hawkins a year earlier and what a blessing that was. She had taken charge, found a house and made all the arrangements.

He stopped at the next red light. No need to touch the gear selector, simply apply the foot-brake and stop, even on a gentle incline and he didn't have to use his left leg at all.

Nowadays the sum that Manchester United had paid for him wouldn't buy a first division player, that's how silly the football market had become. He had tried to get his fellow managers to agree to limit the amount that they would pay for players and the salaries to be paid to players but his proposals had fallen on deaf ears, the cry was that continental clubs like Real Madrid and Inter Milan would offer inflated transfer fees and salaries and all the best British players would go overseas. He couldn't get anyone to face up to the fact that, for the foreseeable future, the number of English players of sufficient ability to attract such offers could be counted on the fingers of both hands and that the players on the continent would have something to say about it anyway. This hadn't gone down too well with the people who managed the player's union, either.

None of them wanted to accept that players in the English leagues were over-paid and under-skilled and, what was more, their work-rate on the field of play and in training, wasn't good enough. Why were so many continental players so willing to join English clubs? Look at the names of the players for the top clubs, hardly an English name among them.

He had to admit that part of the work-rate problem could be laid at the manager's door but people had to realise the difficulty of disciplining players earning over a million pounds a year, many times what the manager himself was getting.

The lights turned green and he moved off without the gentle reminder from the car behind.

It wasn't only players, some of the top clubs had non-English managers. Even the England team was managed by a foreigner. That sparked another train of thought as he drove automatically along the route that he followed every day. He wondered if the European Commission or the European Parliament had passed a law saying that Europeans weren't foreigners? He had to admit that he didn't like calling Europeans foreigners. He was a convinced supporter of the European Community and believed that, certainly within his daughter's lifetime and notwithstanding what the politicians might be saying today, Britain would be pleased to shelter within the trade barriers that Europe would be forced to introduce to provide employment for its citizens and, perhaps, defence barriers, to preserve the Western way of life.

He crossed the Northam Bridge, passed the Meridian TV studios on his right, turned left into Princes Road and then to the right at it's end from where it was a straight run to the ground and he brought his mind back to the more immediate problems with the thought that it was up to the politicians to see to that. This triggered the notion that since the recent public opinion polls showed that the majority of the British population, and indeed the free world's population, appeared to think that their politicians were idiots and not to be trusted, the outlook for mankind looked pretty bleak.

The familiar outline of the stadium loomed ahead and soon he had parked in his allotted spot and walked up to the familiar surroundings of his office to start the day's routine.

He made it his practice to be at his desk by eight-thirty every morning which gave him half an hour to glance through his post before the players were due. He'd had a lot of dissent from the team about starting training so early, the London clubs didn't start until well after ten and then not every day so why didn't they? And so on. They'd taken the matter to the Chairman, a self-made millionaire builder, who'd told them to get on with it or leave, they were lucky not to be starting work at seven in the morning like he had when he was their age.

This morning, because he hadn't had to take Samantha to the university, he was at his desk just after eight o'clock. His secretary, Petra, arrived at her usual time, just after eight thirty.

At five past nine o'clock he went to the player's dressing-room. His assistant coach, Brian Watters was already there. They were all there, most of them were in their playing kit, the last, as usual, being the coloured mid-field player Sylvester Stakes, the one player in the club who had an England cap. Sylvester was a problem. Immediately the club had been relegated he had let it be known that he wanted a transfer to one of the Premiership clubs so that he might continue to play, as he put it, with players of his own quality. Sam would be quite happy for him to go, provided the price was right. The only problem was that his reputation for awkwardness on and off the pitch had preceded him and none of the other clubs wanted him. It was always he who was at the bottom of the player's complaints. He had taken an instant dislike to Bruce Somers and always referred to him as 'college-boy'. The press, of course, encouraged this, it made good copy.

Sam outlined what he intended they should do that morning. Four laps of the ground for a warm-up, followed by a rehearsal of some tactical moves that had been discussed earlier, followed by fifty shots each from various positions on the eighteen yard line at a goal defended by the goal keeper and two defenders. There would be goal-mouth heading practice for both attackers and defenders and then some sprinting with the ball and other exercises in ball-control and passing. When they were changed again, there would be some tactical discussion in what Sylvester called the kindergarten. That understood, he and Brian took them on to the pitch. He didn't know whether his players liked him, he didn't care that much whether they did or didn't, but they'd certainly learn to respect him. Who knows, they might thank him one day for making them better players.

An hour or so later his secretary came on to the pitch, to an accompaniment of quiet wolf-whistles, to say that the chairman had arrived. Sam told Brian to carry on and walked back with Petra. Driving in, he'd decided that he ought to tell the Chairman about the letter.

When they had dealt with the day's mail, Sam showed the Chairman the anonymous letter. The Chairman read it twice then dropped it on his desk and said,

"Another bloody crank, Sam."

"That's what we thought."

"You haven't shown this to anyone else?" said the Chairman, alarmed.

"No, only to Stella."

"What about your secretary?"

"No, only we three, me and the wife and you, know about it," said Sam.

"Good, crank or not, let's keep it that way. There's nothing we can do, let's pray that we don't hear from him again."

Chapter Two

WORD quickly spread through the 'family' that Luigi Coroneli was happy. The 'soldiers' who ran the family's legal and illegal operations only knew it third hand because the lieutenants or caporegime who collected their takings were not their usual demanding selves and their awareness of mafia ways told them that must mean that the underboss and above him the capo, Luigi Coroneli, weren't demanding the impossible, so the Capo must be happy.

The Coroneli family was organised and run on traditional lines. It followed the strict Omerta moral code, never to assist the authorities or seek assistance or justice from them and the caporegime and the soldiers understood that their lives and the lives of their dependants, depended on the maintenance of the denial of any connection with the family, should they be apprehended by the forces of law and order. The family took care of it's own.

Take Michael Bernoulli, for example, found dead with head injuries one dark night outside his house in Lime Gardens, Highgate. More accurately, a short distance from his wife's house in Highgate. The inquest assumed that he had been struck by the wing mirror of a lorry and returned a verdict of accidental death but when Scotland Yard issued a statement that, following the death of Michael Bernoulli they were no longer seeking the murderer of a man and a girl who had been killed one afternoon near to Bournemouth, the soldiers came to realise how convenient his death had been.

Those who knew something of his constant womanising had been surprised when Michael Bernoulli had become one of the small select band of soldiers who provided a body-guard for the Capo and aghast when he was allowed to marry Sophia, the Capo's only daughter. The old man had set them up in a fine house in Highgate and given his son-in-law a legitimate rent-collector's job. All he had to do was to keep his nose clean and have Sophia produce sons, but no, there had been rumours that Michael was also performing away from home. Perhaps they had reached the ears of the Capo.

Luigi was pleased with life. The various businesses in which his mafia family had their murky fingers were prospering and they were at peace with the other two families that operated in the Home Counties, they had all learnt the lesson from their distant relatives in Sicily and the United States, that internecine vendettas benefited no one but the authorities and so far none of them had bid to become the capo dei capi.

Two things were giving Luigi particular pleasure, the killing of his son-in-law and the letter that he'd sent to the manager of Southampton Football Club. The first demonstrated that he still had his ability to deal with critical situations promptly and in person and the second demonstrated his ability to recognise new opportunities when they appeared.

No one knew that he had journeyed out to Highgate that night to kill his son-in-law. Two people were in a position to reflect on the coincidence of him learning that the police were after his son-in-law on a double murder charge and said son-in-law's convenient death the same night; the solicitor who had telephoned him from a public call-box at lunch time to tell him of the police's interest and Luigi's secretary, Maria, who's bed he had shared at least two times each week. In any event she couldn't speak Italian but she may have recognised mention of the name, Bernoulli. He was sure that he could rely absolutely on their silence, they knew that even one word out of place could result in their untimely death. Usually a very painful death.

He liked the football thing. Why hadn't he thought of it before? There is big money in football and they can afford it. Better that it should come to a worthy cause like him than be paid in exorbitant salaries to what he considered to be a collection of under-employed layabouts like professional footballers. Leonardo, his consigliere had put the idea into his head. Leonardo was a keen Arsenal supporter; why? Luigi couldn't understand because he didn't live anywhere near to the gunners north London ground at Highbury. Leonardo had scorned the amount of money that the new owner of Chelsea Football Club (a Russian, would you believe?) was spending on foreign players and had commented that the man must have more money than sense. This had led to the idea that they should seek a way by which some of that money could be made to come their way.

With Salvatori, his underboss, they had sat down and considered the possibilities. Luigi studied Salvatori.. Over the years his face had settled into deep furrows around the eyes and mouth and his hair had thinned. No one would take him for the handsome curly headed young man from Pedara, a village literally on the slopes of Mount Etna in Catania in Sicily who had come to England many years ago to work for Luigi's father. He seldom smiled these days. He was the enforcer who favoured physical action like armed raids on Saturday afternoons to seize the day's gate money. He accepted that what might have been possible five years ago was complicated these days since the threat of terrorism had resulted in a substantial police presence at the big clubs, some of it armed. Leonardo, who's smooth complexion and luxuriant hair contrasted vividly with his colleague, had remarked that they would have to be more subtle, they were in the protection racket, why shouldn't the clubs pay money to prevent some ill-intentioned person from setting fire to property, like their offices and stands? It was then that Luigi had pointed out that the club's most valuable properties were its players.

Thus the idea was born and the more they thought about it the better it sounded. Clubs could employ extra security guards to patrol their offices and stands but they wouldn't be able to afford people to watch over all of their players and their wives for 24 hours a day. Leonardo did a quick calculation that showed that working three shifts for a first team squad of twenty players would not leave a club with any change out of £25,000 a week.

The discussion had then centred on how much and how? Luigi thought that they shouldn't ask for too much to start with, say £25,000 a week, paid electronically into an offshore bank account from which it would move instantly to another and so on, to make it next to impossible to trace. Leonardo produced his pocket calculator and said that with twenty premiership clubs, that would bring in more than 20 million pounds a year. If they all paid.

"The beauty of it is," said Luigi "that, once we get it running, there is very little risk, we send them untraceable letters with the details of the bank account into which the money is to be paid and in due course that money, less the banker's expenses, reappears in an account to which we have access."

"How do we persuade them that we mean business?" asked Salvatori.

"Well," said Luigi, "we send them our first letter saying that we want money, or else their star player gets hurt. Then we send them another letter telling them how much we want with the delivery instructions. Then we make one of their minor players or his wife have an accident after which we send a third letter, pointing out that next time it will be one of their best players and tell them once again where to send the money."

"Why do we have the accident, Capo?" asked Salvatori.

"Because I don't expect them to pay-up until we do, would you?"

"No, I see what you mean."

"Arranging that will be in your department" said Luigi.

"It'll be a pleasure, Capo," said Salvatori, smiling.

"Shall we start with Chelsea?" said Leonardo, hopefully.

"I rather think that we should set our sights a bit lower to start with," said Luigi. "I favour Southampton, they will be desperate to get back into the Premiership and most probably won't be able to afford to buy expensive replacements for star players who have an accident."

"What do you want us to do, Capo?" asked Salvatori.

"I'll handle the letters," said Luigi. "I want you to pick one of your people who's keen on soccer and have him prepare a list of clubs, their addresses, their chairmen, managers, first and second team players and all their addresses. Then I want him to take a look at the grounds and at the places where the players spend their time, that sort of thing."

"From the stories that get into the papers they seem to spend a good bit of their time in nightclubs," said Leonardo.

"More's the better," said Salvatori, "that's where we can hit them if we have to."

"You could well be right," said Luigi. "First get someone to give Maria the name of a key Southampton player."

The first letter had been sent that afternoon, Luigi had had second thoughts and decided to ask for only £25,000 a month to start with.

Detective Inspector Don Donovan did not much believe in coincidences. The untimely death of Michael Bernoulli was a case in point and although Scotland Yard had issued a statement linking him with the murders of Raymond Farrell and Laura Wells in Dorset and that the case was now considered to be closed, he, Don Donovan still had the file in the drawer of his desk because he didn't like convenient coincidences.

That Michael Bernoulli had killed the man and then raped and murdered the girl in Dorset he had no doubt and, as his chief had said when Donovan had expressed his reservations to him, fate had taken care of things and justice had been done. Donovan thought that someone may have given fate a nudge.

The results of the feelers that he had put out during the week preceding the death, that the police were looking for a minor crook called Bernoulli who had been seen by another minor crook who had himself left a partial fingerprint at the scene of the first murder and by no less a personage than the Chancellor of the Exchequer and his wife near to the scene of the second murder, had come in after he was dead. The vice squad knew him as Mick the Knife and there was a strong hint that he was a Mafiosi. Donovan didn't doubt that, now that he knew that the man's wife was Sophia, Luigi Coroneli's daughter.

He was certain that bringing the owner of the Four Oaks Club in for questioning had triggered events. The owner, what was his name? He consulted the file, Guiseppe Maranti. ran the club with his brother Francesco who insisted on being called Francis Martin. Although Guiseppe had been terrified and had steadfastly refused to name the man, he was sure that Bernoulli had been the debt-collector who the club owner had commissioned to recover the money that Farrell had taken from the club. As a result of the questioning, Guiseppe and the solicitor who he had insisted should be present – again he consulted the file -, Silvestro Bessani, that was him, they had both known that the police were looking for Bernoulli. That same night Bernoulli had been killed.

According to the file he had been struck a blow on the back of his head, just above the neck, and had died instantly. It was thought that he had been struck by a projection, such as a wing mirror, of a passing lorry. The coroner had expressed the view that the driver of the lorry probably hadn't known that he had struck anything. What idiots some coroners are, thought Inspector Donovan, the blow necessary to kill a man must have been heard and felt within the driver's cab. But of course there were trees in Lime Gardens and a stranger might have thought that a noise in the dark was due to striking a low branch.

Donovan studied the notes made by the police officers who had attended the scene of the fatality. As usual, they were perfunctory, no one saw any reason to make a Central Criminal Court sort of case out of a simple hit-and-run accident. According to the widow, the victim had gone out after dinner to meet someone and had been found some hours later in the gutter a few yards from the entrance to his own drive. Why had he gone out in the dark? Because he'd taken a telephone call. She thought that he'd said that he had to meet someone called Leonardo. According to the widow when questioned, the only Leonardo that they knew was on holiday in Italy.

No one had asked the obvious question, why didn't he take his car?

There was no bus route along Lime Gardens and the only traffic was largely residents' cars.

Had he been standing on the verge waiting for someone to pick him up, seen lights approaching and stepped off into the gutter expecting the vehicle to stop? In which case why wasn't he struck in the face rather than the back of the neck?

Then there was the question of the wound itself. He studied the file. Bernoulli was five foot six; say five foot seven with his shoes on. The distance from the injury to the top of his head would be about six inches so the object that struck him would have been five feet above the ground if Bernoulli had been standing bolt upright. In Donovan's experience the wing mirrors of lorries were much further above the road surface than five feet.

He thought about that, the powers that be in the Home Office had issued an instruction that metric units be used in reports. Donovan had no intention of complying, five feet meant something to him, a chap could imagine what five feet was. How sensible our ancestors had been to pick units that a person could envisage. 5 feet meant something, 1.524 metres didn't. Honesty forced him to correct himself; to Donovan 1.524 metres meant one and a half yards and a bit, about 5 feet, in fact. So much for the SI scale.

He put the file back in his desk drawer, after deciding that when he had the opportunity he would make some unofficial enquiries. He and his side-kick, Sergeant Sidney Tyler, had more immediate things that demanded attention. He took the top paper from his in-tray, it comprised print-outs from his computer, he preferred to lay out documents on his desk or table and study them as a group rather than bring them up one-by-one on the screen of his computer monitor.

The second letter arrived at the Southampton manager's house exactly a week later. It said,

We are pleased that you had the good sense not to contact the police. Because of that we have decided only to charge you £25,000 a month for seeing that nothing bad happens to your players. You are to send this amount electronically to Account 0007653978 at the Second National Bank in La Paz. Fail to make the payments at your peril.

Stella watched her husband open the envelope and read the contents and said,

"Is that another letter from those people?"

"Yes." He handed the letter across the table.

"What people is that?" asked Samantha who had come down early to be in time for breakfast and in the expectation that her father would provide her with transport into Southampton.

"Oh it's nothing," said her mother.

At nineteen, Samantha could read her parents like a book.

"Come off it, Mummy, Daddy opens an envelope and reads a short note, shows it to you and you both look shell-shocked and you tell me that it's nothing?"

"It's nothing, just some silly crank," said Stella, making to hand the letter back to her husband but Samantha was to quick for her, her long arm was stretched out and she intercepted the letter in mid-air, as it were.

Samantha read the missive and said, more as a statement of fact than a question,

"This isn't the first letter you've had, is it? What's this about nothing bad happening to the players?"

"It's some crank threatening to harm the club," said Sam.

"By injuring the players?" asked Samantha.

"Yes, silly isn't it?" said her mother.

"Now that you've had a second letter are you going to the police?"

"To be absolutely honest, Sam," said her father, "at the present moment I don't know what I shall do, I'll have to discuss it with the Chairman."

"Well, he at least ought to be sensible enough to call in the police and prevent," –she nearly said Bruce – instead she said, "players getting hurt."

Her mother had noticed the momentary hesitation and grinned at her. Samantha added,

"Well, you know what I mean, you owe it to them all, even the ones that aren't very nice, like that Sylvester Stakes."

"I didn't know that you knew him, darling," said Stella.

"Well, I've seen him around and I don't like the way that he looks at me, sort of undressing me, ugh."

"Then stay away from the players and the places where they go in their time off," said Sam.

Stella could see that they were treading on grounds that perhaps shouldn't be uncovered at that precise time and said,

"Never mind about that for the present, it's time that you were both off," with which she stood up and began to clear the breakfast table.

Sam looked at the clock on the wall and said, "Gosh, is that the time. You'll be late for your lectures, Sam."

"It's alright, we're not on until eleven fifteen this morning but before that I've got an exercise to finish. I'll get my things."

She disappeared upstairs.

"You'd better warn her not to mention that letter to anyone else," said Stella.

"Yes, I'll do it on the way in," said Sam senior.

When they were safely on the way, Sam warned his daughter that she mustn't breathe a word to anyone about the letter.

"I won't, Dad, if you say so but has it occurred to you that if you told the media and it was all over the papers and on the television, it might be the best way to clip these people's wings?"

"How do you mean?"

"Well, you'd have several thousand extra pairs of eyes watching over your players, wouldn't you? Everywhere they went someone would be watching."

"I could name one player who wouldn't welcome that," said Sam, Senior, adding, "That wouldn't necessarily stop someone having a go at one of the players near to their homes, say, where there aren't likely to be many people."

"But it wouldn't half increase the possibility of the crooks being caught, wouldn't it?"

"You've got a good point there, Sam, it would be a deterrent, I might suggest it to the Chairman."

They drove on, each busy with their private thoughts. Soon they were across the River Itchen. This time Sam drove straight down Northam Road and turned up Dorset Street and The Avenue and hence to the Highfield Campus to drop his daughter at the entrance and then turned to retrace the route to the Marine Parade and the Stadium. It was a source of some amusement to them that the university website described the Highfield Campus as being 'green and pleasantly landscaped, just a short walk from the city centre.' Green and pleasantly landscaped it certainly was but another page of the web that provided a guide to travel times between campuses, gave the walking time to the city centre as 40 minutes. Hardy folk, these professors.

As he turned into St Mary's Street on the last lap to the ground he mused on the habit that fate had of bringing things in a full circle. When he'd visited Southampton as a player for Newcastle United or Manchester United, the matches had been played at the Dell, on the other side of the city. This had been the home of Southampton Football Club for over a hundred years, since a few years after a group of young men who attended St Mary's church had founded the club in the 1880's to play in the Southern League as Southampton St Mary's. In 2001 the club had moved to the new 32,000 spectator Friends Provident Stadium, just up the road from the St Mary's church where it all began.

He was waiting when the Chairman arrived. The Chairman looked at his face and said,

"What's up Sam, had another letter?"

"Yes Chairman, they want £25,000 a month."

He handed the letter over and waited while his chief read it. The Chairman put it down on his desk and said,

"Fat bloody chance they've got of getting that."

"Do you think that we should go to the police?"

"Nay, lad, let's do nowt and see what they do."

"I don't think that it's as easy as that, Chairman," said Sam.

"Nothings ever easy, what's the problem?"

"Our insurers. Any insurance company would have doubts about meeting any claims that might arise from one or more of our players getting hurt off the field but in our case our insurers are our sponsors. We ought to warn them that some madman is threatening us."

"I see what you mean. They'll say that we should bring in the police, won't they?"

"Yes," said Sam. "There's one other thing…"

"What's that?" said the Chairman leaning back in his chair, smiling and eyeing his manager.

"If we tell anyone, it's bound to get out so why don't we walk along the road to Meridian Television and tell them the whole story?"

"That's what the crank who wrote the letters said we shouldn't do," said the Chairman. "What good would that do?"

"It would mean that the story was broadcast nation wide and many thousands of extra pairs of eyes would be watching out for anyone approaching our players," said Sam. "It's possible that we're not the only club to have had these letters and it might bring things more into the open."

"It's an idea, I'll think about it. Meanwhile I'll think about having a private word with the insurers."

Herbert Jackson was still thinking about it when he went to bed that night, and the next night and Sam continued to fret and look over his shoulder.

Chapter Three

THE manager was not alone in being concerned about the threat to his players; his wife Stella was trebly worried. For him, for the players and for Samantha and the worry didn't go away as the days and then the weeks, passed. She debated endlessly with herself that Samantha should be told that Bruce's name and only Bruce's name, had been mentioned in the first letter.

She worried herself sick every time she knew that Samantha was out with Bruce. She dreaded the arrival of the morning post and she hated answering the phone.

It came natural to her to call her husband Sam and her daughter Samantha. Sam, for his part always called his daughter Sam as did their daughter's friends and now that the male ones, mainly from the university, had manly voices there was sometimes some confusion as to which Sam they were asking for. Stella dreaded getting a phone call from whoever it was writing those letters.

Eventually, after swearing her daughter to eternal secrecy, she said,

"You should know that the first threatening letter that Daddy received mentioned Bruce's name."

"Why didn't you tell me earlier. Has he been told?"

"No dear, Daddy didn't want to worry him, it is probably a hoax and we've tried to ignore it."

"You've made a pretty poor job of that, Mummy, I could see that there was something extra worrying you, you've not been your usual self for weeks. Daddy's shrugged it off better than you have."

"He doesn't know that you're going out with Bruce," said her mother.

"I see," said Samantha, thinking fast, "don't you think that Bruce and the other players have a right to be warned? If the letters are for real, I would think that a player who is injured by these people would have a good case to sue the club for substantial damages for not warning him to be careful."

"Daddy said the same thing to the Chairman but he won't or can't make up his mind to tell the police or the insurance people or the players."

"Well, I'm going to tell Bruce," said Samantha.

"You promised that you wouldn't ever tell a soul," said her mother.

"Don't worry, I'll wrap it up in some way and make him swear that he won't tell anyone."

"Most of all, he mustn't let your father know that he knows," said Stella.

A few evenings later, seated side by side in a restaurant, each conscious of the comforting warmth of the other's thigh, Samantha said,

"You must promise me faithfully that you won't breathe a word of what I'm going to tell you to anyone else."

Bruce turned towards her and grinned, one of her more endearing traits, for him, was her absence of guile. At the moment she sounded like a small girl.

"It depends on what it's about, Sam, if, for example it's that you intend to blow up the Houses of Parliament tomorrow, I might think that they should be warned." He stopped for a minute and added, "On the other hand, it might not be such a bad idea."

"Stop fooling," said Samantha, "I'm serious, Daddy's had some threatening letters."

"What about?" asked Bruce.

"Damaging the club unless it pays them money."

"Has he told the police?"

"No, It's not just Daddy, he showed them to old Herbert and he's still thinking what to do."

"The problem being not to worry the players and the spectators, I suppose?" said Bruce.

"Yes, you see it might be a hoax by someone who wants you to play badly."

"Having a bomb under them might wake some of our team up," said Bruce. He smiled, "It does explain why your father has been warning us to be careful and to watch out for careless people who might cause accidents that would put us out of the game."

"Good for Daddy."

"The lads thought that he was referring to supermarket trolleys," grinned Bruce.

"Promise that you will be extra careful from now on and that you won't tell the other players?" said Samantha.

She looked at him imploringly.

"Yes, Sam, I can see your father's problem and I promise."

She brushed his cheek with her lips and said,
"I knew that you would."

A week later Luigi Coroneli's secretary, Maria, came into his room and said in a hushed voice,
"Senor Alfredo Corleone is on the phone."
Alfredo was the capo of a family that operated south of the M4 motorway. Luigi held sway north of the motorway. Each did his best to avoid treading on the other's toes and it was extremely rare for them to talk.
"Well, put him on then," said Luigi, picking up the phone.
Maria turned and Luigi admired her legs as she went back to the adjacent office; he liked her to wear high heels, it gave her poise. When he heard a click, said into the phone,
"Buon Giorno Alfredo, to what do I owe this pleasure?"
"Ciao Luigi, it's a long time since we spoke, too long, perhaps. I was sorry to hear about the death of your daughter's husband, is she bearing up?"
"Oh yes, Sophia is a sensible girl and she's still so young."
"Perhaps we ought to introduce her to my youngest boy."
"Is that Ignazio?"
"Yes, he's working for an insurance company, doing well, it seems."
"I'm glad to hear that but perhaps we should let the young people make their own choices, shouldn't we?" said Luigi, thinking, if he looks anything like you, my Sophia would run a mile.
"Yes, perhaps you're right. It's not like the old days, is it?"
"No," wondering when the capo of the Corleone family would get to the reason for his call, "Can I do anything to help you?"
"There is just one little thing, Luigi…."
"And what is that, my friend?"
"A little bird tells me that you're interested in football."
Luigi was startled, had the Southampton manager gone to the police?
"In football? What ever gave you that idea, Alfredo?"
"One of my friends tells me that one of your associates is making enquiries about football clubs."
Luigi relaxed.

"Oh, that," he said dismissively. "I gather that he's collecting information for a book or something. Most probably nothing will come of it. Why does it concern you, Alfredo?"

"If that's all that he's doing it doesn't but if, for example, he was planning something I wouldn't take kindly to his doing it to any club south of the M4." He added as an afterthought, "after all, most of the big clubs are in the north, aren't they?"

"I suppose that they are," said Luigi, "now that you've brought it up."

"I understand that your consigliere Leonardo is an Arsenal supporter."

"I believe that he is. One thing I do know is that he doesn't like Chelsea."

"Is he intending to go to Southampton, Arsenal are playing there in the Cup in two week's time?"

"I'm sure that I don't know," said Luigi, his guard up once more. "I should have asked you before, Alfredo, are you a keen football supporter?"

"Oh, I go to Charlton from time to time and to Southampton occasionally and I'd like to see them get back into the Premier League."

"I see," said Luigi. "I must remember that."

"Yes," said Alfredo, "it is good to speak with you, my friend, and I expect that you are busy as always, Caio."

"Caio, Alfredo, we should speak more often."

The line went dead and Maria came in,

"Did you record that?" demanded Luigi.

"Yes, what was it all about?"

"That, my dear girl, is the sixty-four thousand dollar question, how much does he know?"

"And, I would think, how did he find out," she volunteered. "I'll type it up so that you can study it."

"Good and give copies to Silvatori and Leonardo."

He met with his two aides that afternoon. They had read the transcript of his phone talk with the capo of the Corleone family.

"What do you make of it?" he asked Leonardo.

"Well, boss, it suggests two or perhaps three questions."

"And they are?"

"Was he referring to our general enquiries about names and addresses which he could have heard about fairly easily or was it his way of bringing up the Southampton letters."

"And the possible third question?" asked Luigi.

"If so, how did he find out?"

"Good, let's concentrate on the Southampton letters, there's been nothing in the papers or on the TV and that would suggest that the club haven't gone to the police. Agree?"

"Yes boss," said Salvatori.

"Yes," said Leonardo, "that suggests that there's a Corleone in the club."

"It would have to be someone important, they wouldn't leave letters like we sent lying about."

"Or their secretary," said Salvatori.

"Or that secretary's husband or boy-friend," added Leonardo.

"That's very true. Do we know the names of the people who run the club?" asked Luigi.

"We know that the Chairman's called Herbert Jackson, the manager is Sam Hawkins who used to play for Newcastle and Manchester United and his assistant is Brian Watters who used to play for Arsenal," said Leonardo.

"The Chairman made his money in the building trade," said Luigi. "And we don't have a clue who their secretaries are."

"They're called personal assistants these days," put in Salvatori.

Luigi pressed a button on his phone and spoke to Maria.

"Maria, get on to the internet and see if you can find out the names of the secretaries who work at the Southampton club. Yes, I know that it's a tall order but try." He turned to his lieutenants and said,

"The most important thing to decide is whether we call the Southampton thing off and switch our attention to a club north of the M4 or whether we give Southampton a reminder that we expect them to pay."

"Like what, boss?" said Salvatori.

"Like arranging that a member of their reserve team has an unfortunate accident."

"What about the Corleone's," said Leonardo, "is it worth creating bad blood?"

"We've no need to be scared of that lot," said Salvatori.

"It's not a question of being scared but one of business. If they take it as a signal that they can start operating north of the river we could lose more money in the long run than we'd gain from the Southampton club."

"Aw, let's at least do what you said and rough someone up a bit," said Salvatori.

"I think that, in any case, we should send a letter to a club on our side of the river," said Leonardo.

"Such as?" asked Luigi, half knowing the answer and smiling.

"I'd like to say Chelsea but I don't think that would be wise at this time."

"Why so?"

"Because the owner would doubtless bring in his Russian friends and we're having enough trouble from those already."

"So who do you suggest?" asked Luigi.

"Let's go for a club in the midlands, like the Wolves," said Salvatori. "As a kid I always liked the Wolves because they had orange shirts and I liked oranges."

"Do you agree?" Luigi asked Leonardo.

"Yes, but they might be more strapped for cash than one of the Premier clubs."

"Alright, we'll send a letter to Wolverhampton Wanderers and see what comes of it," said Luigi.

"What do we know of what's going on at Southampton?" asked Salvatori.

"Unless the capo knows something that I don't, very little," answered Leonardo.

They both looked at Luigi, who said,

"I know no more than you do but we can infer a lot from the silence, can't we? Like they haven't told their players or the police, nor, I suppose," he added as an afterthought, "their insurers."

"Because one or other of them would have leaked it to the papers?" said Salvatori.

"Yes."

"Is that a good thing or bad, from our point of view?" asked Leonardo.

"On balance, it's good, the players won't be on their guard when we take the next step."

They continued to talk about the options until Maria came in. Luigi asked,

"Any luck?"

"I'm afraid not, all it does is tell you about the club and how they moved into their new Friends Provident Stadium a few years ago and how to get there. It gave the players names but not the secretaries."

Luigi thanked her and she turned to go. He suddenly said,

"Maria, what did you say their new ground is called?"

She consulted her notes,

"The Friends Provident Stadium. I thought that was an insurance company."

"So it is," said Luigi. "If they're the club's sponsors they will most certainly carry the club's insurance and the chairman and manager might think that they had to warn their insurers about the threat, mightn't they?"

"That would widen the field somewhat, wouldn't it?" remarked Leonardo.

"Senor Corleone said something about his son working for an insurance company," said Maria who was still hovering.

"So he did. Clever girl," said Luigi.

She smiled at him at this rare compliment and went back to her room.

"It opens up all sorts of possibilities," continued Luigi. "The son doesn't even have to work for that company, perhaps someone who does was chatting in a bar or at a party the way people do. The question is, they haven't paid any money, do we take the next step?"

Chapter Four

THE letter threatening Wolverhampton Wanderers players with dire consequences if the club didn't pay £25,000 a month into a bank account, the details of which would be given in the next letter, went that afternoon by first class mail.

The next morning Len Girling, the Wolves manager, read it, laughed and threw it into his waste-paper basket. He only wished that he had £25,000 a month to spread around and anyway, he had bigger things to think about than stupid letters from cranks; like what could he do to make his midfield four play better together, and when would the directors give him some money to buy better ones.

The Chairman of the club looked in that afternoon and Len saw the letter as a means of raising the matter of buying new players with him, so he retrieved the crumpled letter, smoothed it out as best he could, and showed it to him. To Len's surprise, self-made millionaire Jim Markham, the Chairman, took it as a serious threat saying,

"Come on Len, you must have wondered as I have, when some clever crook who reads about multi-million pound transfer fees and players getting more pay in a week than the average person earns in a year, would try to find a way of diverting some of that money to himself."

"But we get lots of letters from cranks," said Len, "why should this one be any different?"

"I don't know, but I've got a feeling. What was the postmark?"

"I didn't look. It's in my waste paper basket, I'll go and get it."

He came back a few minutes later and smoothed the envelope out on the desk. They examined it and agreed, it had been posted in London.

"Leave it with me, Len and warn the players to keep their eyes open."

"The papers will get to hear of it."

"More the better," said the Chairman, "we just couldn't afford to chuck away twenty-five thousand quid even if we had it, which we don't, so let them all know."

"We could tell our MP," said Len.

"I might well do that, let's see what our William has to say about it. I pass his agent's office on the way home."

William Davis, the long standing MP for the constituency, and his wife Peggy were friends of Jim Markham and his wife and the MP always did his best to arrange his 'surgery' visits to Wolverhampton on weekends that the Wolves were playing at home. When he had first been elected he'd had a 'surgery' every weekend but now it took all his time to manage once a month, but in between, Peggy went to a number of functions in Wolverhampton on her own, to show willingness.

William and Jim had a lot in common, both had started as engineering apprentices with big companies, William with Vickers Engineers at Barrow in Furness and Jim with British Leyland. William had worked installing the reactors in nuclear submarines and had then become a trade union official while Jim had become a foreman at Longbridge. William had had no political ambitions, like Jim he believed that a worker is entitled to a fair day's pay for a fair day's work. He had become an MP by chance, Wolverhampton North was a trade-union seat, the AEU had always nominated a member of the union for this safe Labour seat and the man so nominated had been killed in a road accident a few days before nominations for the 1992 general election were due. William had been thrust into the vacant spot to avoid the union losing it's rights and had been elected although, some thought against the odds, John Major and the Conservatives had won the election.

This had been all the more embarrassing because his younger brother, Andrew, who had set his heart on becoming a Labour MP, had fought Tunbridge Wells and lost. Andrew had subsequently stood and won Blackpool East for Labour.

Jim Markham had become concerned at the extent to which the unions and workforce of the motor company were being penetrated and manipulated by communist activists and, after trying for months to make his fellow workers see that they would eventually ruin the company and put themselves out of work, he had left. He was convinced that, notwithstanding the perpetual labour troubles at Longbridge, automotive engineering had a big future in Britain and had set up a company to manufacture components for the industry. His company had prospered and nowadays was an important supplier to several motor manufacturers in Britain and on the Continent.

The wives had both been shorthand-typists at the place where their future husbands worked, in Peggy's case, the Accounts Department of Vickers Shipbuilders, and had followed their man. It had been the lovely Peggy who had shouldered most of the burden of their move to the nation's capital, it was she who found the house in Wimbledon, arranged the mortgage and furnished it. She had then started her Public Relations consultancy and had prospered. Jim's wife, Joyce, had stayed at home to look after their two children, who were now grown-up and working in the family firm.

William was a rare thing among politicians, he wasn't ambitious and had no pretensions that he should one day be Prime Minister. Because of his engineering and trade-union background he had been a shadow minister for employment in the 1992 period and when Labour was returned with a landslide majority in 1997 had been made a junior minister in the Department of Employment and subsequently in Trade and Industry. Further ministerial posts had followed in Defence and Trade and Industry (again) until, much to his surprise and not a little consternation, known only to Peggy, he had been appointed Chancellor of the Exchequer following the 2005 election. Andrew was now the Minister of State for the Armed Forces, loyally dealing with the myriad of problems presented by events in Afghanistan and Iraq.

A copy of the threatening letter arrived at the House of Commons in his agent's bag, with a covering note saying that 'Jim Markham wants you to see this. For obvious reasons he hasn't shown it to the police yet but he thinks that it's for real.'

William had his Principal Private Secretary send a copy to the Home Secretary's PPS with a covering note wondering if any other clubs had received similar threats.

The following Saturday, Southampton Reserves played at home and won.

The players showered and changed and went home or went straight into the city for a drink and a meal. They were feeling good, they liked playing at home, they'd won and Saturday was the one night that they could do all the things that young men want to do, without incurring the manager's wrath.

Charlie Parham was nineteen and a fine, strapping six foot two of muscular energy. As a schoolboy he'd played for the Winterborne Whitechurch village soccer team and had been noticed by Will Conway a Royal Marine Commando, when he was home on leave. He had mentioned the boy to one of the PTI's when he had returned to the depot, mentioning that he had thought it remarkable to see a schoolboy holding his own against much older players. He wasn't to know that that particular physical training instructor was an unofficial scout for Southampton Football Club and that his casual reference would lead eventually to the adolescent goalkeeper being taken on the club's books. By the time he was eighteen he was the reserve team goalkeeper, gaining experience fast and attracting attention from other clubs.

Will Conway, young Will to all who knew him, had lived his life in the nearby village of Tolbrite – except for his time in the Marines. He had befriended Charlie and thereafter kept an eye on his progress for he believed that the young man would one day play for England. Will's father, old Will, was the village blacksmith who had followed the onward march of progress and turned his smithy into the village farm machinery repair shop and then into the village garage, only to see his trade disappear as the villagers bought their petrol at the supermarket when they did their weekly shopping while bemoaning the disappearance of the village shop. Will had returned to find himself bound out of loyalty to working with his father in a business that barely earned enough to keep the two of them alive, he was in love with the publican's daughter and not earning enough to support a bride.

The village of Tolbrite was part of the Manor House Estate of six farms, the village and the park in which the house was set. The Hawkridge family had built the house at the beginning of the seventeenth century and had lived there ever since. The family had a military tradition and had a distinguished number of generals in it's family tree. The present squire was General Sir David Hawkridge GCB, DSO, MC, Bart. and the elder son was a lieutenant-colonel in the army following in the family tradition.

The General had retired many years ago and the day to day running of the estate was largely in the hands of his wife, Margaret, their butler Sergeant Hodges, who had been the general's batman/driver, and young Will.

David and Margaret had three children, David – known as David two – in the army and married to an American girl called Sally. They had two children. Next was Timothy who owned and ran a media company, married to Helene who owned French vineyards. They also had two children. The youngest was Elizabeth, a practicing doctor married to the Managing Director and heir to the Hardwick Holdings business.

Running the estate had taken all of the General's and Margaret's money and hadn't been enough to keep up with the maintenance bills. Timmy and Helene had come to the rescue by setting up the Manor House Estate Trust and undertaking to put in sufficient funds annually to maintain the estate. Tolbrite and it's farms were now among the best maintained in the county. Thanks to Helene taking the bull by the horns as it were, the garage was now the estate maintenance depot with old Will as it's caretaker, young Will was the estate maintenance manager and he was married to Gloria and lived in a house a few doors removed from the Tolbrite Arms where she had grown up. She helped her parents in the bar every lunchtime and they both helped in the evenings except Monday when she and Will went into Bournemouth for a meal and a show and for Will to host his hour-long chat-show on Hawkridge Radio Bournemouth. Despite Will's loudly expressed misgivings, his lifelong friend Timmy had insisted that he do this and the slot between ten and eleven on Monday evenings had proved to be one of the station's most popular programmes.

Timmy and Helene worked in London, had a house in Chelsea and spent three weekends out of four at the Manor House. On the middle weekend Helene's mother came to England and accompanied them. On the fourth they went by Eurostar to Paris and then by road to Helene's family chateau where her mother lived with her elderly nurse Matilde amid the vineyards and farms. They were bringing their children up to be naturally bi-lingual.. Helene's mother, Claire-Marie, had married a British air force officer when he was attached to the Royal Jordanian Air Force and she was the daughter of the French Ambassador to Jordan. Their daughter, Helene, was born in Amman and had grown up speaking French, English and Arabic, to which she had added German and Italian at her finishing school in Switzerland. It was her fluency in Arabic that had caused the merchant bank for which she worked to lend her to the Hawkridge Media Headquarters at Canary Wharf to assist Timmy in some negotiations with the crown prince of Qatar concerning a proposed commercial radio station in his country. It had been love at first sight and she had never gone back to the bank.

A minor result of all this to-ing and fro-ing was that Chateau Bouchier wine was now served in the Tolbrite Arms.

Charlie Parham had a flat in Southampton and went home to his parents in Winterborne Whitechurch on most weekends. He had discovered the excellent food served at the Tolbrite Arms and quite often brought his parents to lunch there on Sundays or his current girl friend on Saturday nights. In this way he developed a passing friendship with Will and Gloria and was, in turn, nodded to and greeted by the other members of the group of Timmy and Helene's friends who met at the pub on most Saturday evenings.

It had all started the weekend of the Qatar negotiations when the body of a man had been found on Saturday morning in the Manor House park and the local police inspector – known locally as Clousteau – had treated Timmy as the prime suspect. Timmy and Helene, assisted by Will and Gloria and some private enquiry agents, all of them unmarried at the time, had solved that one. They had then solved a number of crimes, some of which had involved US interests, and earned the nickname of the Irregulars. The private eyes, Fred Smart and Paula Simms had moved to Bournemouth and, with a little help from Timmy, had set up as Southern Enquiries, with an office in the Radio Bournemouth complex. Fred was now married to Angela, the Poole harbourmaster's assistant and a gifted pianist who had since been persuaded to record albums for Hawkridge Media, although the only public performance she would consent to do was to play for half an hour for her friends in the bar of the Tolbrite Arms on Saturdays.

The conversation on Saturday nights always included mention by Fred and Paula of the cases that had occupied them during the week, without names, of course, tit-bits from the estate and surrounding district by Will and Gloria and the progress in the charts of the latest releases under the Hawkridge label. Southern Enquiries was now established and prospering, thanks, admitted Fred, largely to man's infidelity and woman's suspicion of infidelity. Such cases were rarely mentioned.

"You remember that some time ago we mentioned the woman who wanted us to investigate the Council's Planning Department because she said that it's corrupt?"

"Yes," said Will. "She'd had her planning application for a garage turned down and you told her that she wanted a surveyor, not a private eye."

"That's the one," said Fred. "Well, she's been back, even more convinced that there's something fishy going on. She accepts that we're not planning experts and that we're not familiar with the Acts of Parliament, she just wants a second opinion. Paula's been dealing with her."

They shifted their gaze to Paula who took up the story.

"The woman had been to the Planning Offices and obtained copies of the letters from her neighbours, opposing the application and also the internal report by the Case Officer, called the Delegated Report. I have to admit, it does look odd."

"In what way?" asked Timmy.

"To start with the neighbours objections are wildly inaccurate and include comments and gossip which is nothing to do with the proposal."

"Fair enough," said Timmy, "that probably happens in most planning applications, the neighbours aren't lawyers and it's the duty of the Council's planning officers to take note of only those comments that are germane to the proposal."

"That's the woman's point, the Case Officer seems to have repeated the lot in her report. Yes, she's a woman."

"Didn't her bosses cut it out?" asked Helene.

"Oh, it's much worse than that," said Paula. "The Case Officer actually held a meeting on site with the neighbours at which they apparently rehearsed their objections and sent them to the Council the next day."

"Was the applicant there?"

"You're joking, she only found out after her application had been rejected and the Case Officer rudely rejected all requests for a meeting to discuss the grounds of the rejection set out in the Delegated Report."

"But I thought that there were checks on these procedures," said Timmy. "If your client and now Paula could see that the Case Officer had behaved peculiarly, how is it that her bosses and then the Councillors on the Planning Committee didn't pick it up?"

"The whole thing stinks," said Paula. "It's clear that when our client wrote to the Case Officer's bosses, they didn't investigate but simply passed the letter down to the Case Officer to prepare a reply which the boss then signed."

"What about the Councillors, it's their duty not only to preserve the town's architecture but also to look after the interests of the townspeople, to monitor their officials. What did they do?"

"As far as we can tell, very little," said Fred. "We're looking into that."

"I'd like to know how it turns out," said Timmy, "there could be an interesting radio programme here."

They talked of other things and then Paula said,

"And there's also the girl who thinks that her mother's being swindled by a fortune teller."

"I thought that sort of thing only happened in novels," smiled Helene and added, "and TV soap-operas."

"Well, this girl thinks that it's for real," said Paula.

The conversation was stopped when Gloria's mother, Mrs Trowbridge, came in from the kitchen to say that they had just said on the wireless that young Charlie Parham had been knocked down and seriously injured by a hit-and-run driver and was in hospital. It wasn't the sort of news to make the national channels but Jill Jones, the Bournemouth station manager, had picked it up from the wire because the victim was a local boy.

Sam and Stella Hawkins heard the broadcast from the Southampton station. Sam rushed to the phone and called the Royal South Hants Hospital because it was the one closest to the club's stadium. The person who answered the phone had herself heard the broadcast but could find no record of Charlie's admission. Sam phoned the Southampton General Hospital; the person who answered the phone said that they had no record of his admission but that didn't mean that he wasn't there. Didn't the caller know that it was Saturday night? Adding 'they were too busy saving lives to worry much about the paper-work. They'd catch up on that later.'

Meanwhile the Chairman phoned Sam and demanded to be kept informed.

Sam phoned the police and was passed through three different people before he reached someone who knew what had happened. The accident had taken place just after seven-thirty p.m. in the Asda car park at the Marlands Centre in Manchester Street. Charlie Parham had come out of the store and was making his way to where he had parked his car when he was struck by a motor cycle that failed to stop. He had been carrying a shopping bag in each hand and the contents were spilt all over the car park.

Sam was just about to say what the hell's important about what happened to the shopping when the policeperson said that they thought that crushing the shopping against his legs had reduced the severity of the impact. As it was, the victim had been rendered unconscious and taken to hospital, as had an elderly woman into whom the motor-cyclist had swerved and hit after striking the footballer. What hospital asked Sam and was told the General.

The policewoman had added that the young woman who was with the victim, a Miss Jennifer Ridout, had behaved with great presence of mind, she had noted the registration number of the motorcycle and had dialled 999 on her mobile phone and reported the accident. The motor cycle which still bore traces of the victim's shopping, had been found later at the Central Station.

Sam thanked the policewoman for her information and phoned the Chairman while Stella got her car out to drive him to the hospital. They knew that there would be nowhere to park and she would wait in a side street and come and get him when he phoned.

At the hospital Sam couldn't find anyone with the time to answer his questions. The Saturday night procession of real and imagined casualties was just building up, most of them drink related and many of them violent as doctors, nurses and orderlies strove to pick the seriously sick and injured from the human dross that shuffled or was carried in. Sam marvelled at their patience and thought that all the government ministers and all the members of parliament should be made to come and witness these scenes that were doubtless being replicated the length and breadth of England. So much for league tables of hospitals performance, somebody should produce league tables of minister's performance. Thus the hands of the clock crept round until a blessed angel in nurses uniform came and said, "You can see him now."

He found a white-faced Charlie propped up in bed with an attractive young woman sitting at the bedside. His right arm was covered in bandages and strapped across his body. His first words were,

"Sorry Boss. It wasn't my fault. Did you see my Mum and Dad anywhere? Jenny and I are supposed to take them out to lunch tomorrow."

"Don't you worry about anything, lad," said Sam, "except getting better."

"Yes but what about me Mum, she won't be able to get here from Whitechurch at this time of night."

Jenny said, "They're not on the phone and I didn't know what to do so I phoned the pub at Tolbrite that Charlie takes me to and asked them if they could find some way to tell Charlie's parents that I will come out in the morning and take them in to the hospital to see him. The man, Will, said leave it to him, he'd get on to the village pub in Winterborne Whitechurch and tell them."

"There you are then," said Sam, in what he realised was his hospital-talk manner, "they'll be in, in the morning."

After some more meaningless patient and visitor talk, Sam managed to get Jenny outside.

"Do you have any idea what his injuries are?"

"They say that he's got a broken arm and one or two fractured ribs, perhaps more."

Shortly afterwards a nurse asked them to leave. Sam phoned Stella and they gave Jenny a lift to the Asda car park and saw her safely on her way in Charlie's car en route to Charlie's garage and flat, and then went home, with Sam already thinking about a replacement goalkeeper.

In London, Salvatori phoned Luigi and stated cryptically that the mission had been accomplished. "Good," said Luigi, "let's see if they see sense now."

Ignazio Corleone had also heard the broadcast and made a mental note that on Monday morning he would ask if the football club had reported what had happened and how serious the reserve goalkeeper's injuries were. He mentioned it to his mother during his weekly phone call home.

Chapter Five

ON MONDAY morning the Southampton Chairman, Herbert Jackson, and his manager sat down to decide what action to take. The youth team goalkeeper could stand-in next week while they awaited word from the hospital on how long Charlie Parham was likely to be unfit to play. That was the easy part. More difficult was deciding whether this had been an accident pure and simple or whether it had been a demonstration by the writers of the threatening letters that they meant what they wrote, pay up or else! Arising from this was 'shall we tell the police?'

At about the same time, at the insurance company, Ignazio Corleone walked casually past the secretary and into the room of the director who handled sports risks,

"Jeff, have you heard how seriously that Southampton footballer was hurt?"

The director looked up and smiled at his colleague who handled a part of the motoring risks business.

"I didn't know that any Southampton footballer was hurt, did they have to stretcher him off?"

"No, I heard it on the radio, this one wasn't hurt on the pitch, he was knocked down by a motorbike outside a supermarket."

"Oh, I see, you think that it might be your risk?"

"I don't know. I haven't heard anything and I wondered if you had, that's all."

"I'll get on to the club in a minute and I'll let you know what they say."

"Thanks."

Thus it was that while the Southampton pair were discussing the pros and cons of various actions, the Chairman's secretary put her head in the door and said that a director from their sponsors was on the line, asking for a report on the circumstances of the goalkeeper's accident and the severity of his injuries.

"It's no good, Sam," said the Chairman, indicating that she should put the caller through, "we have to put it on the line with our insurers. Quite apart from the fact that we must be above board with them is the fact that if we aren't they might not meet our insurance claims." He spoke into the handset,

"Hello, Herbert Jackson here, I understand that you're asking about the accident to our goalkeeper on Saturday night?"

"Yes," said the director, "is he hurt badly?"

"We're still waiting for the hospital to tell us but on Saturday night they said that they thought that he had a broken arm and two fractured ribs."

"I understand that a motor-bike was involved. How did it happen?"

"He came out of the supermarket and was knocked down by a hit-and-run rider, there is an off-chance that it might not have been an accident."

"Why?"

"I was going to ring you this morning, we've had a couple of letters from a crank threatening to injure our players if we don't pay twenty-five thousand pounds a month into an offshore bank account."

"Have you told the police?"

"No, not yet, they'd have said that it was probably a crank and advised us to keep our eyes open. Now it's different, a player has been hurt."

"I suggest that you do it as soon as possible, there may be a clue somewhere that will quickly be lost."

"If it's in the Asda car park it will have gone already," said the Chairman.

"I suppose that you're right, but you must tell them."

"I'll get on to them now."

"You'll let us have copies of those letters won't you?"

"Yes," said the Chairman, "hold on a minute."

There was a pause, then he said,

"My secretary says that my manager's wife is on her phone saying that what appears to be another of those letters has come in the morning post. Sam's asking her to read it out to him."

Another pause.

"She says it's just one line. *'Next time it will be the first team. Pay the money.'*

"It looks as if it wasn't an accident, doesn't it? You'll keep us informed won't you?"

The Chairman replaced his receiver and asked his secretary to ring the number that the club used when arranging the policing arrangements at the stadium. When the phone on his desk buzzed he picked it up and said,

"Chief Inspector Holland? Good Morning to you too. Peter, we've got a problem."

"How's that, Gordon, I heard about your goalie, bad luck."

"That's what I'm ringing about, we don't think that it was an accident."

"Why so?"

"We've been getting letters asking for money and threatening to injure our players if we don't pay."

"Have you now. Why didn't you tell us earlier?"

"We thought that it was a crank, we get lots of them writing in but this morning we got another, which reads simply, *Next time it will be the first team. Pay the money.*"

"Do you have the letters there?"

"Of course," said the Chairman, thinking does he think that we're daft?

The Chief Inspector reacted to the shortness of the Chairman's reply,

"Sorry, It's just that I'll have to turn this over to the CID and I didn't want them to come over to the stadium if the originals are at Sam's house."

"There's not much to go on," said the Chairman, mollified.

"No but they might take a closer look at the bike and ask about people getting on trains at that time on Saturday, at least it'll be a start."

"Thanks Peter, I knew that you'd get things started. See you next Saturday."

Chief Inspector Peter Holland walked along the corridor and down a flight of stairs to his CID colleagues room, pushed open the door and slumped into a chair. Chief Inspector Valerie Sutton looked up from the papers on her desk and grinned,

"Morning Peter, this is an unexpected pleasure, what brings you to this neck of the woods so early on a Monday morning?"

"It's about that young footballer who was knocked down by the hit and run driver in the Asda car park on Saturday evening, they don't think that it was an accident."

"Who doesn't think that it was an accident?"

"The football club. The Chairman, Herbert Jackson, has just been on to me, it seems that they've had some threatening letters, demanding money or else."

"There's a lot of that about," said Valerie.

"This morning they had one that said Pay up or next time it'll be a first team player or words to that effect."

"I see and I agree, we have to take it seriously. I wonder if any other clubs have had similar letters?"

"One way to find out," said Peter, "would be to tell the press that somebody has been trying to blackmail Southampton."

"I assume that the club has no intention of paying?" asked Valerie.

"Correct."

"Then I would think that they've got nothing to lose by telling the press."

"It might unsettle their players," said Peter.

"They've got to tell them now," pointed out the detective, "the management can't let them be exposed to potential danger without warning them, can they?"

"You're right, as usual. I said that you'd send someone over to collect the blackmail letters."

"Thank you, kind Sir, I'll do that." She thought a moment and said "and I'll also get someone to take a look at the bike and the witnesses statements."

As the result of these high level discussions Detective Constable Chester Hands was given his instructions and told to get on with it.

The insurance director phoned his friend Ignazio and told him what the Chairman of the football club had said about the accident, the footballer's injuries and the threatening letters. Ignazio said,

"Have you got the letters?"

"Give us a chance," said the director, "I was only speaking with him a minute ago. He's going to send us copies and is also informing the police."

"Sorry, I wasn't thinking straight. You say that they haven't told the police?"

"No, they hoped that it was just a crank. Now they know that it isn't."

"It complicates the insurance position somewhat, doesn't it?" said Ignatio. "It's a traffic accident, so it's mine but it appears that it might have been a malicious attack instead of an accident or perhaps some clever lawyer –like we employ – might say that it's an act of terrorism."

"True, but I suppose that, in the circumstances, we'll pay, we're the club's sponsors."

That lunch time, Ignazio went for a walk and phoned his father and told him all that his friend had told him.

"So someone is trying to blackmail the football club," said Alfredo. "I've got a feeling that it's the Coroneli's. I wonder if any other clubs have had letters?"

"What has happened at Southampton will be common knowledge by tonight and that should make other clubs go public if they, too, have been threatened."

"That's true. I'll see what I can find out at this end. Thanks for the call."

In fact the news was broken by the West Midland Police at lunch time in a statement stating that the Wolverhampton Wanderers Football Club had received an anonymous letter threatening to harm its players if a ransom was not paid.

Prompted by this, the Hampshire Constabulary issued a statement that it had learned that day that the Southampton Football Club had received a number of letters threatening injury to its players.

The evening news programmes had a field day.

On the Tuesday morning, Alfredo Corleone was closeted with his two most senior assistants. He said,

"So it seems that Luigi didn't take any notice of our warning."

"He'd probably sent the letters before you spoke with him, boss," said the Underboss

"But not the soldier on the motor-bike," said the Consigliere.

"Exactly," said Alfredo, "he has broken our unwritten agreement, so we can do the same."

"What do you have in mind, boss. Shall we have our boys go up west and teach them a lesson?"

"Yes, but not the sort of open warfare that you have in mind, I intend to move in on his operations and stay there. To do that we have to put some of his money-spinners out of business and have our operations take their place."

"He's big in drugs, protection and prostitution," said the Consigliere.

"We can achieve the most immediate effect by putting some of his houses out of business, it'll take time to re-establish them and meanwhile we'll get a house or two and move some of our girls across the river. At the same time we'll lean-on the pushers that he supplies and have them buy drugs from us at reduced prices."

"The Coroneli's won't like that," said the underboss with evident satisfaction, he handled matters of enforcement in the family, "What do you have in mind for putting the houses out of action?"

"I suggest that we start a little fire," said the capo, "several little fires in fact. One or two of our soldiers go to each house and make use of the girls, there's no reason why they shouldn't enjoy themselves, but each of them will have a small parcel that he leaves close to a lot of curtains or bedding in the girl's room, either with a timer, timed to go off when they've left or better still, set-off by a mobile phone call. The girls will have time to get out but the smoke and fire should put the house out of business for quite a while."

"If we only send two of our people to each house, do you think that two bombs will be enough, boss?"

"It's a question of judgement, if three strapping young men walk in one after another the Madame might smell a rat but she probably won't be suspicious of two."

"They could do it on a Saturday and act like football supporters from out of town," said the Consigliere, on whom would fall the task of organising the operation.

"OK," said Alfredo. "You organise it and let me know when you're ready."

"What about the drug thing?" asked the underboss.

"We have to identify the Coroneli agents and the people they supply. When you can spare them send some people up west to keep their eyes open and their mouths shut and when we know the score we'll send the boys in to lean on people and make them buy from us."

North of the Thames, Luigi Coroneli, Salvatori and Leonardo were also in conclave, discussing the outcome of the weekend's events, the radio announcements that Wolverhampton Wanderers and Southampton Football Clubs had made that they had received letters threatening injury to their players, and the wide coverage that the matter was receiving in the press. Much was being made of the accident suffered by the Southampton reserve goalkeeper, 'was this a warning by the blackmailers that they would stop at nothing'. The

Hampshire police were appealing for witnesses who had seen anyone park a motor-cycle with traces of groceries on it, outside the Central Station after seven o'clock on Saturday evening. The reporters had spoken to the railway staff and it would soon be common knowledge that the police had made extensive enquiries there and so far, had no clues to the rider's identity

Luigi had not been pleased at this latter development but had accepted that there would have been a greater risk of being remembered by a fellow driver and hence laying a trail to the 'family', if the soldier had ridden the stolen motorbike back to London.

"I think that it went well," said Salvatori, "the goalkeeper isn't too badly hurt, nor is the old woman, and the football club know that we mean business."

"But letting the press know is bad," said Leonardo. "Now the clubs will find it harder to pay us."

"Why?" asked Luigi.

"Because public opinion will be 100% against giving in to threats and the police and the anti-terrorist people will be alerted, that's why, not to mention the Corleone's."

"What's it got to do with them?" blustered Salvatori.

Leonardo realised that he must chose his words carefully,

"Alfredo spoke with the capo and warned us to stay north of the M4, didn't he?"

"And we agreed to go ahead, didn't we?" said Luigi.

"Yes," said Leonardo, "from the timing of the announcements it looks as if it was the Wolves who broke the news first."

"They didn't waste much time, did they, they could only have received our letter yesterday morning and it was on the one o'clock news."

"And, according to the news, it was the Chancellor of the Exchequer asked the Home Secretary to follow it up."

"What's it got to do with him?" asked Salvatori.

"He's the MP for Wolverhampton," said Luigi.

"Oh, I see," said the underboss, "probably gets a free seat every week."

"I wish that I could," said Leonardo.

"The question is," said Luigi, "what do we do now?"

"I think that we should show them all that we really mean what we say," said Salvatori, "by putting the wind-up their best player."

"Have you got any ideas?" asked the capo.

"Leave it to me, boss."

Chapter Six

THE incident at the car park had been treated as a routine affair by the traffic police. There were too many youngsters riding around in vehicles and getting involved in accidents. The one who hit the goalkeeper was probably riding a stolen bike with no license and no insurance and had dumped it at the station because lots of buses stopped there and no one would be able to find out which one the rider had taken.

DC Hands obtained a copy of the traffic police report. The circumstances were set out, together with what witnesses had said. Formal statements hadn't been taken but the officers had got their names and addresses. He collected the originals of the blackmail letters from the football stadium, had a brief word with the Manager and drove to the Central railway station.

The big event had been finding the helmet and gloves. It came about as follows. No one at the station could recall anyone suspicious boarding a bus or train on Saturday evening or, put another way by the oldest railwayman questioned, what with spiky, coloured hair, rings through various parts of their anatomy and half naked, they all look suspicious these days. Chester Hands persisted, had there been anything that was unusual that particular Saturday evening, after half past seven?

"Can't say as how there was," said the elderly man.

"Thanks anyway," said the detective and turned away.

"Now if you'd been asking about Sunday morning it would have been different."

DC Hands turned back towards him and said,

"In what way?"

"We found one of them motorbike helmets and a pair of gauntlets in the 'Gents'. They looked brand new."

"Where are they now?"

"In the 'Lost Property' I suppose unless somebody's already claimed 'em."

After some difficulty the Lost Property Office was opened up and the three items produced. DC Hands went back to his car for plastic bags to put them in and gave the railway a receipt. He wrote down the names of the railway personnel who may have handled the items and warned that they might have to have their fingerprints taken for elimination purposes. Privately, he thought this unlikely. What the police wanted was to know who had worn the helmet and gauntlets and there would probably be DNA evidence inside them. The trouble is that the UK doesn't have a national register of the population's DNA but there was an outside chance that the authorities might have a record of a fingerprint.

Back at the nick he reported his findings to his sergeant, they discussed them with the Inspector who told DC Hands to pass the letters, helmet and gauntlets to the forensic scientists. He hastened to comply with the instruction because he rather fancied the new blonde girl; perhaps she'd come out for a drink to discuss her findings.

In London, Detective Inspector Don Donovan decided that it was time that he made a gap in his busy schedule to follow up his misgivings about the 'accidental' death of Michael Bernoulli. He said as much to his friend and assistant, Detective Sergeant Sidney Tyler.

"It was simply too convenient, Sid."

"I'll grant you that, but what have we got to go on?" said the sergeant.

"Two things really, we wanted him for a double murder and he was married to Luigi Coroneli's daughter."

"We haven't got anything on Coroneli and certainly nothing that would connect him with the death."

"Not officially, one of his underlings always takes the blame, but we all know that he's the capo of one of the mafia families operating around here and its unlikely that he'd allow his daughter marry a member of a different family."

"You think that he may have been killed by someone from another mafia family?"

"All the evidence suggests that he wasn't," said the Inspector. "If he had been we could have expected some retaliation by the Coroneli family by now but there hasn't been a thing, the Corleone's continue to operate to the south of the river and the Coroneli's to the north and there's no evidence of gang warfare."

"Granted that there's no sign that either has moved into the other's territory but there has been the occasional killing in south London."

"I gather that informed opinion upstairs is that it's the Corleone's and the Yardies sorting themselves out. I don't think that another mafia family had anything to do with Michael Bernoulli's death."

"You think that his father-in-law had him killed?"

"I didn't say that, Sid, I only said that we don't have to look south of the river."

"Yes but...."

"Think about it. He's married to the capo's only daughter and we're going to put him on trial for rape and a double murder. It would all come out in court and the papers would shout it to the world with hints of mafia connections. What shame to a son of Sicily and his daughter. Luigi would never live it down. And there's another thing..."

"What's that?" asked the sergeant, responding on cue.

"Bernoulli might do a Valachi and betray Luigi's mafia family in an attempt at plea-bargaining."

"All right, I'll ask it, what is or who was Valachi?"

"Valachi was a senior member of a mafia family in New York. The police arrested him and he sang like the proverbial dicky-bird, told the District Attorney all the secrets and crimes of the various New York families who the police promptly arrested and put on trial, lawyers as well. His testimony practically destroyed the Mafia in New England."

"OK," said the Sergeant. "So Luigi wouldn't want his son-in-law to go on trial."

"So what alternatives does he have?" asked the Inspector. "He could either make him leave the country or silence him. If he made him leave the country his daughter would probably go as well, lost to a rotter who has raped and killed another girl."

"We don't know that he knew that, do we Don?"

"We know that the lawyer who came with that fat Italian club owner knew, don't we, 'cos we told them so, didn't we?"

"Yes, I suppose we did," said the Sergeant slowly.

"Well then, he probably tipped-off Luigi," said the Inspector triumphantly.

"So we're agreed that, to a mafia capo's mind, there are grounds for liquidating his son-in-law before the police can take him into custody," said the Sergeant. "But he was killed by a lorry, that would have taken a great deal of arranging and there just wasn't enough time."

"You know that we can drive a horse and cart through that story," said the Inspector, holding up the fingers of his left hand and ticking them off. "First, if someone rang him up and asked him to meet them, why didn't he take his car? Second, there is the injury that killed him, no lorry has got a wing mirror that close to the ground and no car has got one that high above the ground, so what did hit him? And third, it seems as if he was expecting to be picked up in which case he would have been facing the on-coming traffic, wouldn't he?"

"You've convinced me, Don, how do we go about proving it? Remembering that as far as the people upstairs are concerned, the case is closed."

"I think that we start by questioning the residents of Lime Gardens, Highgate, starting this afternoon."

They drove there after lunch and parked where the police report stated that the accident had occurred, a short distance from the house in which the widow lived.

"We'll start with the immediate neighbours and then ask at the houses opposite and sort of work our way out from there. They've all got drives and trees, it was dark at night and it's unlikely that anyone further away would have seen anything."

"Unless they were out walking the dog," said the sergeant. "Do we include the widow's house?"

"I haven't made my mind up about that, Sid, it could stir up a hornets nest."

"You think that she'd protest?"

"She'd tell her Dad and he'd do the stirring. Remember, I'm defying orders in reopening this enquiry and in bringing you here and I'd like to test the water before we stir things up."

"OK so we don't bother the widow but one of the neighbours might tell her."

"We'll tell the neighbours that we don't want to upset her. In any case, in a place like this they probably don't speak with their neighbours from one year's end to the next."

"I thought that they spent all their time sleeping with each other's wives and girlfriends," said the Sergeant.

"You mustn't believe all that you read in the Sunday papers," said the Inspector.

"Only most of it," grinned his Sergeant, "I'll start the other side of the road.

He walked across the road and up the drive of a semi-detached house. An elderly man answered his ring.

"Good afternoon, Sir," said the Sergeant, showing his police identification. "We're just tidying up a few loose-ends concerning the accident that happened here about three weeks ago when Mr Bernoulli was killed."

"Oh yes." said the man, vaguely. "My wife mentioned that somebody had got hurt. Mr Bernoulli, you say. Was he from round here?"

"Yes, Sir, he lived opposite. He was knocked down and killed."

"Was he now, fancy that. It's happening all the time, I hope that he was insured."

"We were wondering if you or anyone else in this house saw anything of the accident?" asked the sergeant, already knowing that this was a waste of time.

"The first we knew about it was when my wife had some reason to come into the front room and saw a lot of flashing blue lights in the road. We never did know what it was all about, we thought that it was probably one of our neighbours had been burgled. It's happening all the time round here, don't get me wrong, I'm not blaming you people, it's the politicians I blame, letting all these immigrants in, I don't know what the country's coming to what with…."

"And neither of you saw the accident or anything else before it?" asked the sergeant, to stem the flow.

"'Fraid not," said the man, beginning to close the door. "We keep ourselves to ourselves these days and our doors and windows bolted. Good-day."

Sergeant Tyler said "Good-day" and walked back down the drive to the noise of bolts being shot in the door behind him.

There was no reply at the adjoining house. He rang the bell and knocked on the door but apart from a dog barking behind the door, there was no response.

He walked down the drive and up the drive of the next house, detached, he noticed. He rang the bell and heard footsteps come along the passage. An elderly female voice said,

"Who's there?"

"The police."

"The police?"

"Yes, Madame," said the Sergeant, waving his identity wallet in front of the brass ring of the spy-hole, "the police, Detective Sergeant Tyler."

The door opened on a chain and a face with grey hair and a pair of gold rimmed spectacles appeared at an angle round the edge of the door. Tyler waved his wallet again and wondered, not for the first time, if any of this was really worthwhile.

"What do you want?" demanded the grey head.

Tyler said his piece about tidying up a few loose ends concerning the accident in which the man opposite had been killed.

"Oh, that," said the woman. "I trust that you arrested the driver of the car."

She closed the door.

The sergeant waited, expecting the door to open. It didn't. He waited, perhaps she had something cooking that would boil over.

Two minutes staring at a closed door seems an eternity, so he rang again. And again. There was the noise of angry footsteps and the door was opened again, still on the chain. The grey head angled round the edge of the door and said,

"What do you want now? I'm busy."

"I'd like you to tell me about the car that you saw, that night."

"I can't, it was dark, I mean the night, not the car."

"Don't you think that it would be easier to talk if you opened the door properly?" said the sergeant.

"I suppose so," said grey head, grudgingly.

She pushed the door too as she unhooked the chain and then opened the door wide. He found himself looking at a woman of perhaps seventy years, with a bright, intelligent face, dressed in a skirt and blouse, regarding him, in turn, through those glasses.

"It's thought that he was struck by a lorry," began the sergeant.

"Fiddlesticks, there was a car stopped there, with its lights on."

"You're sure that you've got the right night?"

"Oh yes. I wrote it up in my diary. A person got out and walked round to the back of the car. I saw whoever it was as they moved in front of the rear lights. After some minutes the near-side rear light was obstructed then both sets of rear lights were obstructed. By this time I could make out the outlines of two people. Then the nearside light reappeared and the number plate light shone as one of the shadowy forms opened the boot. Then the figure seemed to fall down and the boot was closed, the off-side light was momentarily obstructed and a red light shone from half way along the car then went out. It then drove off."

"How did you come to see all this?" asked Tyler. "Your house is surrounded by trees."

"Quite fortuitously, I went upstairs for something. It was dark. I always pull the curtains before I put the light on in case people look in and when I got to the window to close the curtains, I saw the car pull up. We can see the road through a gap in our trees and our neighbour's drive opening."

"I see," said the Sergeant, not really seeing but indicating belief. "What made you watch that car?"

"Burglars."

"You thought that it might be burglars?"

"Yes," said the woman. "Visitors to these houses nearly always park in the drive. If someone is having a party then there's lots of cars parked in the road. Single cars usually denote strangers and single cars stopping in the dark at gone nine at night are suspicious, so I watched."

"You say that you wrote this up in your diary, Mrs er.."

"Mrs Constance Eckhart, Yes."

"We'd like to see that diary"

"In no way, young man, my diary contains my private thoughts."

"I understand," said Tyler, deciding to let his superiors deal with this matter of ethics. "Perhaps we can find a way in which just that entry is copied, say by your vicar."

The moment that he said those words he could have kicked himself.

"Clearly you don't know much about the facts of life, Sergeant, if you think that I'd let a vicar be privy to my innermost thoughts, you don't know much about elderly women. Or vicars." she added with a little grin.

Sergeant Tyler banished from his mind the vision of a vicar meddling in Mrs Eckhart's affairs and said,

"I'm sure that my Inspector will wish to hear what you have told me, Mrs Eckhart, would it be too much of an imposition if I brought him back within the next half-hour, or perhaps you'd prefer to come to the police station and make a statement?"

That always gets them, he thought. It did.

"I've never been in a police station in my life, young man, and I've no intention of starting now. Bring your Inspector person if you must, I'll be here."

He found a dispirited Inspector Donovan coming back down the drive of the fourth house that he had visited without finding anyone who had seen or heard anything that night or any other night as far as he could judge. As they walked across the road and up the drive to The Gables, he explained that the old lady thought that she had seen a car that night at the place where the body was found. He warned Donovan that she was difficult.

Mrs Eckhart responded almost instantly to the door-bell, welcomed the Inspector at the front door and invited them into her sitting room and gave them a cup of tea and a cake as she told her story. The sergeant was amazed at the change in her demeanour, what did Don Donovan have that he didn't? The Inspector questioned her closely but she was sure about what she had seen and, for that matter, what she had not seen. She had clearly thought about the diary which she had ready and she allowed the Sergeant to photograph that particular day's entry.

"In the light of the great importance of your evidence, Mrs Eckhart," said the Inspector, "I'm afraid that there's one other request that I have to make, I'd like you to show me where you were standing when you saw the car."

"You mean you want to come into my bedroom?"

"I'd like to stand at the window that you stood at when you saw the car."

"It was at the side window of the front bay in my bedroom."

"Then that's where I or my sergeant would like to stand and look out as you did."

"You doubt my word?" she said half accusingly, half humorously.

"Not at all," said the Inspector, "but we have to cover every angle. Imagine that as the result of your evidence, we find the driver of that car and arrest him for murder. It comes to trial and he has some clever barristers defending him. You would have to give evidence, the barristers will want to destroy your credibility and argue that you couldn't possibly have seen that spot from your window. We police must be in the position of being able to state categorically that you could. That's why."

She looked accusingly at the sergeant.

"You didn't tell me that I'd have to give evidence in court."

Donovan hastened to say,

"It might not come to that. It's simply that we have to cover every possibility."

"I can see that. Give me a minute."

She hurried out of the room and they could hear faint sounds upstairs. She came back and said,

"Alright, you can come up now, you too, Sergeant, you can both give evidence then."

She led the way up the stairs and into the front bedroom and indicated the window from which she had seen the car. She walked over and looked out and gave a start, saying,

"There's a car parked at the identical spot."

"Yes," said Donovan. "It's our police-car."

"Oh, that's alright then," said the old lady.

The policemen looked out and, sure enough, there was the gap as she had said and there was their police-car parked where the accident or murder had occurred.

"One final thing, Mrs Eckhart, I'd like my Sergeant to take a photo from this window."

"More evidence, I suppose, alright."

They left after congratulating Mrs Eckhart on her vigilance and thanking her for letting them copy the relevant entry from her diary and take photographs from her bedroom.

When they were on their way, the inspector said,

"I thought that you said that she was awkward, she was as nice as pie."

"Must be your charm Don, I had to threaten to take her to the station even to get her to open the front door."

They discussed the implications of her evidence all the way back to Scotland Yard.

The mother of Maria, Luigi Coroneli's secretary, was proud of her daughter and the good position that she held as an important man's secretary. But she had one big disappointment, Maria wasn't married and she was, in her mother's view, running out of time to find a nice husband and produce grandchildren for her mother to cuddle. She had brought her daughter up properly and ensured that she went to church as well as going to the convent school and then a secretaries school; she had grown into an attractive young woman and her mother had expected her to make a good marriage. Instead she had gone to work for Mr Coroneli and seemed not to be interested in men.

Maria had hoped to be swept off her feet by a handsome rich man, marry him and give him children to make their marriage perfect. But until Mr Right came along she had to earn her keep and help support her mother. When she learnt from Delores, the woman who did her hair, that a Mr Coroneli was looking for a secretary, she had applied for the post. The interview hadn't been what she'd expected, it had been concerned as much with her background as with her secretarial capability but she got the job and the small flat in the building that went with it. She hadn't realised until it was too late that she was expected to provide more than secretarial services. To be given a flat as well as a generous salary had seemed to be too good to be true and after she had settled in she found that her employer expected to share her bed whenever he felt like it.

She had been petrified and had refused and had been told that the choice was hers, she either became Luigi's mistress or she would lose not only her job and the flat but her good looks as well. It had been a painful awakening in more ways than one.

She had been brought up a good catholic girl and knew nothing about birth-control except that her church forbad it. She was terrified of having a baby and judged, correctly, that if she became pregnant her days as Luigi's secretary would be numbered. She couldn't ask her mother, the only person in whom she could confide was Delores, who did her hair and talked about men and had recommended the job in the first place.

Delores reaction had been

"I thought that you knew, dear, good jobs like that always have a price ticket. I thought you were on the pill, we must see about that, mustn't we?"

That was four years ago.

Luigi's wife had died two years ago and Maria had hoped that he might ask her to marry him. She had no affection for him but in her view, since he had spoilt her chance of ever marrying a decent man, he should do the proper thing now that he was a widower. Since he made no move she had plucked up the courage one night, after he had sex with her and asked him to marry her. His reaction had been scornful, she should be grateful that she was still his secretary and hadn't been moved to one of his houses in Mayfair to earn her keep like her predecessor had.

She still had her hair and nails and things done every week at the Maison Delores. Delores always gave her personal service and chatted as she cut, washed and set her hair and did her nails. She always asked if Maria had had a good week and if her boss was in a good mood. She expected that, having so many business irons in the fire, he would sometimes be difficult to please and she sometimes wondered how Maria kept up with them all. Maria was careful only to answer in the most general terms, there was no harm in saying whether Luigi was bad tempered or not, was there?

Over the months, Delores had discerned that Maria felt rootless and that she had hoped that one day Luigi would make an honest woman of her. Poor foolish girl, mafia capo's didn't marry the hired help. Two weeks ago Delores had asked Maria,

"What do you do on Saturdays, do you go to the football?"

"No," said Maria.

"Does your boss go? I expect that he supports Arsenal."

"I don't know," said Maria, "but he mentioned Southampton and somewhere in the midlands."

"Birmingham?" tried Delores.

"No, it sounded like wolfs"

"I expect it was the Wolves, Wolverhampton Wanderers," said Delores.

"That's it. I think that it's terrible, the way men shout and sing at football matches these days, and all that violence, it makes me ashamed to be English."

Delores stifled a smile. Maria's parents had both been born in Italy. She steered the conversation back to beauty treatments and body care.

That evening Delores telephoned her sister Carla who lived in Croydon. After the usual enquiries about her children and her sister's enquiries about the state of the beauty salon business, Delores said,

"You asked me to pass on any tit-bits about you know who. I gather that himself has mentioned Southampton and Wolves."

"OK dear," said Carla. "I'll pass it on."

Carla's husband Fred ran one of the legitimate businesses for Alfredo Corleone, collecting rents and information in that order. He passed the tit-bit of news up the chain of command and it reached the South London capo.

Chapter Seven

CHARLIE PARHAM, the local boy, had introduced Bruce Somers to the Tolbrite Arms and it was natural that the latter should take his girl-friend, Samantha, there. He liked the drive through the New Forest, he liked the river that flowed through the village, and he liked the pub and the people who ran it. The food was good and not expensive and it was sufficiently far from Southampton not to be patronised by the general run of Southampton supporters, which included, of course, the team manager, Samantha's dad.

Charlie still had his arm in a sling and his ribs bound and there had been a minor power struggle with his parents who expected him to stay at home with them until he was fully fit again. After a week he had moved back into his apartment in Southampton 'to start doing light training' where his seemingly indefatigable girlfriend, Jenny, drove him around, cut up his food and generally looked after him as well as her job as a teacher in a junior school.

This Thursday Bruce and Sam were meeting Charlie and Jenny at the Tolbrite Arms. Samantha loved the place. That summer they used to park close to the bank in the pub's car park and sit and talk as the river flowed lazily past, or walk, hand in hand along the bank and feed the swans and ducks. It was natural that they continued to park in 'their' place on the bank as the nights drew in. They were already in the bar, nursing half a pint of lager each, when the other two arrived. For players in training, drink was always a problem, not drinking too much but how to drink very little and still be acceptable to the licencee. The four of them had worked it out, they would have a glass of lager or a dry sherry before dinner and a bottle of Chateau Bouchier white wine with their meal, of which the men would have only one glass each, and that would be that.

So it was this evening, they talked and laughed over their meal until just before half past nine when they moved back into the bar, Charlie and Jenny to sit for a while in the cosy atmosphere with a soft drink and Bruce and Samantha to say goodnight to Gloria and whoever else happened to be behind the bar, and then depart so that Samantha wouldn't be too late home. She didn't want her parents to worry and he didn't want to get on the wrong side of the manager.

They came out of the pub into the village street and went round the side of the building into the car park, past the large gates through which the brewer delivered the barrels and crates into the yard at the back and then down the side of the pub's garden in which they had sat and dreamed in the summer-time. There were several more cars; they noted that Charlie's was one of three in a loose row behind Bruce's, parked beside a large Nissan Navara with a double cab.

Bruce opened the door for Samantha and saw that she was properly seated before going round and getting in himself. He buckled on his seat belt, started the engine and switched on the car's side and headlights. He was telling Sam to put on her seat belt when there was the most tremendous impact from the back. They were both flung back and then forward as the car was pushed over the edge and into the river.

Young Will was in the yard. He had just carried a crate of empties from behind the bar and deposited it with the others when there was the roar of engines and the most tremendous crashing noise from the car park, followed by the mad revving of an engine and the scrunch of gravel being thrown aside by racing wheels. The big gates were locked against intruders. Will rejected the thought of climbing over them and raced through the pub along the passage between the usual offices and the kitchen, the dining room and the bar and out into the village street in time to see a large vehicle race out of the car-park and turn east. He couldn't read the number but it was one of those cars with four seats and a pick-up, covered in this car. He noticed it because he had toyed with the notion of suggesting to his employers that such a vehicle would be useful to have for jobs around the estate.

His first thought was that the person in the speeding car was a hit-and-run driver who had hit one or more of the customer's cars and was making off. He ran towards the river looking at the parked cars and then, to his horror, saw something white fluttering and realised that it was someone clinging to the roof of a car submerged in the river, a river that was swollen by recent rain storms and was no longer the lazy stream of the summer. Without a seconds hesitation Will slithered down the bank and waded, then swam, to the car. He recognised the clinging person as Bruce Somer's girlfriend and reached up to carry her to the bank, only to hear her scream at him,

"No, No, I'm alright, find Bruce, I got him half out of the window but couldn't hold him."

Will took a great gulp of air and ducked under the surface. The door through which Samantha had escaped had been shut by the force of the water and he entered his head and shoulders through the passenger door window opening. He couldn't see more than a hands breadth through the murky water but he groped as far as the driver's window, there was no one in the driver's seat and a quick grope told him that there was no one in the back. He surfaced and gulped in great lungfuls of air.

"He's not in the car," he panted.

"I got him out but I couldn't keep hold of him. Someone ran into us."

"Alright," shouted Will. "It won't take a minute to get you ashore, then I'll look for Bruce."

He prised Samantha loose from where she was clinging to the open car window opening and with some difficulty got her on to the bank.

"Wait there, I'll get some help."

"Don't go, look for Bruce!" she screamed.

"That's what I'm doing," said Will. "Getting some more people to look."

He left her and ran across the car-park and into the pub, a dripping figure, shouting,

"There's been an accident, I've brought Bruce's girl ashore but she says that he's been swept away by the flood. They were knocked into the river by one of those hefty car-pick up's. Phone for the police."

Charlie and Jenny led the rush from the bar. Gloria waited until her mother came to watch over the bar and followed. It was she and Jenny who half carried a white faced and shivering Samantha back into the pub.

Meanwhile Mrs Trowbridge had dialled 999 and asked for the police

"You'll want an ambulance," said Control.

"We might when the man swept away by the river is found," said Mrs Trowbridge "and in that case it won't be wanted here, but somewhere closer to where it joins the Stour."

Ten minutes later an ambulance arrived and ten minutes after that a police car driven by a policewoman in plain clothes.

Gloria looked up and said,

"Oh Clare, I'm so pleased that it's you, it's terrible, someone pushed Bruce's car into the river with him and Samantha in it and we can't find Bruce."

"Bruce Somers the footballer?"

"Yes," said Gloria.

"Is anyone looking?"

"Yes, Will and Charlie and Jenny and all the people who were in the bar but he'll have been swept a good way down the river by now."

"I'll get some more help," said Clare and phoned police HQ.

She came back and said, "They'll start at the bridge over the Spetisbury road."

Samantha, now dressed in clothes provided by Gloria, steadfastly refused to allow the ambulance men to take her to the hospital for a check-up and instead, urged them to do something useful and join the search for Bruce along the river bank.

She told Detective Sergeant Clare Thornton what had happened. They had just got into their car to go home when it was rammed from behind and pushed into the river. It had been deliberate, the other car hadn't hit them and stopped, it had pushed and pushed with its engine screaming until they were in the river. She had been saved by not yet having secured her seat belt. Bruce had secured his. He seemed to have been stunned by the initial impact and, she now realised, had made no effort to escape from the flooding car, she had undone his seat-belt and pushed him out of his car window as the car sank, then she'd opened her door and escaped. She had expected to get hold of Bruce again but the current had been worse than she expected and he'd been swept away.

Clare remembered the amount of space the media had given to the threatening letters that had been sent to the football club and asked Samantha once more,

"You're sure that it was deliberate?"

"Yes, it hit us then hit us again and pushed and pushed, Bruce pulled on the handbrake as well as standing on the brake pedal but it wasn't enough. It was deliberate."

Clare went outside and reported what she had heard to police HQ.

Word went out to all cars to watch for a saloon pick-up, similar to a Nissan Navara, with a damaged front-end and to detain the occupants.

Soon the police air-waves were busy with the news that someone had pushed Bruce Somers car into the river and he was missing. The press overheard this traffic.

Jenny reasoned that at times like this a girl needs her mother so she phoned the Hawkins number. Stella answered the phone,

"Mrs Hawkins, this is Jenny James, I'm a friend of Samantha. I was out with her and Bruce Somers tonight. She's fine but there was an accident and Bruce Somers has been lost in the river."

"Stop a minute, you say Samantha is OK but Bruce isn't?"

"Yes, someone pushed their car into the river."

Jenny could hear a man's voice in the background and Stella telling him to shush and that there had been an accident but Sam was alright.

"Yes, they went to get in Bruce's car to come home and another car pushed them into the river."

"Where is she now?"

"At the pub in Tolbrite west of Bournemouth. She refuses to leave while the police are searching the river for Bruce."

"Are the police there?"

"Of course, they're doing all that they can."

"That was silly of me, of course you are. Tell Sam that we'll come and fetch her."

There followed a hectic few minutes during which Sam Hawkins was told to get his coat, that Samantha had been in Bruce Somers car when someone had pushed it into the river, that Samantha was unhurt but that Bruce was missing in the river. By the end of this he was sitting beside his wife in the car, en route to the M27 Motorway. The next five minutes were filled with questions like what was she doing there and did you know and how long has this been going on and why wasn't I told?

Eventually the true import of what had happened struck the manager.

"It was the people who sent those letters."

"Yes dear," said Stella who had already worked that one out.

"Yes dear what?" asked Sam.

"The people who sent those letters and injured your reserve goalkeeper have now injured and perhaps killed your star mid-field player."

"I've got to tell the Chairman," said Sam, taking out his mobile phone. He paused and said "How do I explain what Sam was doing with him?"

"You tell him the truth, that they are both nice young people who enjoyed each other's company and that you didn't know until tonight."

"But you knew?"

"Oh yes, a nice girl like our Samantha has few secrets from her mother."

Sam patted her thigh, "She's lucky to have a Ma like you, luv."

"She's lucky to have us both, Sam."

Sam dialled the Chairman's number. When the other end answered he said,

"Chairman, it's Sam Hawkins here. I'm afraid that Bruce Somers has been involved in an accident and is missing in the river. I'm in the car on my way to where it happened. The police and emergency services are on the spot."

"Slow down Sam. You say that Bruce is in the river?"

"That's what we've been told. Our daughter was in the car with him. They'd been having dinner with Charlie Parham and his girl friend in the village pub and they were just leaving to come home when another car pushed them into the river. Samantha got out. That's all we know at present."

"I expect that he swam downstream with the current and will turn up in due course."

"I can only hope that you're right, Chairman. We think that it might be the people who sent those letters."

"Aw, no Sam, they wouldn't do a thing like that. Let's keep our fingers crossed, let me know how you get on in the morning. Goodnight."

Sam turned to his wife.

"He said that he didn't think that the blackmailers would do a thing like that."

"More fool him," said Stella. "I think that he's got a shock coming to him."

It took them nearly an hour to reach Tolbrite. They couldn't miss the pub, it's car park was lit-up by TV floodlights and there were two television lorries in the street outside. The car park itself contained two police cars, a police van and an ambulance in addition to one or two cars, one of which Sam recognised as Charlie Parham's. A cordoned-off area at the far end was the scene of police (and TV) interest and a vehicle recovery lorry stood nearby. The entrance to the Tolbrite Arms was open and people were going in and out.

Stella and Sam went in and turned to the left into the bar. Samantha saw them instantly and flung herself into her mother's arms, sobbing. Stella noticed over her daughter's shoulder, that both Gloria and Jenny looked relieved, they'd had much more than an hour of trying to comfort Samantha who had convinced herself that she was responsible

66

for Bruce's disappearance – perhaps she should have tried to get him out on her side. No amount of pointing out that she could never have dragged him over the centre console, past the gear lever and handbrake, would console her.

Sam walked down to the cordon where the roof of the car could be seen, level with the surface of the river and thought that surely an athletic fellow like Bruce Somers should have been able to get out of there, his Sam had, and she was on the side where the flow of the river would make it difficult to open the door. What was it that Sam had said, that Bruce had made no effort to unbuckle his seat-belt and she had done it for him and then shoved him half out of his open window. He must remember to ask her just how hard the other car had hit them.

Sergeant Clare Thornton came in and gave a small shake of her head at Gloria's enquiring glance. Stella and Sam were introduced to her and she said that there was no reason why Samantha shouldn't go home, the police and volunteers were combing every inch of the riverbank and she would undertake to tell Samantha the moment that they found anything. She didn't say alive or dead.

The police made two discoveries before dawn, the first was a Nissen Navara Double Cab with a badly damaged front, parked in a street behind Bournemouth station. The second was Bruce Somers body, caught in some tree roots about half a mile before the Spetisbury Bridge. The Nissen was removed to the police garage for forensic examination and the body was taken for examination by the pathologist, Dr Simon Watts, who happened to be Clare Thornton's fiancée.

The Nissen proved to have been stolen a week earlier in Edgeware and the odometer showed that it had been driven a hundred and thirty four miles, sufficient to get to Tolbrite and back to Bournemouth. It had clearly been kept in a garage, out of sight but sometimes people notice strange cars being driven out of lock-ups. The police view was that it would have been garaged in or close to London, which was probably true but of little help in the investigation, the Met would ask around anyway but everyone knew that they had more pressing cases on their hands.

The morning news programmes carried the news of Bruce Somers death, Samantha's rescue and the discovery of the Nissan Navara with a battered front. The media were quick to link the deliberate ramming of Bruce's car with the hit-and-run attack on Charlie Parham and with the threatening letters received by the club. Sam Hawkins and the Chairman were besieged by reporters asking what they intended to do to protect their players. Not only reporters, Sylvester Stakes informed the manager that he would remain at home until the club or the police sent an armed guard to accompany him wherever he went.

Later in the morning, the General Secretary of the Professional Footballer's Union phoned the Chairman to enquire what measures the club was taking to protect it's members who were on the club's books.

"Why are you ringing me?" demanded Herbert Jackson who was in no mood to humour callers.

"Well, it's your players that are being murdered, isn't it?"

"Then you'd better ring the police or the ministers of this bloody government that you're so pally with, hadn't you?"

"I could advise my members not to play for you."

"And I would sue you for every penny your union has. I suppose that Sylvester Stakes has been on to you ?"

"I understand that he has threatened to stay at home," answered the General Secretary, obliquely.

"The next time he rings, tell him that you understand that we have it in mind to play him in the reserves and release him on a free transfer. That should cheer him up, the fellow's a pain in the arse."

"Well, Herbert, I've done my bit and asked the question," said the official. "Personally, I'm sure that the police are doing all that they can and I'm sorry about Bruce, he was the sort of player who would only have brought credit to the game. I'll tell our members to take care but otherwise to carry on as usual."

Samantha was inconsolable, although she had known in her heart of hearts that her career would come first and that her affair with Bruce wasn't serious, she had liked him a lot.

In London, Luigi Coroneli was more angry than he could remember ever being before. He was surrounded by cretins, a legion of cretins, a whole choir of cretins, conducted by that idiot Salvatori. First he picks a soldier who is stupid enough to leave the bike, helmet and gauntlets to be found by the police instead of throwing them in the water – and there's lots of water round Southampton - and then he trusts the same cretin with the Somers job and the idiot goes over the top in a monumental way. When he'd agreed to 'leave it to' Salvatori, he hadn't expected the imbecile to kill the goose that was going to lay the golden eggs.

He spat at Maria "Tell Salvatori that I want to see him, now." Adding as an afterthought "Leonardo, too."

"Yes Mr Coroneli," said Maria, thinking, I wonder if it's anything to do with that footballer from Southampton who the radio news was on about? She went back to her desk and phoned Luigi's two top assistants.

Salvatori was scarcely in the room before Luigi shouted at him, in Italian,

"Are you totally brainless, can't you do anything right, who was it that killed that footballer?"

"Carlo Johnson, capo. I thought that you'd be pleased."

"Pleased?" Shouted Luigi "Pleased? One of your idiots destroys the entire operation and I'm supposed to be pleased?"

Leonardo entered the room and was waved to silence. Luigi repeated,

"One of his idiots wrecks the whole operation and he thinks I should be pleased."

"Aw, come on capo, it's not as bad as that, we've shown them that we mean business," tried Salvatori.

"What was meant to be a quiet shake-down for a few months is now exposed to the world," shouted Luigi. "Do you think that the police and the Football Association and, for that matter, their insurers and public opinion, will let the football club pay us any money now?"

"No, I suppose not," said Leonardo. "Why didn't the footballer get out, the girl did?"

"He did get out," pointed out Salvatori, clutching at straws, "how was Carlo to know that he couldn't swim?"

"What do we do now, capo?" asked Leonardo.

"We do nothing, I don't want to hear the word football ever mentioned again. It's Finito with a capital F. In future we'll stick with doing what we have always done well out of in the past."

Chapter Eight

ALFREDO CORLEONE heard the news of the murder of Bruce Somers with a certain amount of amazement, tinged with satisfaction. He was sorry about the footballer, because he had seemed to be a decent sort of young man as well as a good player and Alfredo liked his sports to be clean. He might earn his living by supplying drugs and catering to man's depravity in other ways but he believed that athletes who took performance enhancing drugs, like the East Germans, the Russians and the Chinese - and a few Americans – had, should be banned for life.

There was no doubt in his mind that the affair was associated with the blackmail letters that someone had sent to the football club and his amazement was that whoever was responsible had taken such a drastic measure to reinforce their threat so early in the game. Like Luigi, many miles to the north at that time, he considered that whoever had done it and invited the intense police and media interest,had blown the whole blackmail operation.

It was the latter aspect that gave him the quiet satisfaction. His 'family' honour would have been demeaned if someone else had devised a new slant on the process of extracting money illegally from the British public.

A successful capo must have an instinct for crime and, it must be admitted, for self-preservation. His instinct told him that somehow his erstwhile friend Luigi Coroneli was behind those letters and, presumably, behind the botched-up enforcement effort. His spies had told him that one of Luigi's soldiers had been asking around the football clubs, collecting information and that Luigi and his senior lieutenants had been discussing Southampton and Wolverhampton Wanderers. He accepted that chance and coincidence played a part in the lives of all great men – modesty was not one of his traits – but, knowing Luigi, he was sure that this was more than coincidence.

Alfredo reflected that in a way, they were now quits, Luigi had strayed in a way into his territory and had been stung. He, Alfredo, could sit on his hands and do nothing, for surely the police would make every effort to catch the murderer and, through him, the blackmailer, so Luigi's troubles were only just beginning.

But his lieutenants considered that Luigi had offended against the brotherhood's code and his lieutenants expected the brotherhood, in

70

this case himself, to take care of it's own. He would wait a few days but meanwhile his lieutenants could order the necessary hardware from the man in Catford who put together that sort of thing. He would stress that they must be incendiary, not simply explosive, he didn't want to hurt any of the girls or their clients.

In Bournemouth Dr Simon Watts the pathologist phoned Clare Thornton.

"Clare dear, it's Simon. I've a spot of news for you."

"What's that?"

"Bruce Somers didn't drown, he was dead before he got into the water. His neck was broken."

"The girl Samantha who was with him said that they were given a dreadful bump but I didn't imagine that it was enough do that," said Clare. "No wonder that she had such a job to get him half out of the window."

"Yes it must have been quite a struggle with the water pouring in," said Simon. "I thought that you'd want to know. See you tonight. Love you."

That evening, in her flat, there was only one topic of conversation. Clare told Simon that the most exhaustive examination of the Nissan Navara had produced several finger prints that proved to be those of the vehicle's legitimate owner and his wife. There was no human hair. There was, however, a half smoked cigarette in the ashtray. This had gone for DNA testing but as Clare pointed out to Simon, that would only be useful after they had caught their man. What they wanted was a finger print or two. He had remarked that, that too, would only be useful provided the villain had previous form.

Simon raised himself on one elbow and said,

"Have you thought of every thing that the villain may have touched?"

"It wouldn't matter what he touched if he wore gloves, would it?"

"No, I suppose not but what I had in mind was anything that he simply couldn't have made work with his gloves on."

"Such as?" said Clare.

He ran his finger down the valley between her breasts and said,

"This for example."

She giggled and said, "Keep your mind on the job, Sir."

"I was," said he.

"No, I mean on what he or she might have inadvertently touched in the car."

"Oh, I don't know, the side-light switch or the radio. Did it have a tape or a CD player?"

"I don't know, I expect so."

"Well, if it was me I don't think that I could have manipulated a CD out of its sleeve, even with surgical gloves on, could you?"

"I don't know, lover but he or she may not have touched one."

"Put yourself in the crooks place, I'll call him he because it's easier and probably 100% correct. He must have followed them from the other side of Southampton to the Tolbrite Arms. He probably put his head in and checked that they were having dinner and he knew that he'd got a wait of two or more hours. He goes back to his vehicle and sits there. He can't put the light on to read so he sits there in the dark, bored stiff. After a while he decides that he might as well listen to the car's radio and casually looks at the CD's in the locker. Perhaps one appeals to him, better than the radio, anyway, so he tries to take it out of it's sleeve and it won't come. So he takes off his glove, takes out the disc and drops or pushes it into the player. Nothing to worry about, thinks he, who would think of testing a CD disc for prints and anyway he only held it for a few seconds."

"You've nearly got me believing it," grinned Clare.

"So the music plays softly and he feels relaxed. What could be more natural than having a cigarette to keep awake. Are you still with me?"

"I'm way ahead of you, my sweet and I'll be sure to ask the forensic people to look at the car's entertainment system tomorrow."

There was a different atmosphere at the Tolbrite Arms that Saturday night. Helene could sense it the moment that she, Timmy and Claire-Marie walked into the bar after dinner at the Manor House. The other members of the Irregulars were already there, on both sides of the bar. There were many faces that they didn't recognise, hardly surprising when the pub had been featured on the TV news and in the press for the past three days and the chap who had gone into the angry river to rescue the girl was there, large as life, serving behind the bar.

Claire-Marie perched herself on the bar-stool that Fred vacated for her, and showed a lot of her legs. The strangers felt that this was an unexpected bonus, a murder in the car park was one thing and now there was a film star – a French film star – showing her legs in the public bar. The men decided that they would come here more often while their wives were deciding that once was enough.

Timmy asked if the police had made any progress in tracing the murderer. Paula answered,

"Not as far as we know. I haven't seen Clare Thornton, she's been too busy but I spoke with her on the phone and she said that the were following-up a couple of leads."

"What about the cases that you're investigating?" said Helene.

"Oh, it's the usual mix of sex, drugs and general cussedness."

"It's the same in France," chipped in Claire-Marie. "Of course, we do the sex bit better than you Anglo-Saxons."

"Well, your men have more practice," said Will.

Claire-Marie gave him a coquettish look with her big blue eyes and said, "Can you blame them?"

Helene decided that it would be better change the subject.

"Have you finished with the case of the girl who thinks that her mother is being taken in by a fortune teller?"

"Not by any means, it could be more serious than we first thought."

"Go on," said Claire-Marie, "tell us about it, Helene's dying to know."

"Well," said Paula, "the girl's mother had her fortune told in the booth on the pier."

"Ooh, Madame Destie," said Gloria, "she's ever so good, she told me that Will and I would be married one day. It was ever so spooky, she had a shawl over her hair and looked into a sort of glass ball."

Paula ignored the interruption.

"This Madame Destie asked her mother why she wanted to have her fortune told and she said that she wanted to know where the old woman had hidden her money. She was talking about our client's grandmother who was quite well off. It appears that the grandmother didn't trust banks and was known to secrete cash away."

"Under the mattress and under the carpet, I bet," said Gloria, idly polishing a glass.

"To make matters worse, the old lady died in hospital and her last words, or the last words they remember, were "My money's in the…"

"Go on," said Will.

"That's it. She didn't speak any more," said Paula, "only those four words, my money's in the…. The girl and her mother practically tore the old lady's house apart, looking for the money and they haven't dared to sell the place in case it's hidden somewhere they have missed, so what with the funeral expenses, they are considerably out of pocket. That's why the girl's mother consulted Madame Destie."

"She told the fortune teller all this?" asked Timmy.

"Yes," said Paula, "and a lot more."

"I bet that the fortune teller told her to come back tomorrow," grinned Helene.

"No, she didn't," said Paula, "she invited her to come to her studio in the evenings for a proper consultation. What annoyed her daughter, that's the dead woman's grand-daughter, is that this went on for a number of weeks and her mother didn't breathe a word to her of what she was up to until it was too late, which was when she, the grand-daughter that is, came to us."

"Too late?" queried Timmy.

"Yes, she'd parted with the money."

Gloria was conscious that a hush had descended on the bar, she looked at the clock and then at Angela, saying,

"I think that they'd like you to play for them, Angela."

Paula said in an aside to Timmy and Helene, "I'll continue the witches story next week."

At about an hour later than the time that Timmy and Helene arrived at the Tolbrite Arms, two men walked up the two steps and into the foyer of a house in Clarges Street in Mayfair. The muscular young man who's duty it was to preserve the decorum of the establishment by keeping rowdy and potentially damaging people out, saw no danger from these two, obviously they were from out of town bent on sampling the delights of the nation's capital and, perhaps, doing something that they wouldn't dare to do back home.

They were allowed through into a tastefully furnished salon and after a short discussion with a charming lady, were taken upstairs.

The same sequence of events was taking place at a house in Half Moon Street, where two smartly dressed, yet nondescript men also disappeared upstairs.

All four men had left the houses well before ten o'clock and repaired to a hostelry in Shepherds Market where they met for a drink after their labours and, naturally, to share something of their experiences. At half past, exactly, the oldest member of the group said that he had to make a phone call. He dialled the number, listened for a moment and said,

"No reply, we may as well go home."

"Can't we stay and watch the fun?" said the youngest.

"No, you know what the boss said, 'Get the hell out of the West End.' "

"He need never know."

"For all you know he might be outside himself, mightn't he? In fact I would expect him to be but you can expect him to make himself scarce the moment anything happens. Like now."

The sound of sirens came over the night air.

"Sounds like there's a fire somewhere," said the leader. "Come on, it's time we made ourselves scarce."

At the house in Clarges Street and that in Half-Moon Street, pandemonium reigned. In each house two beds had suddenly burst into flames. The occupants, in each case an attractive young woman and an older man, had leapt up and rushed into the passage screaming and shouting fire. The noise on two floors had brought the occupants of other rooms into the passage, usually the girl clad in a lingerie while their male customers stayed for the most part in the room scrambling into their clothes and wishing that they were anywhere other than where they actually were at that precise moment.

Those who did come into the passage beheld two naked girls and two naked men, scared out of their wits. The other girls hastily provided their friends with something to cover their nakedness and together they rushed screaming down the stairs and into the foyer. The two naked men were torn between going back to get their clothes, dodging into a girl's room on a lower floor and grabbing something to wear, or arriving in the foyer in their birthday suits. One went back and found the room an inferno, the fire beneath the bed had ignited the carpet and had already spread to the curtains and diverse articles of clothing – there was nothing to be saved and worn. Both arrived downstairs wearing only a bath towel.

The charming lady who greeted new arrivals had dialled 999 and the only-to-be-used-in-an-emergency number she had for the man who came to collect the money. The custodian had gone upstairs with fire extinguishers. Most of the girls went upstairs and hastily dressed and collected what they could, those who couldn't reach their rooms borrowing clothes from those who could. The men who managed this came down and disappeared out of the front door and into the night, sadder and wiser men, but the girls could muster nothing better than dressing gowns for the two naked men, dressing gowns that were too small and made the retention of the bath towels vital.

When the noise outside heralded the arrival of the London Fire Brigade, the firemen found the girls huddled in a foyer that was beginning to fill with smoke from the fire that had taken a firm hold on the upper storeys. They were all ushered out. The fireman in charge, who knew a thing or two about what went on in certain houses in Mayfair, asked them if there was anywhere that the girls could go.

"Yes," said Madame, "24b Half Moon Street."

The fireman said,

"I'm afraid that 24b Half Moon Street is also on fire."

The man who collected the money phoned Leonardo and told him that he'd had calls from both the Mayfair houses to say that they were on fire. Leonardo immediately realised that the fires must be deliberate, two accidental fires occurring at the same time in Coroneli's best properties stretched credibility. He said,

"Get down there and take care of the girls."

"Where shall I take them?" asked the man.

"I don't know, take them to hotels and explain what's happened. Give the girls enough money to live on and to buy some outdoor clothes tomorrow and arrange a place where we can all get together sometime tomorrow. Meanwhile we'll find new properties to set them up in business again."

"I don't think that I can lay my hands on that sort of money at this time of night, boss."

"You get down to the houses and I'll meet you there within the next hour with the cash. Can you call the receptionists on their mobiles?"

"Yes, they're all in the street."

"Well get on to them and tell them what we've arranged."

Leonardo phoned one of Luigi's mobile numbers.

Luigi replied after about four rings. He sounded breathless. Leonardo told him the bad news and what he had done. He had to have some cash for the girls, now.

"I'll meet you at the office in a quarter of an hour," said Luigi.

Ahem, thought Leonardo, he's there already, well, not exactly in the office, more probably in Maria's bed.

When Leonardo got there Luigi was fully dressed and Maria was in her dressing gown. Like a good secretary who had just been roused from her beauty sleep.

"I've been thinking," said Luigi as he produced bundles of notes from the safe, "this is arson."

"Yes capo, most certainly arson."

"Who do you think it can be, those Russians or the Albanians?"

"I don't see why they would do this, there's plenty of trade for all of us," said Leonardo. "I think that it's someone with a grudge."

"Who do we know who could have a grudge and is clever enough to set two fires?"

"At the same time," added Leonardo.

"Well, who?" demanded Luigi.

"I can only suggest one name who might think that we've offended him and that's Alfredo Corleone."

"My thought exactly," said the capo. "Off you go to do what you can and we'll get together in the morning."

Leonardo met the man who collected the money and gave him the large sum of money to get the girls housed and dressed.

The London Fire Brigade had already decided that the two fires were arson. In their experience it was not unknown for the arsonist to return to the scene of the fire to view and perhaps gloat over the results of their crime. For this reason they and the police kept an unobtrusive watch around suspect incidents and photographed the people who lingered. Thus it was that, unknowingly, Leonardo was photographed by an infra-red camera, giving a wad of money to another man. Both the man and Leonardo were followed to their homes that night.

Chapter Nine

ALFREDO CORLEONE was elated, it had gone absolutely according to plan. How he wished that he could have been there and seen it. It had been too late for the morning papers but he guessed that the morning TV and the mid-day editions would make a lot of it. They did; fires starting simultaneously in two bedrooms in each of two houses, houses, they hinted, occupied by several attractive girls who worked mainly at night, was enough to sharpen the interest of even jaded reporters and to make the national headlines.

The fires had been brought under control before midnight and the residents of the adjoining houses allowed to return to their smoky abodes. As soon as there was sufficient light the next morning the arson teams began a meticulous examination of the premises. They knew from the girl's statements that in each case the fires had started under their beds and they started their search in what was left of those rooms and the rooms below.

In Scotland Yard, Assistant Commissioner David Vowles, formerly the head of the Special Branch and now the head of the Anti-terrorist Branch, phoned his assistant, Detective Inspector Tom Burton, said that he was sorry to disturb him so early on a Sunday and asked him to come to the office. When he arrived, he said,

"Tom, did you see those Mayfair fires on the TV?"

"Yes Gov, someone had it in for somebody, didn't they?"

Vowles decided to ignore the inspector's unintentional double entendre

"There's an off-chance that it could be our lot."

"Terrorists Gov, you're joking? The al-Qeada frown on Western decadence."

"All the more reason for setting fire to it, then," said his chief.

"Do we know how the fires were started?"

"It says here," he waved a message slip, "that the girls said last night that the fires started under their bed."

Tom decided that now was not the time for jokes about some girls being hot stuff in bed and said,

"Then someone must have put the device there and he must have been a customer and I don't think that the Islam fundamentalists do that sort of thing here on earth, that's why they are so keen to get to Paradise," said Tom.

For his part, the Assistant Commissioner decided not to pursue the metaphysics of terrorism and said,

"I understand that the experts have found the remains of electronic things at the site of each fire."

"That's a start, Sir, there might be a lead to who assembled them although the work is more difficult these days, the insides of radios, mobile phones, iPods, computers and the like, all have the bits that could be assembled to trigger an explosion or a fire."

"Yes, I suppose that they do. Anyway, the arson experts think that they know how the deed was done. I want you to go and see them and also interview the people who were in the houses when the fire started."

"The girls, you mean?"

"Any men who were daft enough to give their names," grinned Vowles, "and the girls. I won't tell Kim."

Kim was Inspector Tom Burton's partner, to be precise Sergeant Kim Bourne of the Army's Corps of Military Police, currently serving in the Ministry of Defence's Special Investigations Unit.

Tom decided that the walk would do him good and set off across St James's Park and Green Park to Piccadilly and to the house in Half-Moon Street and then to Clarges Street. At each house he listened to what the firefighters had to say about the origin and nature of the fires, asked them if they knew where the residents had spent the night and thanked them for their help. He then took a cab to the laboratory where the arson investigators were examining the material they had collected at the fires. Tom said,

"I know that you're still collecting the evidence but is there any hint as to how the fires were started?"

The scientist smiled at a recollection, and said,

"Each of the young ladies said that there was a small pop sound and smoke and flames shot out from under the bed, so they ran out of the room."

"Clearly someone put something there," said Tom. "My job is to find out who and the nature of the device might give us a lead on that."

"There is no trace of any clockwork mechanism," said the scientist "That and the fact that, as far as we have been able to establish, all four fires started at the same instant, would indicate that they were triggered by radio, probably by means of a mobile phone call."

"Did you ask the girls who their previous, er, visitors were?"

"No, my job's the how, the who and the why are your department, Inspector."

Tom made his way to the address of the first small hotel in which some of the girls had spent the night. He found that the Clarges Street girls were staying there and that the Half-Moon Street girls were in a similar hotel just round the corner. At the first place the receptionist said that they were all still in bed and that she had instructions that they were not to be disturbed. She had been instructed by Ms Redfern, who was also staying there and who looked after them, to refer all callers to her. The receptionist lowered her voice.

"That man over there," she indicated a young man who was sitting on one of the few chairs in they foyer, "is also waiting for Ms Redfern."

Tom looked across at the youngish man who chose that moment to fold the newspaper that he was reading, get up and walk out of the hotel.

"Well," said the receptionist, "he's been here ever since I came on duty."

"Never mind," said Tom. "I think that, fire or no fire, Ms Redfern has had long enough, please ring her room and say that the police would like to speak with her."

"Oh, I don't know if I should, she left strict instructions...."

"Tell her that either she speaks with me, now, or I have them all round at the nick. The choice is hers. Give her ten minutes to come down or I'll be going up."

The receptionist grinned at him, said "Better you than me," and dialled a number on the internal phone. Tom heard her explaining that the police would like her to come down. Ten minutes was mentioned.

It was a good quarter of an hour before a slender woman with black hair and what he would call a sunburned complexion, came down the stairs, came up to Tom and said

"I'm Sylvia Redfern, I understand that you wish to question me. You are?"

"Detective Inspector Tom Burton from Scotland Yard." Waving his identity badge.

"What do you want to know? I told them all that I knew last night."

"I want statements from the two young ladies in who's rooms the fires occurred."

"They know nothing about it. One minute they're, er, well, one minute they're resting on their bed and the next minute it's on fire."

"What are their names?" asked Tom

The woman thought about that for a moment and said,

"Greta Johansson and Beulah Morris."

Tom turned to the receptionist, who was an interested spectator, and said, "Please ring the rooms occupied by the Misses Johansson and Morris and tell them that the police are here and that they are to come down into the lobby, now."

He turned to the indignant Ms Redfern and said, "I've no objection to you being present."

"I should hope not."

They moved into the salon.

In a short while a noise from the stairs heralded the arrival of Greta Johansson. Tom thought that she looked ravishing, even in the clothes that her friends had provided. A tall willowy blonde with a flawless complexion and remarkably blue eyes, who smiled at him in a totally unaffected way and said in an attractive accent,

"You wish to ask me some questions, no?"

"Yes," said Tom. "About what happened last night."

She started to grin.

At that moment Beulah Morris came down the stairs, a dusky beauty with laughing eyes and a generous mouth. Greta said,

"This nice policeman wants to ask us some questions about what happened last night."

Beulah grinned at her and said,

"About us rushing about with no clothes on?"

"I suppose so, he looks human, doesn't he?" said Greta in that accent.

Tom decided that, diverting though the thought of these two beauties rushing about with no clothes on might be, he'd better endeavour to do what he'd come for. He said as much,

"Look girls, if you don't look out, I'll do a Hercule Poirot and make you stage a dramatic reconstruction." He paused and they grinned at him. He got the impression that they wouldn't mind if he did. He went on, "The fires were obviously part of a well planned operation and the devices must have been put under each of your beds by someone who came to your room. I want each of you to describe everyone who came into your room during the day and who might have had the opportunity to put something under the bed."

Ms Redfern said, "that's none of your business."

"Don't be silly, Sylvia, of course it's the police's business," said Greta.

"Well, don't mention clients names."

"We don't usually know their names," pointed out Beulah, "and you only know those who pay by cheque or credit card."

"Most men pay cash," said the downright Greta.

Tom said, "You first Greta, what did you do yesterday?"

"I got up at ten o'clock and did my exercises. Then I had a shower and breakfast. Sally came to tidy up my room and then I read for a while. In the afternoon I went out and got back about five. I went out for a meal with one of the other girls and we were back by half past six."

Tom interrupted her and turned to Ms Redfern,

"Who went into Greta's room when she was out?"

"No one."

"Could one of the other girls have done so?"

Ms Redfern looked startled, then annoyed,

"Of course they could but they wouldn't, the suggestion's ridiculous."

"I didn't suggest anything, I simply asked, in a roundabout way, if Greta and Beulah's doors were locked."

Ms Redfern snorted. Tom turned back to the blonde Swede.

"Now please talk me through your evening up to the fire, Greta."

Greta was entirely unabashed at being asked to describe the way she earned her living. She had come to London to earn sufficient money in the shortest possible time in order to put herself through university in Sweden and achieve her ambition to become a lawyer.

"My first client arrived at seven. He asked for me. He is a regular and calls in on the way home from his office in the City. He's lonely, sometimes he just sits and talks with me. He would like to be married but is frightened that it might end in divorce like his parent's marriage did. He said that his mother was always shouting and crying. I don't know where he will go now."

"About last night," prompted Tom.

"Oh yes," she made a small gesture, dismissing the banker's troubles. "Last night was not a talking night. He put his briefcase on the chair and I saw him take it away afterwards." She added, "He sometimes gives me Stock Exchange tips."

"You never told me that," snapped Ms Redfern. Greta ignored her.

"I washed and freshened myself and the next client arrived before eight. He was young and wasn't carrying anything and he put his top-coat on the chair. He was a quickie, I think that it was his first time. He was gone by eight fifteen."

Tom noticed out of the corner of his eye that Ms Redfern had glanced at the hotel entrance. He turned and saw that the man who had been there before was lounging in the foyer. He judged that he was out of earshot and said to Greta, "Please continue."

She gave him an old-fashioned look and grinned.

"My next client arrived at a quarter to nine. He was tall, well built and, I would say, had some Italian ancestors. He fancied himself, he was a dominator and tried it on a bit but I don't permit any of that sort of thing. He left before half past. I noticed it because he kept looking at his watch, a big fancy looking watch."

"Did he leave anything behind?" asked Tom.

She started to grin and Tom hastily said, "did he bring a briefcase or package?"

"No."

"Did he do anything unusual?"

"Well, as I said he tried to do something kinky and I...

"No,"interrupted Tom, "I mean, how can I put it, well, out of bed?"

She thought about that. "One funny thing, though, he dropped his top-coat down beside the bed. I didn't think anything of it at the time because some of the clients are practically undressing as they come through the door."

Tom thought about that and asked,

"Did he touch it at all while he was on the bed?"

"No."

"I know that this sounds silly, but was he ever alone in your room?"

"Only for a moment when I got him a glass of water." She put her hand up to her mouth and said, "Oh no."

"Mine did the same," said Beulah, "dropped his coat beside the bed and then asked for a glass of water."

"Which required you to go into your bathroom," said Tom. "That's probably when the switch was made."

"That was my last client before the poor man who lost his clothes," said Greta.

"Mine too," said Beulah, "and nobody is going to willingly burn up his clothes and things, is he?"

"No," said Tom. "I think that we can safely leave them out of it. I'd like you to think hard about the man who came to you just before nine o'clock last night. What did he look like, how tall he was, was he fat, did he have whiskers, was his hair curly, what were his clothes like, did he wear jewellery? That sort of thing, nothing is too small to help us. We might ask you to come to the police station to make an identikit picture."

"That's a good idea," said Sylvia Redfern, realising that the people who owned the houses might also welcome such a picture.

Tom turned to her and said,

"You know the lady who occupies your position in the house in Half-Moon Street. I'm going there now to ask her and her girls the same questions that I've asked you. Will you please phone her and tell her that I'm coming and that I'm seeking descriptions of the two men who, at about nine o'clock last night, came to the rooms that were subsequently burnt."

He turned to Greta and Beulah and said,

"Afterwards I shall come back here and collect what you have both remembered about the two fire raisers, Ms Redfern's recollections, too."

They promised to do their best.

His experience at the other hotel was similar. Here too, there was a man hanging about in the reception area. Tom thought about that. He was certain that some of the girls would have photographs of themselves in their handbag. He'd like to borrow one or two for a couple of days. He accepted photo's from the two girls whose rooms had been burnt, each had apparently rescued her bag. On the way out he thrust a shiny picture at the loitering man and said,

"Good looking, aren't they?"

The man instinctively took the photo, looked at it, grinned at Tom and said,

"Yes."

Tom took the photo back and walked out of the hotel, taking care not to touch it more than was absolutely necessary. When he was round the corner he slipped it into a plastic envelope.

He repeated the procedure when he arrived back at the first hotel, presenting the second photograph to the second man. Greta and Beulah came down into the salon and told him all that they could remember about their nine o'clock visitors.

Tom thanked them and took the four descriptions and the two postcards with the watcher's fingerprints back to the Yard. Cars would collect the four girls that afternoon to take them to the police station to have a shot at preparing identikit pictures of the suspects.

Chapter Ten

TOM BURTON reported to David Vowles in the early evening. He laid the four identikit pictures on the Assistant Commissioner's desk and said,

"It's not a terrorist effort. These are the four men who got into the girl's rooms and, we think, left incendiary devices under their beds. The experts say that they were probably set off by radio, possibly by a call from a mobile phone. They're working on that."

David Vowles picked up the pictures one by one and said,

"Have we got any idea who they are?"

"They might have a connection with Italy. One girl said that her visitor was sunburnt colour like an Italian and the other, Beulah, who comes from Jamaica, said that her visitor said that he had always wanted to have a black girl because his grandfather had said how willing the girls in Abyssinia were. That's Ethiopia today."

"Yes I know. Mussolini invaded the place in the 1930's. His grandfather couldn't have been very old at the time. So it could be the mafia. "

"It looks very much like mafia versus mafia, Sir. I got the prints of the two men who were hanging around the hotels where the girl's are staying and they've got form. But it's better than that. Last night the fire brigade spotted a man dishing out wads of money to another man who then gave it to the two Madams, presumably to look after their girls. Our people followed the man who brought the money to his home and it turns out that it was Leonardo Bianci who is Luigi Coroneli's right hand man."

"So someone is trying to muscle-in on Luigi. It's about time, he's got his tentacles into a lot of filthy crime."

"And we can now tie the men who's dabs I got, and their associates, to the Coroneli family and try to lay some of the blame on Mr Big for a change," said Tom.

"Who do you think is trying to muscle-in, the South Thames lot?" asked Vowles.

"That's my guess, they're the only family big enough to try."

"Some of my colleagues would say let them get on with it, if crook kills crook who are we to care, but in the long run that's the way to lose control of events. What do you suggest that we do now?"

"I agree with your colleagues, Sir," said Tom and added hastily, "But only up to a point."

"And what's that point?" smiled Vowles who had chosen Tom Burton to be his assistant because they thought alike.

"Let them bring each other out into the open, then we hit them. Probably help us solve half the crimes in London."

"So what do we do, Tom?"

"Give these pictures to the media, Sir."

Thus it was that the following morning neither Alfredo Corleone nor Luigi Coroneli was a happy man.

Alfredo had been basking in the recollection of a job well done. In the light of his success in putting two of Luigi's houses out of business, he had instructed his consigliere to make a move to replace the Coroneli family in the drug and protection business north of the Thames and, unusually for him, he had interfered in his subordinate's conduct of the day to day business; he had suggested that the 'boys' who had done such a good (and enjoyable) job the night before should be used, 'to get them used to working in the West End.'

Then this morning he had opened his newspaper and found their features looking out at him under a banner headline that asked 'Do you know these men?'

He read the text. Following the bald statement that the police wished to question the men in connection with the mysterious fires that had gutted two rooming houses in Mayfair two nights ago, the writer had mentioned that the rooms were occupied by attractive young ladies and as good as accused the men of attempting to injure, if not kill, these innocent females by starting the fires.

And he had dispatched them to operate in the Piccadilly area.

To say that Luigi Coroneli was upset would be a great understatement. First there had been the football fiasco. How was he to know that the fools would kill the player and wreck everything? He was beginning to think that his Underboss, Salvatori, should be retired. Perhaps he ought to go back to Sicily. In a casket. As regards the fires, he was shattered, perhaps more by the realisation that someone should dare to do this to him, than by the financial loss entailed, although that would be considerable. Somebody would be made to pay.

He'd had great difficulty in getting insurance cover for the houses, no one offers cover for brothels. So with a great deal of nudging and winking, they had been insured as hotels, at considerable cost. But there was bound to be an argument in the present circumstances that the policies didn't cover deliberate acts of arson.

Luigi was not pleased and the only person on whom he could vent his bad temper was the unfortunate Maria. Nothing that she did was right, she fetched and carried, she typed and she took phone calls but nothing, it seemed, would please her boss. She did her best to keep out of his room but he kept shouting for her to complain about something. She knew what the burnt properties were used for and was half inclined to envy the girls who lived and worked, if that was the right word, there. She felt that she was little better than they were, after all, she wasn't married to the man who she didn't love and who demanded sex with her two or more times a week.

He had to raise the funds to buy some new properties for use while the old ones were repaired. He'd decide later what to do with those, to sell them or to re-furnish them and put them back into what he called the male entertainment business. He'd have to use some of his property as surety for the new loans. He opened the big safe for which only he knew the combination and spread his portfolio of property deeds on a side table. He took up the deeds for the house in Half-Moon Street and carried them to his desk. After a while he shouted for Maria and when she was standing before his desk, said,

"Where are the deeds for the house in Clarges Street?"

"With all the others, I suppose, Mr Coroneli."

"I couldn't see them."

"Well, no one else can get into the safe, so they must be, unless you've put them somewhere."

"Don't be stupid, why should I do that? You have a look for me."

He must really be upset, thought Maria, to let me see the deeds, so she went over to the side table and sorted through the pile of deeds, one by one, with her back to him. She knew most of them, from time to time she had typed correspondence about them, they were all occupied or let to ostensibly legitimate businesses and generated a fair income. She came to a set that she hadn't seen before. She knew better than to comment on the fact. They were for a garage in Welbeck Mews Lane, wherever that was. She put them on the pile and soon found the deeds for the property in Clarges Street. She turned and placed them on his desk, saying,

"Here they are."

"I knew they must be there somewhere," he grunted. Then he looked up and said,

"Haven't you got any work to do?"

Maria left the room. One day she'd have a look at the garage in Welbeck Mews Lane.

Meanwhile Leonardo was looking after the girls and looking for suitable houses to rent or buy. Sylvia Redfern had kept him informed about the police activities and it was she who had reported what the girls had told the police and she, too, had got hold of copies of the photofit pictures that had appeared in that morning's papers.

Sometime after she had gone back to her desk, Leonardo Bianci phoned and asked to speak with the boss.

"Capo, you've seen those pictures in the paper, haven't you? Well, several of our people say that they recognise them, they're part of the Corleone mob."

"The bastard," said Luigi, "this means war. Tell your people to look out for any of the South London mob in our territory and if they see one, to make sure that he won't come back. Come and see me when you're free."

This wasn't to be the end of the shocks for Luigi that morning.

The receptionist at the Four Oaks Club in Mayfair rose at her desk and said "Excuse me," as four men entered the club and walked past her. She was torn between ringing the director's secretary to warn her that interlopers were approaching, or chasing the quartet. She opted for the latter and hurried round the desk and repeated her cry, "Excuse me," only louder.

She might as well have saved her breath for all the effect it had.

She thought that they looked familiar, she'd seen those faces somewhere. Recently, too.

What should she do? The proprietors prided themselves on the unruffled atmosphere of the club where nothing was allowed to disturb the members and their willingness to pay for the privilege. But this was different, it was morning, she hadn't seen any members come in. If he had been in, she would have asked Mr Francis.

The club was owned and run by two brothers, both of whom had been born in Naples. They were quite unlike each other, Guiseppi Maranti the round, fat and very Italian one, was the worrier. It was he who ran the restaurant, ordered the food and wine, charmed the clientele, engaged the staff and worried about profitability. The other brother had been born Francesco Maranti but had changed his name to Francis Martin. He was married with two children who went to good schools, lived in the Home Counties and effected to be an English gentleman. He looked after the gaming room and what went on upstairs. He was seldom at the club much before lunch time.

The four men walked into Guiseppi's secretary's room and straight through into the partner's room with the secretary and the receptionist following, protesting. One of the men turned round, placed the palm of his hand over the secretary's face and pushed her, and the receptionist, back out of the room and closed the communicating door. The girls huddled the other side of the door and wondered what to do.

"What is the meaning of this?" stuttered Guiseppi

"We're your new insurers," said the man who seemed to be the oldest of the group.

"We've got all the insurance that we can afford," said Guiseppi, pressing the alarm button under his desk.

"You don't seem to understand what we're talking about, we will prevent any nasty person damaging your club, like this, for example," with which he picked up a chair and slammed it down, crippling the two back legs. The girls heard the sound of breaking.

"But we already pay for that sort of insurance and we can't afford any more," whined Guiseppi.

"That's just the point," said the man. "You don't pay them any more, you pay us."

"Mr Leonardo isn't going to like that."

"He's not going to have any choice, is he old man, or would you like us to wreck your restaurant next?"

"I only said that he wouldn't like it. It's no skin off my nose who we pay for protection, why don't you have the thing out with them?"

"Come on men," said their leader, "let's show this fool that we mean business."

"No, no," screamed Guiseppi, "alright, we'll pay you in future."

"What shall we do boys? Lets break up a few more chairs."

There was the noise of breaking.

The receptionist said, "I've heard enough and I've just remembered where I saw those men before, their picture's in today's paper, something to do with those fires, I'm going to call the police"

She went back to her desk and did what she'd always wanted to do ever since she was a small girl – she rang 999. When asked which service she required she said, "Police" and soon she was explaining that the men who the police wanted in connection with the Mayfair fires were now wrecking the Four Oaks Club in Jermyn Street.

The first police car was there in three minutes. The receptionist pointed towards the back and the officers hurried past to where the frightened secretary pointed mutely at the door. They burst in. One of the men was in process of smashing a standard lamp across Guiseppi's desk. All four turned and stared at the police.

"What's going on here?"

The man who had done the talking, recovered first.

"Nothing, officer, we were just showing this gentleman the poor quality of his furniture that we intend to replace." He turned to Guiseppi. "Weren't we Sir?"

"Er, yes," said a startled Guiseppi who could see that this development could result in these dreadful creatures coming back later to really turn the place over.

"You don't sound very sure of yourself. Do you wish to make a complaint?"

"Er, no," said Guiseppi, "it's as he said, just a demonstration."

At that moment the two officers from a second patrol car arrived. The first police officer, who knew full well what was going on, said,

"Very well then Sir, you don't wish to press additional charges."

The crooks began to smile in a self-satisfied way, only to find that the policemen had grouped around them and the first officer was saying,

"We are taking you into custody on suspicion that you were responsible for causing the fires at premises in Half-Moon Street and Clarges Street, two nights ago."

The startled crooks were handcuffed and led out of the building, where they were snapped by a free-lance photographer who made it his business to follow police cars.

When he had stopped shaking and could think coherently, Guiseppi had his secretary get him the man to whom he paid the protection money and told him what had happened. He even summoned up the courage to complain that the man had failed to provide that protection.

The money-collector phoned Leonardo and Leonardo phoned Luigi. That completed Luigi's unhappy morning. The bright spark was that four of the Corleone mob had been arrested but even here Luigi's satisfaction was tinged with regret, he would have preferred his soldiers to have despatched them for good.

In Bournemouth Clare Thornton had asked the forensic experts to look at the CD player that was installed in the Nissan Navara and they had found a partial finger print on the playing side and a partial thumb print on the reverse side of a CD that had been inserted back in its sleeve and put back in the storage space provided. Prints that weren't the owner's.

The prints were forwarded to Central Criminal Records and identified as those of a minor crook called Carlo Johnson who had a previous conviction for living off immoral earnings and two for assault and was thought to have connections with the mafia.

Word went out that he was to be brought in for questioning.

He was arrested by the Metropolitan police three days later and taken to Bournemouth where he was processed and his DNA taken. It was identical with that found on the cigarette and human hair found in the Navara. It was also the same as that of the hair found in the helmet recovered from Southampton railway station. The next day Carlo Johnson was formally charged with causing the death of Bruce Somers and injuring Charles Parham.

He stoutly denied the offence, claiming never to have been in the vehicle and that the CD was one that he had lost and which the owners must have found somewhere. He was asked if they had also followed him around and picked up his discarded cigarette ends?

Clare recited all of this to her friend Paula Simms when she called in at the Southern Enquiries office for coffee on the Wednesday morning. She rather liked coming to the radio station complex where something always seemed to be happening. Furthermore there was a place to park her car. The two girls were firm friends and exchanged information on enquiries in which they were engaged, a process that had benefited both the police force and the private-eyes without infringing any honest person's privacy.

"The trouble that we have," said Clare, "is that so far we can't see any logical reason why he did what he did. Admittedly there were those threatening letters sent to the football clubs but that shouldn't have led to murder."

"Perhaps that's because we're too close to it," said Paula diplomatically.

"What do you mean?"

"Perhaps it wasn't meant to be as serious as it was," said Paula.

"You mean that it went wrong?"

"Yes, my thought is that he was sent to put the wind-up the football club by banging into their star player's car, you know the sort of thing, we've done this, next time it could be for real."

"And the problem is that it was for real," said Clare. "What we have to do is to find out who is behind it. We're sure that Carlo what's-his-name didn't think the idea up on his own. We think that it's the mafia."

"Then you haven't got much hope of getting him to tell you, have you?" said Paula. "What about the London end?"

"There have been some interesting developments there. You saw that the Met had arrested the four men that they wanted for setting fire to those two Mayfair brothels, didn't you?"

"Could hardly help it from all the coverage that the media gave it," said Paula.

"Well, they've got a positive lead that they are part of the mafia family that operates south of the river. The Met also believe that the mafia north of the river ran the two brothels and so it looks as if we have a case of mafia families falling out, on our hands."

"Does the chap who you have under arrest come from the north or south?"

"The last address that the Met have for him is in Cricklewood and it's unlikely that a south London mafia soldier would, as it were, live in alien territory, isn't it?"

"So we have a mafia soldier from north of the river arrested for a murder that happened when enforcing a blackmailing action south of the river," said Paula. "I wonder if that has any significance?"

"You mean that he was operating in the other lot's territory?"

"Yes, and shortly afterwards we have four mafia suspects from south of the river setting fire to two houses run by the mafia from north of the river. I don't know much about the mafia but they had some bloody shoot-outs in New York when one mob moved in to operate in another mob's territory.. Who's handling it in the Met, anyone we know?"

"Yes, Tom Burton and Don Donovan," said Clare. "Tom because at first it was thought that terrorists might have started those fires, so Tom was the first one in and when they arrested those four suspects and

Scotland Yard realised that it was probably a mafia thing, Don took over."

"I don't think that I've met Don Donovan," said Paula.

"He's nice," said Clare, "he helped us with those two murders in the summer."

"The gambler in the boat and the croupier in the river?" said Paula.

"Yes, and then the man who they were seeking was killed by a lorry outside his house," said Clare. "It came out that he was married to the daughter of the man who the Met think is the boss of the north London mafia."

"It looks as if all roads lead to Rome," commented Paula, "or perhaps, to be more accurate, to Sicily."

"How are you getting on with the planning thing?"

"Not very far, I'm afraid, there certainly appears to be something peculiar about the way they work but it's difficult to move without showing our hand and if we did that the whole scam would probably disappear for ever," said Paula, and added, "Or until they thought that we'd lost interest."

"What have you got to date?"

"Well, the decisions of the council's Planning Committee are put in the local paper, so I went to the Council offices and said that I was from the university doing a bit of research on local government and the employment opportunities that arise in local industry from it's decisions, in schools for example and particularly in the building trades and that I'd like to see the sort of things that people seek planning permission for."

"Were they helpful?"

"Yes, the front office people couldn't have been more helpful, they produced volumes of decisions. I spent two days there, not looking at the detail but simply going through the decisions. There were a few large projects but most of the applications were for building or extending individual houses, adding garages, building or knocking down walls and the like. The most compelling evidence that something odd is going on is the thing that brought our client to us and that's the very randomness of the planning decisions."

"They always have been," said Clare.

"That might be so," said Paula, "but I think that it goes deeper than that."

"How so?"

"Well, a proposal for a garage in a suburban street A might be approved and separate proposals for identical garages in adjacent streets B and C refused. House X wants to knock down their front wall and pave their front garden for parking. Not approved but House Y in the same street is given the go-ahead. These aren't isolated cases, there have been literally dozens of them during the past eighteen months."

"Is there any common factor?" asked Clare.

"That's where it gets interesting," said Paula, "and I'm still trying to get the information that I want out of the Planning Office without revealing the true purpose of my enquiries."

"You really can be the most annoying person, Paula. What sort of information?"

"Who made the decisions," said Paula.

"I thought that the Planning Committee made the decisions," said Clare.

"So do most people but that could be far from the case."

"In what way?"

"I'm still trying to find out what happens in Bournemouth but I know from Gloria's friend, Liz Mitchell, what happens in Bath and it could be the same here. In Bath they have a thing called Delegated Approval under which the decision to approve or not to approve a proposal is made by a council planning representative who prepares the Delegated Report."

"Doesn't it go to the Planning Committee," asked Clare.

"No."

"I thought that they were there to protect the ratepayer's interests."

"In theory, yes but most of them are there on an ego-trip," said Paula, "and nowadays being a councillor is a well paid job."

"You're joking, I thought that they stood for the council out of public spiritedness, not financial reward."

"Well, according to Gloria, payments to the councillors in the Bath area cost the ratepayers nearly a million pounds last year."

"I wonder if it's the same here in Bournemouth?" said Clare. "But, getting back to this planning thing, surely it was ratified by the representative's superiors?"

"That is questionable," said Paula. "Liz Mitchell knows of at least one case in which a young planning officer broke all the department's rules in rejecting a proposal for a garage in a cul de sac."

"And you think that a similar thing might be going on in Bournemouth?"

"That's what I'm trying to find out. Remember the department makes dozens, perhaps hundreds, of good sensible decisions every year. I'm just looking into a set that seem to be odd But that's enough about planning, we've had another enquiry that might interest you, a daughter who thinks that the fortune teller on the pier is trying to get money out of her mother."

"I thought that was what fortune tellers did to everyone," said Clare, grinning.

"I know but in this case it's not just the price of admission, it seems that Madame Destie is after more than that."

"In what way?"

"The mother was deeply upset when her mother, her daughter's grandmother, died and she decided to consult a fortune teller in the hope of being able to communicate with the old woman. She went to Madame Destie on the pier and the fortune teller claimed to be a medium and persuaded her to attend séances. She convinced her that she, that is Madame Destie, was receiving messages from the other side that her mother needed some money to get past Saint Peter. So she gave Madame Destie £500 and asked her, while she was about it, to ask the old lady where she had put her money."

"I don't believe it," said Clare, "the mother must be mad."

"Fred thinks that Madame Destie might be sailing close to the wind but since any right minded person knows that all this fortune telling business is a load of codswallop and she didn't force the mother to hand over the money, she probably would get away with it."

"I'm afraid that's so. She'd be warned to be careful in future. What do you intend to do?" asked Clare.

"I thought that I might become a rich young widow and have my fortune read."

"I will await the next instalment with considerable interest," laughed Clare.

She left soon afterwards.

Chapter Eleven

DETECTIVE Inspector Don Donovan observed to his sergeant and friend, Sidney Tyler, that in this detecting business it never rains but it pours. Here they were quietly looking into the circumstances of the death of Luigi Coroneli's son-in-law's, in their own time and then two houses that they were sure that he owned, went up in flames. Scotland Yard had long suspected that Luigi was the capo of the north London mafia family with a finger in most forms of vice. The problem was proving it. Every time they thought that they had a lead, it had petered out when someone with no discernable link with Luigi, stepped forward and admitted guilt.

This time they had film that showed one of his senior lieutenants giving money to the victims at the scene of the fires. That confirmed the link of the north London mob to the houses. Then four members of the south London mob were identified as the fire raisers and were arrested when, according to the receptionist at the Four Oaks Club, they were clearly trying to intimidate the owner of a Mayfair club into paying protection money.

Donovan was sure that the owners of the place were already paying protection money to Luigi. He was aware that it had been the club that had asked Luigi's son-in-law to try to collect the money that one of its ex-employees had stolen. How else would they have known that he was in the debt collecting business? This commission had gone horribly wrong and had resulted in the killing of the ex-employee and the raping and murder of his girl-friend and, Donovan thought, eventually to the execution of the son-in-law to prevent a scandal that would involve Luigi's daughter. Between them, the Dorset and Metropolitan forces in the persons of Clare Thornton and Don Donovan, had assembled sufficient evidence against Michael Bernoulli to have secured a conviction. Donovan was fairly sure that he had been killed to prevent the story coming out in court, meaning that it had to be a member of Luigi's mob, a very trusted member of Luigi's mob, who had done the killing. Donovan had his suspicions.

Then there were the two unexplained murders of young men who's bodies had been found in back alleys in Soho. Neither had any form of identity and each had been killed by stabbing with a long slender blade. Whether the same long slender blade had been used to dispatch both victims, the pathologists couldn't say. Their pictures, fingerprints and DNA were with the experts. Scotland Yard thought that the murders might have some connection with the recent upsurge in mafia related events.

Donovan went over the ground once more with Tyler and concluded that shortly they could well have a full-scale gang war on their hands.

"Good," said the sergeant, "let's hope that this time they all kill each other."

"The MP's and the media will scream about innocent civilians getting into the line of fire and point out that we're paid to maintain the peace," said Donovan.

"Then they should come and do it for a change, instead of just preaching," said Tyler.

"Come, come, Sid," grinned Donovan, "you're speaking of those whom the people have chosen to govern us."

"People have chosen, my foot," said Tyler, "they have to vote for the idiots who some even bigger idiots at party headquarters have selected to stand in their constituency. The whole thing stinks."

Donovan had heard Sid on this topic many times before and decided to change the subject before his friend deployed the full range of his complaints about the democratic system of government in general and the present government in particular. For his part, Donovan was willing to concede that governing a nation might be more difficult than the man on the Pimlico bus might imagine and that the Chancellor of the Exchequer, who had gone into the river near to Tolbrite to recover the girl-friend's body, had seemed to be a nice enough chap. And his wife was smashing. He tried,

"What do we do now?"

"We grill the four who we've got, separately of course. One of them is bound to say something eventually and then we build on that and meanwhile we question the man we and the Bournemouth police think pushed the footballer and his girl into the river."

"Carlo Johnson, yes, I agree, then we'll be questioning mafia prisoners from both sides of the river. I wonder if any of the southern lot will know Carlo Johnson?"

"I'm going to enjoy this," said Donovan "We'll bring him here and make sure that they all see each other but not in a situation where they can speak or shout to each other. We don't want one lot reminding the other of the mafia code."

"That means that we mustn't put Carlo in the same cell block or prison van as the others."

"Correct," said Donovan, "then in our questioning we'll imply that we know more than we actually do by mentioning Coroneli and the capo of the southern lot."

"Corleone, Alfredo Corleone, lives in Croydon," said Tyler. "He's a Chelsea supporter."

"How on earth do you know that?"

"A few years ago when football hooliganism was at it's height, some of us were drafted in to help the people who were trying to prevent undesirables travelling to English clubs away games in Europe. Our job was to sift through the lists of names of people who had applied for tickets. One of us was from the vice squad and when we were looking at the lists provided by Chelsea of applicants for a Chelsea versus AC Milan match, he noticed Corleone's name and made a comment about him going home to recruit some more Mafiosi, him being the head of the mafia south of the Thames."

"Interesting but not likely to solve our crimes," said Donovan.

"Well, this did start with some threats against two football clubs, didn't it Don?"

"Yes and that reminds me," he consulted his diary and phoned a number.

"Hello, is that Detective Sergeant Thornton? Good, nice to talk with you too, Clare. How are things in Bournemouth?"

He listened for a short while, then said,

"We would like to borrow the chap you identified as the driver of the Nissan, name of Carlo Johnson. I was wondering if you could let us bring him up here. We've got the four thugs who set those fires in Mayfair and we'd like to play your man off against them."

He listened, then said,

"Your man comes from north of the river and our four are from the south and we could have the beginnings of a mafia war on our hands."

More listening.

"Well, somehow it didn't get to me, Clare, doesn't do to rely on e-mails these days. Thanks for your help."

He turned to Sergeant Tyler and said,

"She said that the DNA from the helmet that was worn by the motorcyclist who injured the other footballer, matches that from the cigarette found in the Nissan. I wonder why on earth Luigi's mob picked the same chap to do both jobs, Sid. Even more reason for bringing Carlo Johnson to town. There is one other thing that we might try."

"What's that?"

"I'll have a word with Tom Burton and get him to ask the AC if he could stretch the anti-terrorism remit a bit and authorise, or have authorised, a tap on Luigi Coroneli and Alfredo Corleone's phones."

"If they've got any sense they'll be using their mobiles," said Tyler.

"We can but try," said the inspector. He disappeared upstairs to have a word with the anti-terrorist people and Sergeant Tyler went back to his desk to start the process of borrowing Carlo Johnson for three days.

Luigi felt that he should be doing more than he had done to date. Not personally, of course, capo's didn't get their hands dirty. His soldiers would expect it. They would share his pleasure that the police had been smart enough to catch the four men who had set fire to his houses and that one of his 'family' had killed two of the other mob who had been foolish enough to venture north of the river and offer cut-price supplies to a couple of the people who distributed their drugs but his soldiers would still expect him to carry the war into the enemy's camp.

He met with Salvatori and Leonardo to consider what they might do.

"First," said Leonardo, "we have to tell all the people who pay for our protection that they must tell us the moment that anyone else tries it on. Salvatori and I have put all our men on the street to visit all of them and our dealers and reassure them that we are about. We might also find out that some of our pushers have bought stuff from the Corleone's on the quiet."

"If they have, you know what to do. Make an example of them," said Luigi, "we mustn't have a repetition of what happened at the Four Oaks Club. How is old Guiseppi?"

"Still shaking like a leaf."

"Be sure to make him understand that he is to make no reference to the family, to both families in fact, in the evidence he gives to the police."

"I've already done so," said Leonardo.

"What are we going to do in return, capo," asked Salvatori, "we can't let Alfredo get away with it."

"The wisest course would be to do nothing at the present time," said Leonardo, "he's already lost six men."

"I can see that," said Luigi, "but it's cost me a lot of money and somebody must be made to pay. Furthermore, our soldiers won't understand it if I take no action, they'll take it as a sign of weakness. What do we know about his operations south of the river?"

"Largely the same as ours, capo except that the balance will be different."

"In what way?" asked Salvatori.

"To put it crudely, he doesn't have the same class of customer, so he makes it up in volume, more hookers on the street, more protection of small shops and much, much more in drugs, there's a lot of blacks down there."

"So there are likely to be fewer places to hit?" asked Luigi.

"No, he's got several but nothing like your houses in Mayfair."

"Then what do you suggest we do?"

"Send the boys in and carve them up," said Salvatori.

"That might have to come later," said Luigi. "First, I think, we have to learn a lot more of how they organise things, like how do they get their supply of drugs? If we could seize or burn a consignment it would cost him, wouldn't it? So I want you to send the boys in as spies, not soldiers, got me? I'll give you a week to spy-out his scheme of operations."

"We did it about three years ago, capo," said Leonardo, "when we were deciding whether to extend our area southwards."

"So we did. I was looking at it some months ago," said Luigi. He pressed a button and Maria appeared in the doorway.

"Maria," he barked, "there's a report in the files, in a dark red folder, all about whether we should extend the business south of the river."

She disappeared. They continued chatting about possible lines of action.

Maria reappeared and said,

"I'm sorry, Mr Coroneli, it isn't in the files. You asked for it some time ago and I haven't seen it since."

"Of course you have, I sent it out."

"You can't have done, there's still a note on the file that it's charged out to you," said Maria.

"Don't you understand plain English, woman, I haven't got it. You must have put it somewhere."

"Would you look in your desk, Mr Coroneli, I haven't..." began Maria.

"Of course you have you stupid cow, I can see that there will have to be some changes around here. Get out of my room and try to do your job properly."

Maria closed the door behind her. Leonardo looked embarrassed.

Luigi turned to his henchmen and said,

"She's hopeless, I shall have to get a new girl." He grinned wolfishly and added, "a young one. Perhaps I'll try a blonde one next. You can have this one, Leonardo."

"I don't want her, capo, I look after my own affairs. I suggest that you keep her, she knows your ways."

"A new girl will soon learn my ways," snapped Luigi.

"I'll have her," said Salvatori, "then she can go to one of the houses."

"We'll see," said Luigi.

He didn't know it, but the intercom between his desk and Maria's was open and she had heard the whole of this exchange.

When they came out of the room Maria kept her head down. Leonardo thought that she'd been crying. He gently touched her shoulder as he passed.

Maria hardly noticed their going, her mind was in turmoil. So he was planning to get rid of her, was he? She'd have something to say about that! But she'd have to be careful. She searched in her drawer, what was the name of that nice policeman who had come here when Mr Coroneli's oily son-in-law had been killed?

She found his card in a visiting card holder, under the D's, where it should have been. She was proud of her filing system and knew, she just knew, that the dark red folder that Mr Coroneli had made all that fuss about was still with him. In one of his drawers probably.

She looked at the man's name, Donovan, Detective Inspector D.C. Donovan of New Scotland Yard. He didn't look the sort of man who would call an attractive girl a silly cow and certainly not in front of other people. What tit-bit would excite his interest? She didn't know much, she knew that her boss ran some sort of Italian organisation and that parts of it weren't entirely honest but Mr Coroneli was careful not to give too much away, she'd say that for him.

She'd hear him jabbering away in Italian. When he'd interviewed her for the job, all those years ago, he'd asked her if she spoke any Italian and she'd thought at the time that it would count against her that she couldn't. But she'd got the job, she knew now that he'd been more interested in her body than in her mind. She'd come to realise as time passed that he didn't want her to understand what was being said. Actually, with the help of her mother's language coaching and unbeknown to Mr Coroneli and Co, she now understood a lot of what was being talked about in Italian. She knew that in addition to his overt business of money lending and debt collecting, he derived money from prostitution, a form of blackmail called protection and drugs and she knew that it was as much as her life was worth ever to admit to such knowledge.

If the police raided the office everything that they would find related to the lawful business. She had never seen anything relating to the other things. She wondered who kept that set of books and how the profits reached Luigi Coroneli. Probably paid into an offshore account. He went abroad several times a year.

Maria went to the cinema that evening. It wasn't one of 'his nights.' She watched the film but her mind wasn't on it. She kept coming back to the same subject, how to land Luigi Coroneli in it? She grinned in the darkness, she didn't know the Italian for that, perhaps capo would become crapo.

She would write an anonymous letter, on that she was resolved. She would type it and the address and post it on Sunday afternoon on her way to visit her mother. The problem was what to put in it. She mustn't put anything that only she and Luigi would know about. The deeds to the garage in Welbeck Mews Lane kept coming back to her. She wasn't supposed to have seen those but if Mr Coroneli thought hard enough about it, he might realise that there had been the one occasion when his guard had slipped and the only person present had been Maria. On the other hand, sometime ago there must have been a lawyer who knew. But so what, the garage might be empty.

It would have to be something known to others, like Leonardo and Salvatori, but mere generalisations wouldn't do, the police probably suspected that Luigi Coroneli was the boss of a mafia family. It would have to be something more specific.

Of course if it was something that had only been discussed in Italian she wouldn't have understood it, would she? That was it, she'd listen and try to remember key words.

Delores had been primed by her sister. When Maria came in for her weekly wash, trim and set and they had exhausted the usual topics she casually remarked,

"Weren't those dreadful, those fires in Mayfair, I expect that your boss was mad."

Maria had no idea that it was public knowledge that Mr Coroneli owned the houses and replied, she thought neutrally,

"He was awfully upset about it."

"I should think that he would be, must be costing him a packet," said Delores. She lowered her voice, "Losing all those girl's earnings. The insurance wouldn't cover that."

"They said on the radio that the fires were started deliberately and that the police had arrested four men," tried Maria.

"They'll get away with it, clever lawyer and all that, you see," said Delores. "Do you know if he has bought anywhere else?"

"No, I don't know, the last that I heard was that Leonardo, he's the nice one, was looking."

"He's the nice one, is he? What's the other one like, always swearing revenge?"

"Something like that," said Maria and steered the conversation into what she considered to be safer channels.

That night Delores phoned her sister in Croydon and reported that Mr Big was mad as hell, hadn't found new premises yet and that the other one, not the one called Leonardo was swearing revenge. Carla's husband passed the message on.

Alfredo Corleone received the message. He already wished that he hadn't started this mob war; the family had been doing quite nicely south of the river despite the trouble from the Afro-Caribbean gangs. The arrest of Carlo Johnson had been sufficient to convince him that the north London mob had been behind the attempted blackmail of the football clubs. That was now a failed scam, but as the result, he had lost six soldiers and Luigi had lost two houses.

He didn't much like the notion that Salvatori was out for revenge. Salvatori had a reputation in mafia circles for violence and ruthlessness, woe betide those who got in his way. Alfredo decided to do nothing provocative in the hope that Luigi would feel the same.

Chapter Twelve

MARIA was surprised when Luigi told her to get Alfredo Corleone on the phone. She knew the number, of course, because she had checked it when Alfredo had telephoned her boss and talked about football.

Corleone was as surprised as Maria when his girl told him that Senor Coroneli wanted to speak with him. He grimaced, it could only be something bad, and picked up the phone,

"Good morning Luigi, what a pleasure to talk with you."

"I hope that you'll still think the same when you've heard what I have to say, Alfredo."

"And what is that, Luigi?"

"My price is a million pounds."

"Your price for what, Luigi,"

"For the damage that your people did to my houses in Mayfair."

"Oh yes, I heard about that. Bad luck, my dear friend. What makes you think that I had anything to do with those fires?"

"The men who caused them were yours."

"I'm sure that they haven't said that," said Alfredo, not being able to hide the hint of satisfaction in his tone.

"I'm sure that they haven't, if they know what's good for them but we know that they are yours and I repeat, my price is a million pounds."

"Even if I knew what gives you this ridiculous idea my friend, I haven't got a million."

"Then I'll have your houses in Croydon and Sutton."

"I only rent them," said Alfredo in the tone of someone trumping an ace.

"Then you had better get a million Alfredo, hadn't you?"

"And what is supposed to happen if I don't give you this million pounds?"

"I'll take it out of your skin, my fat friend and parade you past your posh friends in Croydon."

"You and who else?" scoffed Alfredo, his Sicilian dander up.

"So you want to do it the hard way?"

"Since I don't know why you are blaming me for what four strangers did to your property and I haven't got a million pounds to give you, I suppose that's how it will have to be."

"You could always ask for police protection," said Luigi and he put the phone down.

Maria had listened to the whole exchange.

Dressed in a black costume and clutching a small white handkerchief, a slender figure walked along the pier and hovered close to Madame Destie's small cabin, clearly trying to summon up enough courage to go in. Madame Destie's son, who acted as her assistant, watched as she walked past for the third time. He thought that this one looked different from the usual run of giggling girls and middle-aged matrons. Black suited and slender, the high heels did wonders for her figure. When she came past for the fourth time, he stepped out, as Paula expected that he eventually would, grinned at her in a toothy way and said,

"What's up, love, can't you make up your mind? Madame Destie won't bite you."

Paula pretended to be surprised and said,

"Oh, I don't know what to do," she dabbed her eyes with the wisp of a handkerchief.

The toothy young man realised that the girl wasn't dressed in black just because it suited her. He pulled the curtain aside and gestured for Paula to enter. She went into the dimly lit room and was guided to a chair by the now rather over-attentive young man. As her eyes adjusted to the near-darkness she was aware of the figure on the opposite side of the table. The outline was by no means clear, a head with glinting black eyes set in a lined face surrounded by a headscarf. A deep voice said,

"Good morning my dear, you've come to consult Madame Destie."

"Yes," said Paula, momentarily wondering if this was yet another assistant, this time without the groping hands.

"What do you want, a usual consultation or a deep consultation? The usual one is five pounds and the deep one is double that sum."

"Ten pounds?" said Paula.

"Ah, you'd like a deep consultation," said the voice, "very wise."

Smoothly done, thought Paula, who was of the opinion that she'd asked a question, not made a decision

"I'll have to have something of yours to hold," said the voice.

Like all my money, thought Paula, fishing in her handbag, black of course, for her powder compact that she passed across the table.

"Now tell me your name."

"Paula Simms," said Paula, truthfully, adding untruthfully, "Mrs Paula Simms."

"Ah," said the fortune teller, "you are having matrimonial problems."

"Yes," said Paula, resolved not to help the woman, "in a sort of way."

"Your husband is being unfaithful?"

"No," said Paula "never that."

"He's keeping you short of housekeeping money?"

"Oh no, I'm not short of money," said Paula wondering if that was a sharp intake of breath that she heard from somewhere behind her.

"Then your mother-in-law is interfering," tried Madame Destie "that's it, isn't it?"

"No," said Paula.

They sat and looked at each other for several tens of seconds while Paula made small dabs at her eyes with the hanky. In the end the woman said,

"Well, what is it about your husband that is troubling you, my dear?"

"He's dead," said Paula.

"Oh I am sorry," said Madame Destie, sounding anything but sorry "How old was he?"

"Only sixty-one," lied Paula. "A very young sixty-one. His family say that I married him for his money but I didn't, we were truly in love."

"When you say his family do you mean that his mother and father are still alive?"

"His mother is."

"What family are you referring to, then, my dear?"

"The children from his first marriage," lied Paula.

"And they are contesting the will?" tried Madame Destie.

"Oh, no, nothing like that, his will is watertight, they each got two million pounds and the rest came to me. If they had contested it they would have automatically lost their share."

"So you were left a tidy sum?" tried the fortune teller.

Paula hoped that the voice recorder that she always carried in her bag or pocket, was getting all this and said,

"Why are you asking me all these questions about money? That's not what I thought you people did. Why don't you tell my fortune?"

"What in particular do you want to know, then, my dear?"

"Whether he is happy."

The fortune teller dropped her voice and said,

"You mean on the other side?"

"Yes," said Paula in equally sepulchral tones.

"That's not fortune telling, my dear, the secrets that you are seeking can only be vouchsafed by a trained medium and then only when the correct atmosphere has been established."

"Oh," said Paula, gathering up her handbag and starting to rise. "I'm sorry to have troubled you. Perhaps you would be good enough to give me back my compact that you put under your cloak."

The woman produced the compact and put it on the table beside the glass ball, saying,

"Not so fast, my dear, you're fortunate in contacting me because I happen to be a trained medium and I can arrange a séance during which my spirit guide might be able to contact your departed husband. What did you say his name was?"

"Bertram," said Paula.

"Bert Simms," mused the fortune teller, "that name has a familiar sound."

"You mustn't call him that," said Paula, in feigned alarm, "he'd turn over in his grave if he heard you call him Bert, except, of course, he was cremated. He always insisted on being called Bertram and I agreed with him." Paula was beginning to enjoy herself but feared that her ten pounds-worth would soon be up. Without the fortune teller saying anything meaningful.

"When could you come to a séance, my dear?"

"Here on the pier?"

"Of course not. At my home where all my spiritual wants are available."

Paula wondered if that meant where the bottle of gin was. The would-be medium handed Paula a card and said,

"Would Friday evening suit you, at say, half past seven?"

"That will do fine," said Paula, picking up her compact and rising

"You realise that it will cost a lot more that today's ten pounds, my dear."

"Oh yes," said Paula and added, "spirits are always more expensive." Then she could have kicked herself for bordering on the flippant, so she dabbed her eyes like a widow should and bade them good morning.

As her trim figure disappeared shore-wards, Madame Destie joined her son at the mouth of the kiosk.

"There could be some good pickings there, my boy."

"Not only in money, either, Mum."

"You keep your hands off her, she's still grieving for her husband."

"She might be missing what he can't give her. Fancy a bird like that marrying an old man of sixty-odd."

"What's wrong with that, he wasn't what you'd call old, was he?"

"I wish that dad had left me two million," said the boy.

"Your father isn't dead yet, so far as I know," said the woman.

"No, I meant when he went off with that blonde."

"She wasn't a real blonde, it came out of a bottle," snapped his mother.

The son, who had been required to listen to the catalogue of the blonde girl's real or imagined demerits for the past decade, judged that it would be wise to change the subject.

"What about this séance, same as before?"

"Yes," said his mother. "We'll invite our usual four supporters and give them a belly-full of drink before she arrives to get them in the right humour."

"And dull their senses," said her son.

The four prisoners being held on arson charges were brought into the station and placed in separate rooms with half-glass inner walls. Donovan was in the corridor when Sergeant Tyler brought Carlo Johnson along and appeared to introduce him to the Inspector. Donovan shook the prisoner's hand and to the watchers in the rooms, appeared to engage him in friendly conversation before allowing Tyler to lead him away.

Some five minutes later, Donovan and Tyler were sat at the table in the interview room when a constable brought the first arsonist in, saying "Francis Delegan, Inspector."

"Sit down, Delegan," said Tyler.

Tyler made the necessary introductions for the recording machine.

"Now, Mr Delegan," said Donovan in a conversational voice, "tell us what made you set fire to that young lady's bed?"

Delegan looked down at his hands.

"Come now, Mr Delegan, we don't think that it was because you didn't like the girl." He consulted the paper before him. "I see that you're a married man, was she better looking than your wife?"

No answer.

"Perhaps your wife doesn't know the facts behind your arrest, that you had just spent half an hour in bed with a beautiful Swedish girl and then tried to burn her to death. Was this because she rejected your attempts to do things that no decent man would do? Do you think that your wife will enjoy it when it all comes out in court and all your neighbours know the sort of man she's married to? And, of course, all the kids at school. You do have children, don't you?"

This provoked the prisoner,

"Don't tell me that there's something that you bleeding rossers don't know."

"We only know what people like Carlo tell us," said Tyler

"And, of course he's got it in for you lot," put in the Inspector. "Got good reason to, hasn't he?"

The prisoner looked down at his hands. Had Carlo Johnson committed the unpardonable sin of helping the authorities?

Donovan guessed at what was going through the prisoner's mind. He said,

"We now know a lot about your capo as well. I expect that you four are pretty fed up with our Alfredo, him sending you up West on the morning that you're photo's were plastered all over every paper and TV screen in the nation. Great error of judgement that but then, he's not very clever, is he?"

"He's cleverer than you lot."

"You mean clever enough to send you four guilty fire-raisers out to get caught. He made you sacrificial lambs, is that it?"

"I dunno what your talking about. Who is this Alfredo something?"

"He's the chap who employs you, remember? The person who sends you out to be caught so that your wife and kids will suffer."

"He'll take care of them," blurted out Francis.

"Oh, I'm sure that he will. Tell me, I don't think that you answered my question, is your wife good looking?"

"It's none of your business. Why don't you shut your face."

"You will also have to face charges relating to your attempt to extort money at the Four Oaks Club."

"Where's that?" said the prisoner, and foolishly added, "Old Guiseppi had better keep quiet if he knows what's good for him. Anyway, you've got no right to ask me these questions without a lawyer. I know my rights."

"You'd be surprised at what we can do in terrorist cases like this, Mr Delegan," said the Sergeant.

The prisoner appeared to find this amusing.

"Terrorist, I'm not an Arab"

"You committed a seemingly random attack on innocent people, that's terrorism."

"I'll go to the European Court, you'll see, that'll put you in your place."

"Will that be before or after you complete the long sentence that awaits you?" asked the sergeant.

The prisoner realised that he was talking too much, looked down at his finger nails and said,

"I refuse to answer any more questions."

Donovan asked a few more questions, largely going over ground already covered, and the prisoner sat and looked at his hands.

The next prisoner was the older of the two men who had enjoyed the favours of young women at the house in Half-Moon Street before setting fire to their beds. He refused absolutely to say anything in the absence of his solicitor, other than to confirm his identity.

The third man to be questioned was the second man from Clarges Street, the one who had chosen to be entertained by Beulah because of his grandfather's experience with coloured girls when serving in Mussolini's army in Ethiopia. He too, refused to answer any questions.

The fourth prisoner was the youngest of the lot. He slouched in the chair provided and pointedly examined his finger-nails.

"Sit down, Mr Petrelli," said Donovan, "ah, I see that you already have. Now we'd like to ask you some questions."

Petrelli continued to examine his nails.

"You understand the seriousness of your position, don't you? There'll be a whole list of charges before we're through. Unless you're sensible, that is."

"You can't question me without my brief," said Petrelli.

"You'd be surprised at what we can do in cases of suspected terrorist activities."

Petrelli digested this in silence.

"We understand why you don't bother to explain your actions, you will probably get a life sentence anyway, so what's the good of talking. Mr Corleone certainly knew what he was doing when he picked you."

Silence, but the prisoner had lost a little of the arrogance he'd had when he entered the interview room.

"I expect that you enjoyed having sex with that attractive girl," said Sergeant Tyler. "There'll be none of that where you're going. I don't think that I could stand it, locked up with one or two other men in a tiny cell for over twenty hours each day for years on end, dreaming of all those lovely girls you would have known if Mr Corleone hadn't set you up."

Petrelli thought about this and said, "I want a lawyer."

"In cases of terrorism we don't need to stick to the rules," said Donovan, with his fingers crossed under the table.

"What do you mean, terrorism? All we did was to set fire to a few beds, you can't blame us if the fire brigade let the houses burn down, can you?"

"I very much doubt if the jury will see it that way," said the inspector, "four men deliberately cause fires which endangered the lives of thirty to forty innocent people, people who they didn't know, that's terrorism. You're no better than the al-Qeada."

"You won't be able to make that stick."

"Believe me, we will, Mr Petrelli, and then there's the matter of demanding payment for protection from the owners of the Four Oaks Club, the job that your capo set you up with."

"Why would he want to do that?"

"To distance himself, personally, from blame for those fires. He knew from the moment that your pictures were plastered all over the TV and papers that your usefulness to him was finished, so he got rid of you. He thinks that none of you will have the guts to tell it as it is, so you'll go to prison for life while he continues with his life of luxury in Croydon."

"Luigi Coroneli will know the truth, he owned those two houses and he'd tried to pull a scam south of the river."

"That's as may be," said Tyler, "but it doesn't get you off the hook, does it?"

"The capo will get us out."

"You're joking," said the inspector, "more likely he'll make sure that you never come out – alive. You said that the fires were started because the Coroneli mob had pulled a scam in your territory, what scam was that?"

Petrelli could see no harm in answering that, the capo wouldn't mind him dropping the other mob in it,

"The football scam."

"Demanding protection money from Southampton?" asked Donovan.

"Yes and dusting-up their players when they didn't pay."

"You call murdering Bruce Somers a 'dusting-up?" asked Tyler.

Petrelli relapsed into silence. Donovan searched his mind for something on which to keep the conversation going. He said,

"Did you know Michael Bernoulli?"

"You mean Mick the Knife, who was married to Coroneli's daughter and was killed outside their house?"

"Yes," said Donovan, "we think that it was a bit of luck for the Coroneli family that he should have been struck and killed by a lorry."

"I would have thought that even the police wouldn't believe in coincidences like that."

"We think that a car was involved," said Tyler.

"Cars have garages," said Petronelli. He paused for half a minute and then muttered.   "Someone mentioned a rumour about Welbeck Mews in Highgate to me." He then realised, too late, that he had broken the mafia rules. He said, "You won't tell anyone that I said that, will you? In any case, I don't know what it means."

"No Mr Petrelli, your secret is safe with us," said Donovan, thinking I wonder why the Corleone family should be concerned with a place in Welbeck Mews?

They questioned the prisoner some more but learned nothing further.

Back in his office, Donovan reviewed what they had learned. Very little. They had an open and shut case against the four in respect of the arson and demanding money with threatening behaviour and against Carlo Johnson for murder or perhaps, for manslaughter. Fine, but he felt that he was no nearer to being able to nail the men behind them. The only new thing that had been mentioned was a reference to a Welbeck Mews in Highgate. What was the significance of that chance remark? He asked his sergeant,

"Have you got any idea where Welbeck Mews is and what's in it, Sid?"

"No, but I can soon find out," and he left the room.

He was back inside a quarter of an hour.

"There's a Welbeck Mews Lane in Highgate, but only just. It's quite short and the only buildings in it are ten lock-up garages."

"Good man, at least that sounds right. I'd like to know who garages their car in each of them."

"Do you want to advertise the fact?"

"What do you mean by that?"

"Well, Don, we could station a constable there and ask everyone who gets a car out who they are and do they own the garage."

"That might take three days or more. Surely there is a record of ownership in the council offices?"

"You mean, who pays the council tax?"

"Something like that," said Donovan who left paying all that sort of thing to his wife.

"We could ask the Land Registry who owns them?" said the sergeant.

"Those would do for a start, Sid."

Two days later the sergeant presented the Inspector with a list of the people who paid the council tax for the garages in Welbeck Mews Lane. The names of the owners registered at the Land Registry would take longer to obtain.

"But that doesn't mean that the people named, garage their cars there, some of those names are property companies who doubtless rent them out."

"We've got to get a look at the vehicles, haven't we Sid. Got any ideas?"

"The most reliable way would be to go there at midnight and open up each garage, most of the cars should be back by then."

"What excuse could we offer?"

"When I was with the vice squad we pulled a stunt like this, using the fire brigade to search some lock-ups using the Dangerous Substances Act or Regulations or whatever it's called today."

"That sounds a good idea, have you got any pals in the London Fire Brigade?"

"We don't really need them, do we?"

"Oh yes we do," said Donovan, "we play it by the book, fire tender as well. We'll all look for dangerous substances and in passing, you and I will note the vehicle registration numbers."

Chapter Thirteen

THE following night a small fire appliance and a police car arrived at Welbeck Mews Lane exactly at midnight and their occupants proceeded along the row of garages, opening the up-and-over doors with keys provided to the public services for every eventuality and examining the contents. The fire officers knew that all that the police were really interested in was the cars within but nevertheless the officers made a proper search. One garage did not contain a car, it's contents were boxes containing new laptop computers, Donovan judged that there must be well over a hundred. All of the same well-known make and all stacked neatly in rows. The name on the garage owner's list didn't ring any bells as an electrical wholesaler so Donovan immediately informed colleagues at Scotland Yard.

They collected the registration numbers of the nine vehicles in the other garages, thanked the firemen for their help and watched them depart. Less than five minutes later a second police car arrived containing the officers who would enquire into the ownership of the computers.

The following morning the details of registered ownership arrived from the Land Registry, the owner of garage No 6 was stated to be a Mr Luigi Coroneli. Sergeant Tyler consulted the computerised vehicle registration information and identified the keepers of all nine vehicles. Six were registered in the name of individuals and three were registered in the name of companies. The sergeant methodically went through them all, checking that the addresses and other information given on the vehicle documents, the council tax records and the garage ownership details was factual. It was, in all cases except for Garage No 6, for which the Council tax and car tax were paid by a company. He reported as much to Inspector Donovan.

"You'll never believe this, Gov, Coroneli owns Number 6."

"Interesting," said Donovan. "Are the others all above board?"

"Seems so, except the lot with the laptops could have some questions to answer." The sergeant paused and thought, "there was just one thing, although the Land Registry report says that Luigi owns the garage, someone else owns the car and pays the Council Tax. Of course it's not unusual for a property owner to let out a garage, it happens quite a lot I expect, but this one was, well, a bit different."

"How different?"

"Well, when I phoned to double check the ownership detail, one company took some time to latch on to what I was talking about. I could hear the chap on the other end of the phone shouting to someone else."

"Probably nothing in that, Sid, companies have lots of vehicles and can't remember all the detail."

"Big companies have transport departments who's duty it is to know who has their vehicles and little companies have so few cars that they can remember where each one is."

Donovan grinned at his friend and said,

"This is probably a medium sized company that has trouble remembering anything."

"It isn't a company I'd heard of before," said the sergeant.

"Then go and check it out, Sid, goodness knows, we are clutching at straws."

He was back by late afternoon, beaming all over his face. Donovan took one look at him and said,

"Good news?"

"It might be. The address given for that company is an accommodation address and the name on the vehicle registration document is the name of one of the three chaps who run it. He says that he's never seen the car or the garage or signed any documents."

"Let's take this slowly, Sid," said Donovan. "We have a vehicle with false ownership documents. What about the garage? You know, paying the Council Tax, that sort of thing?"

"They said that a man comes in once a year, at the time the notices go out, and gives them the full amount, in cash, plus a hundred quid for themselves, to pay the tax."

"Could they describe the man?"

"Vaguely, wears a black beard and dark glasses, about five-six tall and not fat, that's the best that I could get. I got the impression that they're not too keen on helping the Met."

"They probably rely on borderline scams for a good part of their income and have got a whole lot going on at the present time," said the inspector. "They wouldn't want the word to get around that they've shopped a client, would they?"

"No, I suppose not. What do you intend to do now?"

"I'll have a word with the chief and then we'll bring that car in for examination. With luck the forensic scientists may let us get it back in the garage before anyone knows that it's missing."

"Why not do the examination on the spot, Gov?"

"I considered that and decided that there's more chance of someone seeing what's going on if we have the garage open all day for a couple of days than if we remove the car for two days and leave the garage door shut."

"What happens if the rightful owner decides to take the car out for a spin?"

"If he complains, we discover who this mysterious person is. If he doesn't complain we'll know that he's up to no good."

"I suppose that you'll want me to arrange a tell-tale to tell us whether the door's been opened so that we will know that he's been there."

"Of course," said Donovan.

"Of more immediate interest, Gov, when you go upstairs you won't overlook the fact that we're not supposed to be working on this case, will you?"

"They wouldn't have stumbled on the computers if we hadn't," grinned Donovan.

"You've been a copper long enough not to expect thanks, Don."

"I know but I just can't stop hoping," was the reply.

Paula's taxi arrived at the fortune teller's house a few minutes before seven thirty. She walked up the short drive – long enough to park a car but no more – and was conscious of the sound of cheerful voices and laughter within the house. She rang the bell and the noise instantly ceased. The fortune teller's son opened the door. He was dressed entirely in black. With his hand in the small of her back, he guided her along a passage and into a sitting room. En route he said,

"Madame Destie told you that arranging a séance would cost money, didn't she? It's best to get these things settled beforehand. Do you have your cheque book?"

Not likely, thought Paula. She said,

"No, but I brought some cash."

"How much?" blurted out the son.

"A hundred pounds."

"That'll have to do for starters then, it's bound to take more than one sitting."

He took the hundred pounds, counted it, pushed it into his pocket and asked her to follow him. He led her back along the passage and stood in the doorway as he ushered her into a dimly lit room. Paula did her best to avoid rubbing against him.

When her eyes adjusted to the light – or lack of it – she saw that there was a round table in the centre of the room around which five people were sat, two on each side of the central figure which she recognised as the fortune teller. But this was the fortune teller with a difference, instead of the black head-scarf, her face was framed in black hair that hung almost to her shoulders with a bandeau round her forehead. Her dress was black.

"Come in my dear," said the fortune teller cum medium, "sit opposite to me."

Paula shook off the hands that touched her from behind and sat herself between two women.

"I asked some true believers in the occult to come to this séance, Mr and Mrs Smith and Mr and Mrs Jones. I hope that their presence will assist me in making contact," the voice dropped an octave, "with the other side."

"I see," said Paula. "Good evening." She wondered what were the real names of Messers Smith and Jones. She would have thought that Madame Destie would have had more imagination than that. She said,

"Which is Mrs Jones?"

"I am," said both women, who each then said, "Sorry, she is," gesturing towards the other. Paula effected not to notice their confusion and Madame Destie ploughed on,

"It's usual to deal with financial matters before a séance. There have been instances in which the enquirer has left before contact can be established, sometimes attempting to evade payment. I understand that my son has dealt with this sordid but necessary, detail."

Paula wondered how she knew. Perhaps he would have spoken out if she hadn't. The medium continued,

"I'll explain what will happen. We six will join hands around the table. It's important that there are six in the ring, six has a particular significance in occult circles. We join hands and in a little while I will fall into a trance. There may be noises and things may move, I can never tell what the spirits may decide. It's their world that we are attempting to look into and sometimes they resent it and try to break the circle. If we are fortunate, my spirit guide, Passing Cloud, may come to me tonight and ask me what I want. Remind me, my dear, you want to know if your husband's happy on the other side?"

"Yes," said Paula in what she hoped sounded a meek enough tone, "will Bertram talk to me?"

"Oh no," said the medium, "you wont be able to speak directly to the dear departed but only to pass messages through my control, Passing Cloud."

"Oh," said Paula, sounding very disappointed. "I would have given a lot to be able to speak to my darling Bertram."

"However," said the medium quickly, "it has been known in exceptional circumstances, where two people were desperately in love, for instance, for the spirit world to relent just a teeny-weeny bit and allow just a few words. Of course voices sound different across the great divide."

"Of course," said Paula, regretting that she hadn't pretended that her 'husband' only spoke Serbo-Croat.

"Very good then," said the medium in her lowered voice. "I will try to contact the other side."

She began to breathe deeply and the lights got dimmer and dimmer and nearly went out.

After some minutes, the side of Paula's nose began to itch and she tried to take her hand away to scratch it. The woman on her right grasped her hand even more tightly and Paula sensed that she was vigorously shaking her head.

Low moaning noises came from the medium.

After a few minutes there seemed to be a rap on the table. Or was it from somewhere behind the medium? She said,

"Passing Cloud, are you there?"

Five minutes passed. Paula thought that this must be the longest ten minutes she had ever wasted. And her nose was still itching!

There was a loud double rap. Madame Destie said,

"Is that you, Passing Cloud? I have a message for you. Tell me if you're there."

There was another loud double rap and a blinding flash of light. Before she involuntarily shut her eyes Paula was aware that a black figure was standing behind the medium. Thinking about it afterwards, she realised that both women who were holding her hands had tightened their grip immediately before the flash. They'd known that it was coming.

119

When her eyes recovered and adjusted to the dim light over the table, Paula saw that the medium was moving so violently in her chair that the men on either side had difficulty retaining a grip on her, she moaned, she writhed and she sobbed. Then she said in a deep voice,

"Good, thank you for coming tonight."

There was another double rap. Paula was relieved that there wasn't another flash.

"Yes, I have a request and it concerns Bertram Simms who passed over on 21st June."

Another double rap, quieter this time.

More writhing and sobbing, then she said,

"His wife, Paula wants to know if he's happy on the other side."

More writhing and sobbing, then,

"You say that he's not happy, why?"

Loud rap, more heavy breathing.

"Oh dear me, I see, that's most unfortunate, isn't it?. Don't go Passing Cloud, I have some more questions. Oh, no, you've gone."

Madame Destie slumped down in her chair, breathing heavily and sobbing. The women relaxed their grip on Paula's hands and she rubbed them together to restore the circulation before scratching her nose. After some minutes the medium opened her eyes and the lights got brighter. She looked at them as if seeing them for the first time and asked,

"Did I make contact?"

"Yes," said the Smiths and Jones's in unison.

"What did he say?"

Paula thought that this was a bit steep since the medium was the only person to have spoken for the past half an hour.

"You said that something was most unfortunate," said Mr Smith. Or was it Mr Jones?

"Ah yes, it's coming back to me," said the medium.

Paula thought that it was time she said something, after all, she was funding this farce.

"Did he say that my Bertram is happy?"

"No," said the medium, "he's not happy."

"Oh dear, did he say why?" asked Paula.

"Passing Cloud said that he hadn't been allowed to cross the final barrier to the other side."

"What does that mean?" cried Paula.

"It means that he's one of those unfortunate souls who are doomed to spend the rest of eternity in limbo."

"Is that bad?"

"It means that he'll be condemned to live alone in space, not on earth or in the other place, until the day of resurrection," said the medium. "When you die and go to heaven, he won't be there."

"Oh dear," said Paula in a suitably grief stricken tone. She thought that perhaps it was about time that she asked the question that she was obviously being primed to ask. "Why can't he get into heaven?"

"Passing Cloud said that he hadn't given enough money to charitable causes in his younger years."

"Oh dear," said Paula, "that must have been before he married me. If I give a lot to charity now and say that it's in his name, will that make it alright?"

"Oh no, to count, the gifts will have to be made through the spirit world," said Madame Destie.

"But I don't know how to do that," cried Paula.

"Perhaps, just perhaps, if Passing Cloud will help, I might be able to arrange something."

"Oh, I'd be ever so grateful if you could."

Paula blushed inwardly, never before in her life had she uttered such rubbish. Surely this old woman would see through her.

Not so, or if she did she Madame Destie was a consummate actress. The important aim of the evening accomplished, she stood up slowly to indicate that that was the end of the performance. The Smiths and Jones's gathered round Paula and congratulated her on her good fortune in having Madame Destie to intercede in the spirit world on her behalf.

The son brought their coats and with many thanks for an interesting evening, they departed. Madame Destie sat down again. Now, thought Paula, I suppose that we get down to the sordid matter of money. She said,

"You said that you might be able to arrange something?"

"It might prove to be costly," said Madame Desti.

"How costly, how much do you thing that the spirits will want?"

"Well, your husband was a very wealthy man and those on the other side know it. I could start by offering Passing Cloud ten thousand."

"How on earth will you get it to him?" asked Paula. "He's a ghost, I think that I saw him beside you tonight."

"Ah," said the medium, "you used the right word, it won't be by earthly means but through the occult."

Paula couldn't resist it,

"Do they take MasterCard?"

The woman's son, who had re-entered the room and was standing inside the door, tittered. Whether it was at the thought of settling heavenly debts by credit card or at Paula's apparent stupidity, Paula didn't know or care.

"Oh no," said Madame Destie, horrified.

"Well, I can't draw ten thousand pounds out of the bank without them asking politely what I want it for. Something to do with money laundering. Do I tell them about you?"

Madame Destie made a show of recoiling in horror and said,

"Oh no my dear, that would spoil everything. This has to be our little secret."

"You mean that I shouldn't tell Mr Swain?"

"Who is Mr Swain?" asked the medium.

"He's the solicitor who's handling my affairs," said Paula.

"Good Lord no, no-one must know, only we three, otherwise the transfer won't be possible."

You can say that again, thought Paula. She asked, innocently,

"Will a cheque do?"

"I suppose that it'll have to," said Madame Destie.

Paula was enjoying this.

"Who do I make it out to, I can't just write God on it, can I? Do I put Passing Cloud?"

"You had better make it out to me and I'll see that it gets to the right place."

I bet you will, thought Paula.

"So I make my cheque out to Madame Destie?" said Paula.

"No dear, that's just my professional name. You must make it out to my given name, Alice Timpson."

"And you're sure that the money will go to Bertram in heaven or wherever he's waiting?"

"Yes, my dear, your money is destined for heaven."

"Can I come and see you pass it over?"

"Oh no, that's a sacred rite known only to those, like me, who have the gift of special powers and it's not possible if a stranger is present. I'd lose all my gifts if I allowed it to happen."

"Oh I see," said Paula. "Do I bring my cheque here?"

"Better to drop it in on the pier or send it by post, my dear."

"Alright, you shall have it early next week," said Paula, "probably on Monday."

"You won't tell a soul about this, will you, otherwise it will spoil everything."

I bet it would, thought Paula, aloud she said,

"Oh no, they might think that I'd gone mad."

"You're very fortunate to have come to me. If I'm able to pass your money across to the other side on this occasion, Passing Cloud may be able to let you speak with your dear departed on a future occasion."

"Ooh," said Paula. "I'd be ever so grateful."

Madame Destie stood up again to indicate that this was the end of the discussion and after a few pleasantries, Paula made her escape, avoiding the attentions of the son in so doing.

When they were alone, the son said,

"You're pushing it a bit, aren't you Mum? Why didn't you string her along for a couple more séances before raising the question of passing money to the other side?"

"You trust your old mother, my boy, I know what I'm doing. She's a good-looking, rich young widow and how long do you think it will be before some young man catches her eye and she starts to shake off her sense of loss or, worse still, she mentions us to that solicitor she spoke about. Strike while the iron's hot is my motto."

"I think that we should have had her along some more," said the son.

"Well, I know what I'm doing and you keep your hands off her when she comes to the kiosk next week, I've seen you groping."

Chapter Fourteen

IN LONDON, Detective Inspector Donovan had been given grudging approval to continue with the investigation into the death of Michael Bernoulli. He hadn't spelt out exactly what steps he intended to take in the near future, only that there were grounds for suspecting that this was a mafia crime and might be related in some way to the recent fires in Mayfair. His chief knew better than to go into details.

He and Sergeant Tyler were present when the car in the lock-up in Welbeck Mews Lane was pulled up on to the back of a low-loader and departed for forensic tests at the police garage and they were at that garage to explain to the experts why it was imperative that the car be back in it's lock-up within two days.

Before the first day was up, their leader phoned Donovan.

"Don, you were right, this car's got some secrets. There are hidden compartments in the inside of both front doors."

"Drugs?" said the inspector.

"No trace of drugs but a largish sum of money in US dollars and Euro's, mainly Euro's and some identity papers and passports, all with the same man's picture. One of the passports is an Italian one."

"Well done Tony," said Donovan. "Any fingerprints?"

"Loads of them, all the same person's. I've sent them off to Criminal records."

Donovan played his hunch,

"Be a good chap and have a look for bloodstains in the vicinity of the boot."

The answers had come the next morning. Criminal records identified the photo in the passports as none other than Luigi Coroneli, the capo of the North London mafia family. This was good news enough but Donovan's cup was filled to overflowing when forensics reported that they had found minute specks of blood on the carpet in the boot. They had been lifted using a revolutionary new technique and sent for DNA testing. Donovan told them to place the car under wraps and not to return it to its garage in Welbeck Mews Lane.

Sergeant Tyler took copies of the passport photo's to Crown Holdings, the accommodation address to which correspondence pertaining to the garage had been sent and the occupants agreed that they might, just might, be pictures of the bloke who came in once or twice a year to collect his mail and pay the bills.

Later in the day forensics phoned to say that the passports were forgeries.

When Luigi arrived home that evening and went into what he called his wife's sitting room, he noticed that the light on 'her' phone was flashing. To say that this was unusual would be an understatement; the line was the one that his late wife had used, it was unlisted and only her friends knew it. There had been a few calls in the weeks following his wife's death but nothing since. He picked up the receiver and pressed the 'play' button. A man's voice that he didn't recognise said,

"Roger Judd from Crown Holdings here, Gov. We pay your bills. You gave me this phone number to ring in an emergency. It probably isn't an emergency but I thought that you might like to know that we had a policeman in here this morning with a picture of you, asking if we recognised you as the guy who drove a car kept in the garage in Welbeck Mews Lane. The boys said no. I thought that you might be interested."

Luigi was thunderstruck. How on earth had the police connected him with the garage? Had they found his 'get away' car?

Apart from the three men at Crown Holdings only he and, he supposed, the solicitor who had dealt with the purchase, knew that he owned the garage. There was nothing to connect him with it. Unless, he realised, they had found the secret compartments and the passports with his picture in them. He was sure, absolutely sure, that the car bore no traces arising from the murder of his son-in-law; he'd taken it to a car-wash within days and had them give it the full cleaning treatment.

He thought on and always came back to the basic question, why had the police searched his garage? He then realised that he was, perhaps, putting two and two together and possibly getting five. All he knew was that the police had his photograph and were asking questions. He corrected himself, what was it that chap had said?

He pressed the play button once more. There it was,

'..if we recognised you as the guy who drove a car kept in the garage in Welbeck Mews Lane.'

He went over the arrangements. There weren't any records, it all had to be in his head. The car was registered in the name of one of the chaps who ran Crown Holdings and the same chap paid the council tax.

Luigi's name didn't appear anywhere. He thought about that and realised that there was one place where it did, on the title deeds to the garage and hence in the Land Registry documents. Locally, only himself and the solicitor had seen those deeds, they were locked up in his office safe to which only he had the combination.

He realised that although that was literally true, there was a million to one chance that his daughter's curiosity might have made a chink in this armour. Had she peeked inside the sealed envelope that he had left with her to be opened only in the event of his death? He went suddenly cold, what a fool he had been, had that wretched son-in-law of his got hold of it and taken a look at the contents? What a blessing that he had killed him.

He picked up the handset and dialled his daughter's number.

"Hello," came his daughter's voice, "Sophia Bernoulli here."

Luigi had been trying without success to get her to use her maiden name.

"Its Popa here baby, are you alright?"

"Yes, fine Popa, what can I do for you?"

"I just want to ask you a question, you haven't opened that envelope that I gave you, have you?"

"Of course not, Popa, fancy you asking me that, you said not to open it until… well, you know, I don't want to think about it. Why do you ask?"

"Don't give it another thought baby, it's just that something's come up and I had to check."

"There's nothing wrong with you, is there, you're not ill or anything?" suddenly worried.

"No, it's just a business thing."

They chatted some more and rang off. He was left with the problem, how had the police come to associate him with the garage. There was another problem, why had the police gone looking at the garage?

The only connection that he could think of was the deeds and they had never left the safe.

He thought about deeds, he'd had to look at the deeds for the houses in Clarges Street and Half Moon Street that had been burnt. He'd opened the safe and taken them all out and put them on the side table. He'd then picked out the two sets that he wanted and put the remainder back in the safe. Hold on a minute, Maria had been in the room and he'd asked her to find one set of deeds hadn't he? To do that she'd have had to sort them out. That was it, Maria had seen the deeds for the garage and had told the police.

He'd kill her!

In an icy rage he went through the communicating door that connected his house to it's garage, started his car and drove to his office building. There was a light in Maria's flat. He ran up the stairs and hammered on her door.

"Who's there?" came a voice.

"It's me, the capo."

"Oh."

The door opened and he stormed past her, shouting,

"You bitch, you told the police about that garage."

He went into the centre of the room, spun round and struck her viciously across the cheek.

Maria, who was undressed and wearing only a light dressing gown, fell back against the closed door. She was doubly stunned, by the blow and by the accusation. She'd thought about telling the police that day when Luigi had called her a silly cow but she hadn't.

"I don't know what you're talking about Mr Coroneli."

He took her by the shoulders and shook her angrily. The dressing gown slid back from her shoulders to reveal her breasts.

"I'm talking about my garage in Welbeck Mews."

"I didn't know that you had a garage in Welbeck Mews." She almost said Lane.

"Well I have and you saw the deeds and told the police."

"I most certainly didn't tell the police anything." Indignantly, struggling to get the front of the dressing gown together.

Luigi was becoming calmer.

"Then why were the police poking about there, tell me that?"

"How should I know?" said Maria, feeling a trifle bolder.

"Well, they were and now they're asking questions about my car."

"You've got a car in the garage?"

"Yes," said Luigi.

"Now you come to mention it, there was something about Welbeck and garages in last night's paper. They found a lot of stolen computers in one of them."

"Have you got the paper?"

"Yes, its in the bag for recycling."

127

"Get it!"

Maria nearly said 'please' the way her mother used to when she was a small girl and forgot her manners, but didn't. Being hit once and shaken like a rag doll was enough for one night. She went out to the cupboard beside the washing machine and reappeared with a folded newspaper. He snatched it from her, put it on the table and turned over the pages. He came to a small article headed, 'Big Computer Find.'

The substance of the article was that in conducting their annual examination of premises for dangerous or inflammable substances in accordance with the regulations, the London Fire Brigade had found a large number of laptop computers stored in one of the ten garages in Welbeck Mews Lane. They had informed the police and the police had quickly established that the computers were part of a large consignment of computers that had been stolen from a warehouse close to Heathrow. In the circumstances they had felt it prudent to search the other garages. They were continuing with their investigation.

Maria had also been re-reading the article and said,

"There you are, Mr Coroneli, it was a routine fire inspection."

Sicilian men never admit that they could be wrong. Luigi said with ill grace,

"That's what they told the press. Let this be a warning to you."

He stood and looked at her. He knew that she didn't like having sex with him, she never had. Should he complete her humiliation by forcing himself on her tonight?

He reached out, grasped the lapels of her dressing gown, tore it open and allowed it to fall to the ground so that she stood naked before him; repeated "let that be a lesson to you," and slammed out of the flat.

Maria hastily put on the robe and bolted the door. If he changed his mind he'd have to break the door down. What a loathsome creature he was.

Reflecting on his visit afterwards, Maria realised that things might soon come to a head. She was pleased that she had already taken precautions.

The next evening, being Saturday, Paula recited the story of her encounter with the confidence tricksters to her friends in the saloon bar of the Tolbrite Arms. They were amused and horrified in turn.

"Have you told Clare Thornton what you're doing?" asked Helene.

"Not in detail," said Paula, "but she knows that we have a client who considers that she was ripped-off by Madame Destie."

"The law knows, of course, that fortune tellers are getting money by false pretences," said Timmy, "but as long as the sums involved are small and gullible fools are prepared to pay, it turns a blind eye."

"It's part of our history," said Fred, "there's always been fortune tellers at village fetes and fairs and things."

"Gypsies," said Gloria.

"Not always welcomed by the church," said Angela.

"For good doctrinal reasons, I'm sure, but there have been prophets, seers, visionaries and the like all through the ages," said Helene, "just as there have been spiritualists who believe that there is a reality independent of matter."

Timmy grinned at his wife, she really was lovely, she had a law degree and she was clearly serious about this spiritualist thing. He prompted her,

"Would you say that all the great philosophers have been spiritualists, Angel?"

"We're dealing with words that have different meanings to different people and in different ages, so it's dangerous, perhaps inadvisable would be a better word, to stick labels on people and things. Let me put it this way, since the beginning of time, philosophers have been grappling with the idea that a person has a soul independent of their body."

"And the concept of a soul or spirit reads across to spiritualism?"

"Yes," said Helene, "there are records going back to the fifth century BC that suggest that a person's soul has its origin with the Gods and exists separately from a person's body. The Greeks also wrestled with the subject and, in this sense, Plato and Aristotle were spiritualists. And so on down the centuries."

"So it's not just a dirty word?" said Will.

"Only in today's society where, in ignorance, people associate the word with quackery and fortune tellers like your Madame Destie."

Timmy decided that the conversation was getting a bit too metaphysical for Saturday night and asked Paula,

"What do you intend to do now?"

"I'll answer that," said Fred. "To really nail Madame Destie on a charge of obtaining money by false pretences, we have to actually give her the money, so Paula will give her a proper cheque for ten thousand pounds which we will then tell our bank to stop."

"Will the grieving widow ask Madame Destie for a receipt?" asked Helene of Paula.

"I would like to but the old woman might smell a rat."

"I would think it better not to," said Helene. "I assume that you recorded everything that was said on the pier and at the séance?"

"Yes," said Paula, "it's all on tape and I've prepared transcripts."

"Then I suggest that you give her the cheque in an open envelope, insist that she checks it to make sure that you've spelt her name correctly and record it all," said Helene.

The conversation turned to other things until Will, as usual, asked Timmy if there was any subject or topic that he would wish him to mention in his weekly chat-show on Monday evening?

"Nothing in particular, Will, you'll have to stick with the old faithfuls to get it started."

"How about fortune tellers, you know, what do people think of them, has what they said ever come true and have they been ripped-off by one?"

"You'll have to remind the listeners not to mention names."

"Jill takes care of that," said Will, "but people are usually very good."

"They drop hints," said Gloria, "like, 'that one on the pier, who's name I mustn't mention', that sort of thing."

"It would be a change from the local football club, the impossibility of parking in town, student housing and country bus services," said Will.

"Sounds OK to me," said the owner of the Hawkridge network, turning to Paula. "Will it affect you if Will airs the subject on Monday night?"

"Why should it?" asked Paula.

"Well," said Timmy, "if one of the people who call in talks about being ripped-off for a sum of money by a spiritualist, Madame Destie might fear that you will have heard the broadcast, fear that you will seek advice and drop the whole pretence that she can transmit money to the spirit world."

"You mean that she could say that she had had another visit from her control, Passing Cloud, during the weekend and he had told her that there is no way that money will buy peace for my dear departed husband, Bertram?"

"Yes," said Timmy, grinning, "that sort of thing."

"Then Paula had better deliver the cheque on Monday," said Fred.

"You are sure that she won't be able to cash it?" asked Angela, who suddenly had visions of a bankrupt Southern Enquiries.

"Yes," said her husband, "and to be absolutely sure, Paula's going to tell Clare about it when they have their usual Sunday morning coffee date tomorrow."

"What can she do?" asked Will. "Arrest the old lady on the way to the bank?"

"Not likely," said Fred, "she must be known to have paid the money into an account. Then she can be arrested. What we will ask Clare to do is to use her authority to ask the bank manager to confirm that the cheque was presented and paid into an account belonging to what-ever she calls herself."

"Alice Timpson," said Paula.

"You've got it all worked out, haven't you?" said Gloria from the other side of the bar.

"We hope so," said Paula.

"That means that you will have to keep an eye on Madame Destie and her son from the moment that you give her the cheque, doesn't it?" asked Will.

"I suppose it does," said Fred.

"You don't seem too sure of it," said Will.

"Well, I was relying on the bank manager picking it up and telling us or Clare."

"She might have an account in another town and take it there or send it there by post."

"I get the point, yes, we'll have to follow her and see whether she, or her wretched son, hurries off to a bank."

"Or the post-box," said the ever practical Gloria.

"I'm sure that she'll take it to the bank," said Paula, "she'll not be able to resist getting her hands on the loot as soon as possible."

"Will and I can help you follow them on Monday," said Gloria.

"I intend to take the cheque to her in the morning to give her the chance of depositing it during the lunch hour and Clare the opportunity of arresting her that afternoon," said Paula. "I'm keen to get it over with."

"Take it to her at half past eleven," said Gloria, "and I'll be watching from somewhere on the pier,"

The conversation turned to other things and at about half past nine Gloria asked Angela if she would play for them.

Chapter Fifteen

PAULA explained what she intended to do with Madame Destie to her friend Detective Sergeant Clare Thornton over coffee in their usual sea-front café the following morning. Clare listened in silence then said,

"You're sailing fairly close to the wind, you know. These days we wouldn't dare to mount a sting operation like that, knowing that the CPS would refuse to prosecute on the grounds that some smart civil-rights lawyer would claim entrapment and cite every human rights act known to man."

"You're not saying that we shouldn't do it?" asked Paula.

"Oh no, you can give her the cheque and on the way home have second thoughts or meet your vicar or someone who tells you not to be a fool, no one can pass money to a ghost, so you stop the cheque and inform the police."

"And then you can act?" asked Paula.

"Oh yes, we would take the line that she was attempting to obtain money from you by false pretences."

"But it would come out in court that I'm not really a widow and had deliberately set out to trap her," said Paula who was beginning to see the possibility of a messy court case with mounting costs and wonder if it was such a clever scheme after all.

"Your counsel would argue that you had acted as a concerned citizen, determined to show the fortune-teller up as a cheat and in so doing protect the general public from being ripped-off by charlatans like her."

"So we go ahead?"

"You should know better than to ask me that, Paula," grinned Clare, "but it'll be good publicity for Southern Enquiries, won't it?"

At Scotland Yard, on Monday morning, they got the result of the DNA test of the minute blood spots found in the boot of the car, it matched that of Michael Bernoulli. Inspector Donovan and his sergeant took their findings to their Chief Inspector, who summarised the situation as,

"So you think that the car belongs to Luigi Coroneli?"

"Yes," said Donovan.

"Because you found three forged passports, each with his picture in it and a large sum of money hidden in secret compartments in the doors?"

"Yes and he's been sort of identified as the person who provides the cash to pay the council tax for the garage."

"OK," said the Chief Inspector. "It seems that he's certainly got some explaining to do on the subject of possession of the forged passports."

"Then there's the bloodstains," said Donovan.

"Ah yes, the bloodstains, what do you make of those?"

"Well, we have a witness who, on the night in question, saw shadowy figures hovering over the open boot of a car parked at the spot where Bernoulli's body was found. We think that it was this car and that he was struck down by Luigi Coroneli."

"And the reason?"

"Because Coroneli had learned that day that we were going to arrest his son-in-law and charge him with double murder and rape," said Donovan.

"And the theory is that he did it to avoid the attendant disgrace touching his daughter?"

"Yes," said Donovan, "we understand that his daughter, his only daughter, is the apple of his eye and they both knew by now that marrying Bernoulli had been a mistake."

"You're not suggesting that the daughter had any part in this?"

"No, Chief, we have no evidence that the daughter was aware of anything."

"So the murder charge rests on circumstantial evidence?"

"More than circumstantial evidence, what about the bloodstains?"

"A clever lawyer would contend that the blood spots were caused when Michael Bernoulli had borrowed the car and accidentally cut himself removing something from, or putting something into, the boot."

"We think that they were caused when Luigi killed him," said Donovan, indignantly.

"I expect that they were," said the Chief Inspector, "but it's not what we think that matters, is it? It's what the jury will think and they have to be convinced beyond reasonable doubt."

"We can't just let him get away with it, Chief."

"I'm not suggesting that we should, Don, I'm simply pointing out that there's a lot more investigating to do before we can be sure of making the murder charge stick."

"But meanwhile we bring him in on the forged identity papers count?" said a slightly depressed Sergeant Tyler.

"Yes, sergeant and the beauty of this one is that we've got him, the capo himself, he can't get some unfortunate mafia soldier to take the rap for possessing them. The unfortunate thing is that he'll have his lawyers get him out on bail before you can say Jack Robinson."

"So we bring him in this afternoon?" said the sergeant.

"There are one or two things that I'd like you to do first," said the Chief Inspector, "like checking up on exactly who's citizenship Luigi Coroneli actually has. Is he British born or naturalised British or Italian? Then there's the question of his mafia family, who are his senior aide's and is there a chance that we might arrest a few more of them so that the leaderless mob loses its way and does something stupid and we can then break it up."

"That'll be the day," said Donovan.

"We can but try, Don, off you go and do what you can."

"I've impounded the car. If Luigi goes to the garage to get it or somebody tips him off, he could do a bunk."

"That's a risk that we must take. Do your best to find out all that you can as quickly as you can. Now push off, I'm busy."

As they walked down the stairs the sergeant muttered, "Filling in his football pools, I expect."

At just after eleven-thirty and dressed once more in her widows weeds, Paula walked along Bournemouth pier towards the fortune teller's kiosk. She wasn't surprised to find that, as she approached, the fortune teller's son detached himself from the kiosk and came towards her. He had evidently been on the look-out, she wondered, girl-like, whether it had been for her or simply anything in skirts. For her part, she had set the time of her handing over of the cheque close to noon in the expectation that the old woman would deposit it during the lunch hour. The son fell into step beside her and made small talk as he led her to the kiosk, succeeding in placing his arm around her in the process.

Mrs Alice Timpson, alias Madame Destie, was sat in her usual place in the dim interior. She motioned to the seat opposite.

Paula sat down, put her handbag on the table and folded her hands on her lap. Then she slowly lifted the edge of the black table cloth and firmly pressed to the underside of the table, the small cube that Bert Smith had provided.

"Good morning my dear, did you have a nice weekend?"

"Yes thank you," said Paula.

"I hope that you kept our arrangement a secret?"

"Oh yes," said Paula, "you said that I mustn't tell anyone."

"That's alright then. Did you have any trouble with the cheque?"

"No, why should I, I only had to write it, didn't I?"

"I suppose that you did," said Madame Destie, to whom giving away ten thousand pounds would have been a mind numbing event.

Paula took the envelope out of her handbag and placed it on the table, saying, "I hope that I've made it out properly, please check it."

"Oh, I'm sure that it's alright," said Madame Destie, picking up the envelope, taking out and studying the cheque. "Yes, that's right, ten thousand pounds, made out to Mrs Alice Timpson and dated and signed correctly. That'll do fine."

"You are sure that you will be able to give the money to my dead husband in heaven, aren't you?" said Paula.

"Oh yes," she lowered her voice, "with Passing Cloud's help."

"When will you, er give it to your spirit? I do wish that I could be there."

"You don't realise how much mental energy on the astral plain it takes to summon my control, it takes me days and nights to prepare for a normal séance and material transfers take several times as long. As for you being there, as I explained last time, the spirit rules simply won't allow it."

"But I'll have to be there when Bertram speaks with me, won't I?"

"True, that's why it will be so costly, it will take an awful lot of preparation by me here in the material world and by Passing Cloud in the spirit world."

"But I will be able to speak to him?" persisted Paula.

"Yes, if I can arrange it but remember what I said last time, voices from beyond the great divide always sound different."

"How long will I have to wait?"

"At least a month," said Madame Destie, torn between not contradicting her remarks about the time and effort required for preparation and eagerness to get her hands on more of this sucker's wealth. "I'll ring you when I've made the arrangements with the other side."

"Well, I'll just have to accept it," said Paula. "I'm sure that Bertram will think that it's money well spent."

"Yes, I'm sure that he will," said the fortuneteller.

"Is that all, then?" asked Paula.

"Yes my dear. I'll make the necessary arrangements with the other side."

When she left the kiosk the fortune teller's son accompanied Paula nearly to the entrance to the pier, preventing her from having a word with Gloria who was sitting nonchalantly on one of the benches. Gloria was wearing a headscarf as a protection from the breeze and to conceal the tiny earphone. Her recorder was in her pocket.

Gloria watched the son leave Paula, and turn to retrace his steps. While he was still on the landward side of her she stood and went along to the kiosk, pushed the curtain aside and said,

"Anyone in?"

"Come in, my dear," said Madame Destie. "You want to have your fortune told?"

"Yes please."

"I'm afraid that I won't have time to give you a lengthy consultation, only a five pound one."

"That's alright," said Gloria.

"Tell me something about yourself, why do you want me to tell your fortune?"

"I'm 24, I work for the radio station and I've fallen in love with one of the producers."

"That sounds good," said Madame Destie. "I suppose that you want to know how it will turn out?"

"Yes," said Gloria. "He says that he loves me but there's only one snag, he's married to my boss."

"Oh, I see," said the fortune teller, not really knowing on which side of the fence to come down on; should she counsel breaking off the relationship or tell the girl to fight for her man? Someone else's man, actually. While she was having these thoughts, the entrance darkened as the son returned. His mother spoke to him over Gloria's blonde head.

"All well?"

"Yes, she went off as good as gold. No one was waiting for her."

"I think that we've got it made, the cheque's a good one with her name printed on it. I'll take it to the bank this lunch time."

She turned back to Gloria and said in her fortune-telling voice,

"I see you journeying through a tunnel. It's dark and sometimes it all seems to be too much for you but you go on towards the light at the end of the tunnel where your lover awaits you. It won't be easy for you or for him." She paused and looked into her crystal ball. "There is a dark and empty space. Oh, I see, what it means, you will lose your job." She paused again. "And so will your lover, but don't worry, he will obtain his freedom to marry you." She consulted the crystal ball again, "I don't see any riches, from then on life will be hard and you will have to be the breadwinner but at least you will have each other."

Madame Destie sat back, she felt that she'd done a good deed. The government should pay her for her social work such as this. If this silly young girl still went with the married producer after all that, she deserved all she got. Like that bitch who her husband had gone off with, she would have discovered quite quickly that he was just a lazy sod who expected women to keep him. She was welcome to him. In the semi-darkness she covertly studied Gloria's hair, it didn't look as if it came out of a bottle.

"Oh," said Gloria.

"Yes," said the fortune teller, "and you will have to bring up his children by his first wife as well as your own."

"Oh," said Gloria once more. She was almost believing her own lies. Wait until she told Will about it.

"What will you do?"

"Oh I don't know, it's all so difficult the way you tell it."

"Then go and find yourself a nice boy who isn't married."

"Like me," came a muttered comment from somewhere behind.

Madame Destie indicated that that was as far as a fiver would get her and Gloria regained the fresh air, being required to squeeze past the son in the process.

She walked back to the bench on which she had sat before and recorded the talk between mother and son that was largely expressions of mutual satisfaction and self-praise at how easy it had been to fool the widow. It wasn't more than five minutes before mother and son emerged, locked the door and walked towards the shore. Gloria rang Paula's number and told her that they were on their way. Paula phoned Clare.

Chapter Sixteen

SERGEANT TYLER consulted his friends in the police units that dealt with vice, drugs, prostitution and the like and using their information on Luigi Coroneli. updated the Bernoulli death dossier. For good measure he put in the same sort of information on Alfredo Corleone as well. Both were known to the officers dealing with vice to have mafia connections although both had escaped conviction to date.

Coroneli lived in Highgate and ran a legitimate money-lending and debt-collecting business. He had been born in Palermo and had been brought to Britain at the age of six. He had Italian citizenship by birth and British citizenship by naturalisation. His wife, also the daughter of parents who had come from Sicily, had died two years earlier and they had one daughter who lived in Highgate and had been married to Michael Bernoulli.

He was thought to be the head of a mafia gang that was deep into the vice industry in the City and the West End and was known to have two close associates, Salvatori Donanti and Leonardo Bianci and a secretary called Maria. The latter lived in a small flat in Coroneli's office building. Salvatori was the hard man, the enforcer, and Leonardo was the accountant.

Corleone lived in Croydon and also ran a debt-collecting business. He was married to an English girl and they had two married daughters. He was thought to be the head of the mafia operating south of the Thames. His mafia family was not as prosperous as that north of the river and was constantly at odds with rival gangs from other ethnic groups, mainly Afro-Caribbean's. He had a similar organisation as Luigi and recent events had shown that he and his principal lieutenants would like to have a share of the better paying business to be had on the other side of the river. Whether his rank and file 'soldiers' still shared this ambition now that two of them had been killed and another four were facing long jail sentences, was now a moot point.

He took his findings to Inspector Donovan. Who said that he'd like to sleep on it.

Luigi Coroneli had driven away from his office building (and Maria's flat) in a rage. He was angry that the police had found his 'get away' car and traced it back to him. He didn't for a moment believe the

138

story printed in the paper. The fire brigade didn't go round looking in private garages. Filling stations, yes, but lock-ups, no. On the other hand, the present government was issuing new regulations all the time and so was the mayor of London. Perhaps it was just bad luck and they were looking in lock-ups. More jobs for the trade union boys.

He thought about what they might have discovered. On the surface there was nothing to connect him with the car, it wasn't registered in his name. So they must have searched it. Had they tested it for fingerprints and found his or had they searched more thoroughly and found his passports and other documents. Was there a law that said that a person couldn't have passports in different names? He wasn't so sure about different nationalities but, he consoled himself, in any case it would only involve fines.

By the time he had arrived home and garaged the car he had calmed down. That left Maria, he was getting tired of her. He had to admit that she was a good secretary and she didn't discuss his affairs with anyone else. As far as he was aware, after more than five years she didn't seem to know anybody or visit anybody except that mother of hers. In any case he always discussed his real business in Italian and she didn't speak Italian. But she didn't give him what he really wanted, all she did was lie in bed and let him have sex with her, to use her body. That had been sufficient when his wife was alive but now he wanted something more, he craved for affection, he wanted a girl who would make love willingly and with fire, like a Sicilian girl, who had the privilege of attracting the capo's eye, would. He toyed with the notion of going back to Palermo and bringing one back with him. He smiled inwardly at the thought that then he'd have to conduct his illegal business in English and then realised that it wouldn't matter, he would be proud to have such a bed-mate share his secrets. A Sicilian girl would be a part of the family.

So he was back with the question of what to do about Maria?

Meanwhile, Salvatori and the more militant members of his 'family' were waiting for him to take retaliatory action against the South London mob. They had done their homework, yesterday Leonardo had reported on the results. Alfredo had four brothels, four that they knew about, anyway, all in the more affluent outer suburbs. In addition there was a large number of girls on the street who gave their immoral earnings to his pimps and other soldiers saw to it that across the region, small businesses paid protection money.

Leonardo had been adamant in recommending that they shouldn't attempt to take over any part of the Corleone empire. He had produced arguments and figures purporting to show that the cost would exceed the benefits. Salvatori had argued that they should at the very least, repay like with like, nothing subtle like putting incendiaries under the girl's beds but good old-fashioned Molotov cocktails thrown into the entrance foyers and a few pimps put out of action and into hospital.

Luigi had agreed and his lieutenants were due to bring him their proposals in the morning. He'd sleep on it.

In Dorset, Detective Sergeant Clare Thornton and her boss, Inspector Wyatt went to the police headquarters at Winfrith Heath to report to their boss, Detective Superintendent Harding. At the conclusion of their report on current cases, Clare mentioned the sting operation that Southern Enquiries had conducted against the pier fortune-teller.

"You're saying that they tricked the woman into accepting a cheque for ten thousand pounds which they then stopped?"

Clare was surprised that the usually reasonable Super should take this view.

"No Sir, they had a client who's elderly mother had been persuaded to part with her hard earned five hundred pounds allegedly to be sent to heaven to make her dead mother happy. This was so evidently a con. that Southern Enquiries set out to allow themselves to be conned while recording the whole thing and photographing the confidence trickster paying the money into her bank account."

"We wouldn't have been allowed to do that," said the Super.

"No Sir, that's why Southern Enquiries did it."

"They're friends of yours, aren't they?"

"Yes and good friends of the police, too," said Clare.

"Tim Hawkridge, General Hawkridge's son, the one who owns all those radio stations, is behind them, Sir," said Inspector Wyatt.

The Superintendent's face brightened,

"The one who has that absolutely gorgeous French wife?"

"Yes Sir," said Clare. "Actually she's half French, her father was in the RAF."

"I've got them now, the General's a magistrate. They all came to the last Police Ball, brought her mother too, she was the life and soul of the party. Produces wine in Burgundy. It's a small world these days isn't it?"

"Yes Sir," said Wyatt. "About the fortune teller…"

"Ah yes, d'you think that it'll hold up in court?"

"Oh I would think without a doubt. I propose that we arrest both the mother and son."

"What will be the charge?" asked the Super.

"Obtaining money by false pretences."

"The old woman may swear that she can transfer money to heaven."

"Then I will willingly give her five pounds in court and invite her to prove it," grinned Clare. She went on, "There were four other people at the séance, they called themselves Mr and Mrs Smith and Jones and they must have known that it was part of a con, should we charge them?"

"Only you will know whether there is enough evidence to charge them with aiding and abetting but bring them in for questioning. Even if we don't charge them we can hang them out to dry in court, can't we?"

"Very good Sir," said Wyatt who knew that his wife in Bournemouth had plans to go out that night and was now anxious to get away, "I'll put it in hand sometime tomorrow."

Monday night was Gloria and Will's night off from helping her parents at the Tolbrite Arms. She had grown up in the pub and naturally helped out in the bar and dining room when she was old enough. She had always liked Will and had always been there when he was helping his father at the garage across the green from the pub. Will had gone off and served for three years in the Royal Marine Commandos and when he came back he realised that the gawky kid with fair hair who was always hanging around the garage had grown into a most desirable and shapely blonde young woman. There had followed a frustrating two years. The garage did not make enough profit to enable young Will to support a bride and showed no sign of recovery as people bought their petrol and accessories from the supermarkets in Poole and Bournemouth when they did the weekly shopping. Eventually Helene had taken the bull by the horns and closed the garage – the Hawkridge Estate owned all the village of Tolbrite, including the church, school and the pub – turning it into the Estate Maintenance Depot with Will as the salaried Maintenance Manager and Old Will, his father, as the caretaker. Will and Gloria had wed and moved into the house that had once been occupied by the antique dealer. Tim Hawkridge, Will's lifelong friend, had insisted that Dorset born and bred Will should host a chat-show on the newly opened Hawkridge Radio Bournemouth and despite Will's misgivings, the ten to eleven spot on Monday evenings was now one of the stations most popular programmes.

On Mondays they usually went to a cinema or theatre, had a leisurely meal and were at the radio station by a quarter before ten o'clock for a chat with the station manager, Jill Jones, before going to the small studio for the broadcast, where Will sat one side of a console and Jill and Gloria sat on the other. Jill's role was crucial, she decided which calls to put through to Will and hence to broadcast and she operated the short delay system by which she could prevent obscene or libellous comments going out over the air.

All the UK Hawkridge stations broadcast the news from the London headquarters every hour on the hour. They waited until it was finished and Jill played the introductory music then cued Will. By now he was an old hand at it.

"Hello listeners, Will here, hosting your weekly chance to share your views with others. As usual the past seven days seem to have sped by as if I was talking to you only yesterday. They say that this shows that you must be happy, I must be very happy."

He looked across the low glass screen and grinned at Gloria.

"In the past years we've talked about most things on this programme but I don't think that anyone's ever mentioned fortune telling. Do you think that some people are born with the gift to look into the future? Looked at another way, if it is possible, would you want to know what's in store for you next week or next year? Let's hear your views with the usual proviso please, no names. If you do, my producer Jill, who manages this station will cut you off the air."

He took off his headset as Jill played the music. She already had some callers waiting for her to call them back, callers who probably hadn't heard Will's introduction because they had all been warned that, for technical reasons, they shouldn't have their radio on when talking to Will. After little more than a minute she cued Will. He put on his headset and said

"Hello caller, what do I call you?"

"Fred," said a gruff voice.

"Hello Fred, we've talked before, haven't we? What's on your mind?"

"This opening of the pubs 24 hours a day. I think that it's mad."

"The government tell us that letting people drink until all hours will reduce drunkenness in the streets."

"They don't know what they're talking about. It's just a way to increase the brewers profits. How much have the brewers give to the political party funds, that's what I'd like to know. You'll note, Will that I didn't name names but we all know who I mean, don't we?"

Fred was consumed by mirth.

"Thanks Fred," said Will *"that's certainly a topic on which our listeners will have strong views."*

Will took off his phones. Good old Jill, she had picked out a good question to start things off. The music played and then on with the headset,

"Hello caller, what shall I call you?"

"Cynthia. I was going to say the same as the last caller. We live opposite a public house and already we're kept awake until gone midnight every night. They're supposed to shut at eleven but they're still in their finishing their last orders at half past. Then they're out on the pavement, shouting singing and screaming, the girls are as bad as the men and they're usually half naked."

"What do the police do?" asked Will.

"They do their best to break up the groups and get them on their way but it doesn't stop the shouting and swearing. If anything, it's noisier."

"And you think that extending the hours could make things worse, Cynthia?"

Will grinned at his wife. Ever since he had been told off for calling a woman by the wrong name, Gloria had written the caller's name in black on a white board.

"Stands to reason doesn't it? A few of them may go home before midnight, shouting and singing, then a few more who have drunk some more, then a few more and so on keeping the neighbourhood awake all night."

"It's a problem, isn't it? Thanks for your call", another glance at the board, *"Cynthia."*

More music and then,

"Hello caller, what's your name?"

"You may call me Beatrice."

"Very well, Beatrice, what do you want to talk about?"

"Mystics."

"You mean fortune tellers?" said Will.

"Mystics," insisted the caller.

"You're obviously interested in mysticism," said Will, rather pleased with his use of the word. Both girls were grinning at him.

"The occult has always interested me."

"Perhaps you would give the listeners an idea of your views."

"There are more things in heaven and earth than most people believe. Some of us have the gift of being able to look beyond the boundaries of this mortal coil."

"So you believe that it's possible to tell fortunes," said Will, trying to make the caller come down to cases.

"That's what I said, the gift of second sight."

"Could you give the listeners an example of where you were able to predict someone's future?"

"I was able to tell an unfortunate woman that her marriage was likely to fail."

Oh Lord, thought Will, I could have hoped for a happier example. He said,

"And did it?"

"Yes, he stayed with the other woman and never came back to her."

He grinned at the girls and said,

"Thank you for that most interesting contribution, Beatrice."

There was a slightly longer musical interlude and then Jill gestured that he should don the headset.

"Hello caller, what do I call you?"

"Greg."

"And what do you want to share your opinions about, Greg?"

"Fortune tellers, it's all a load of malarkey."

"You don't think that people can see into the future?"

"Not for one minute and a good job to."

"How's that?"

"When the good Lord made man he programmed the human brain to discount bad news because it would be bad for us to keep remembering all the bad things."

"That's an interesting idea, Greg, why do you think that?"

"It's obvious, isn't it? Put on the television news and it's all bad news, someone's blown up twenty people, a million are about to starve *or die of AIDS in Africa, there's been an earthquake in the Indian sub-continent and a plane has gone down in the jungle in South America. And that's just one night's ration of bad news."*

Will was struggling to keep up with this and said,

"So you don't think that people can foretell the future?"

"Of course not."

"Thanks for your call, Greg."

Will took off the headset and wiped his brow. Jill played the music and then,

"Hello caller, what do I call you?"

"Miriam," said a voice that Will could scarcely hear.

"What do you want to tell us, Miriam?"

"I think that your previous caller was wrong, it is good to be able to foretell the future."

"Why do you say that, Miriam?"

"My friend Alice can tell fortunes, she's ever so good."

"Has she told your fortune?"

"Oh yes, she gives me all sorts of good advice."

"What sort of advice, Miriam?"

"Well, after my husband Cedric died she told me that I should sell my house and move into a flat."

"Did you?"

"Yes, but my children were ever so angry. They said that I should have consulted them before I invested it."

"Where did you invest it?"

"My friend Alice did the cards and advised me of a good place to put it."

"That's very interesting Miriam, I think that I know someone who would be very interested in knowing all about your experience."

"I'm sure that my friend Alice would be pleased to help them as well."

"Thanks for your call, Miriam."

The remainder of the hour produced a crop of comments on fortune tellers, and the old favourites, student housing, rural bus services, football and television programmes.

They cleared up, asked Jill to give a recording of the last call to Paula, said goodnight and drove contentedly homeward.

Chapter Seventeen

THE following morning the players in the drama all woke determined upon action of some sort.

Detective Inspector Donovan resolved to have Luigi Coroneli brought in to explain the forged documents found in the car in the garage in Welbeck Mews Lane and his connection with what went on in the two houses that he owned in Mayfair that were used for prostitution. That would do for starters.

Detective Inspector Wyatt decided over breakfast to tell Clare Thornton to arrange to question the fortuneteller and her son, bringing them into the station if necessary.

Madame Destie told her son at breakfast that she would buy him the small car that he was always on about. Second hand and costing not more than a thousand pounds. She also informed him that she was taking ten days off for a holiday in the Seychelles; everyone said that it was heavenly so where better to spend some of the money that that girl had donated to heaven. She was so amused at this thought that she spilled her tea. Later she was to remember this bad sign in the mystics lexicon.

Alfredo Corleone woke up hoping that Luigi Coroneli had forgotten his demand for a million pounds damages and would consider that the sacrifice of six of Corleone's soldiers was sufficient to atone for burning his houses. But he doubted if it would be. One of his soldiers thought that he had spotted one of the northern family driving in a car in Sutton and another had seen one in Richmond. He wondered if they had been seen in Bromley and Croydon as well. There was no need to warn his chaps to be alert, with two of their colleagues already stabbed to death, they were alert enough.

Luigi Coroneli woke resolved to side with Salvatori and carry the war into the Corleone's territory south of the Thames. The latter had rejected out of hand his claim for a million pounds in damages and had claimed to have no knowledge of the four men who had caused the fires. Very well, he had waited long enough, today he would let Salvatori off the leash.

Fred Smart took his wife Angela to her place of work as Assistant to the Harbourmaster at Poole and then made his way to the office in the Hawkridge radio complex where Paula was already opening the morning mail. They discussed the cases upon which they were engaged and the need to interview the old lady who had spoken about investing on Will's chat-show the previous night. They would get a copy of the tape from Jill. Paula wondered when the police would move against the fortuneteller.

Detective Sergeant Clare Thornton woke up and nudged the young man sleeping beside her. Doctor Simon Watts, the pathologist, was a heavy sleeper, as bright as a button until after midnight but difficult to rouse the next morning. They had been engaged for nearly a year and he was the nicest thing that had ever happened to her. Over breakfast they talked shop and Clare told him that she expected that today would be the day of Madame Destie's arrest, or at least, her first interrogation. He called it Destie's day of destiny.

Maria had spent a sleepless night. She was conscious that a watershed had been crossed in her relationship with her employer. It was not only the fact that he had struck her, his whole demeanour had changed and her thoughts kept going back to the day when she had overheard him telling his henchmen that he wanted to be rid of her. She would willingly leave today but she knew that he would want to dictate the time and manner of her leaving and that if she walked out he would hunt her down.

She was at her desk when he came in. He walked straight through her office and into his own without a word or glance in her direction. Leonardo and Salvatori arrived soon afterwards, both spoke to her before they went on into Luigi's room. She could hear them talking Italian and it seemed that Leonardo was arguing with the other two, something about Salvatori starting a war that they would come to regret. She heard him say that the football fiasco was bad enough but this could be worse.

The visitors left about an hour later, Salvatori all smiles and Leonardo solemn. She assumed, correctly, that the former had prevailed in whatever it was that they had been discussing. Leonardo gave her a sad smile as he closed her office door.

At precisely eleven, two uniformed police officers came into her room and politely asked for Mr Coroneli. A surprised Maria gestured towards the communicating door and they went in with Maria fluttering behind them.

"Mr Coroneli?" asked the first policeman.

"Yes, I'm Coroneli, what do you want, bursting in here like this." He turned on Maria, "Why didn't you stop them?"

"They didn't give me a chance, Mr Coroneli, they simply walked straight in."

"We'd like you to come down to the station with us, Sir," said the officer.

"What for?" said Luigi.

"To answer some questions, Sir."

"What about?"

"They don't tell us things like that, Sir. All that we were told was to bring you in."

"I refuse, you have no right to question me."

"You'll find that we have, Sir. Now what's it to be, are you coming quietly like a good citizen or do we have to take you out in handcuffs?" Like the crook you are, thought the second officer, removing the cuffs from his belt in readiness.

"I'll have the law on you, I'll write to my MP, I'll…I want my solicitor."

"By all means, Sir, your secretary can call your solicitor and ask him to come to the station as well. The more the merrier." He turned to Maria, "We'll call them if you like, do you have the solicitor's number?"

Maria looked at Luigi for instructions. He barked,

"Get on to Bessani, tell him what's happened and tell him to come to the police station at once. Tell him that I'm going to sue the police."

The officers had heard it all before. It was always the ones with something to hide who made the most fuss.

"Come on then Sir," said the first officer, "we'd like you to accompany us to the station. Let's go."

Luigi took his time, locking his desk drawers and placing his glass paperweight in the centre of the top of the blotter, before putting on his top-coat and preceding the officers across Maria's room. She was already tapping-out the solicitor's number. He shouted at her,

"Tell him that I want him there at once, not in half an hours time."

"He might be out…." started Maria but Luigi was already out of the door.

Mention of the Coroneli name got her straight through to the senior partner, Silvestro Bessani. Maria explained what had happened and that her boss wanted him at the police station at once.

"Did they say what they wanted to question Senor Coroneli about?" asked the lawyer.

"No, the policemen said that they didn't know, only that they had been told to bring Mr Coroneli to the police station, in handcuffs if necessary."

"I see."

Silvestro Bessani was worried. It was he who had tipped-off Luigi that he had learned that the police intended to arrest the capo's son-in-law and charge him with a double murder and rape. The son-in-law had been killed that same night. Bessani had felt like the angel of death. Was it this that the police wished to question the capo about?

Maria was also worried. The capo's glass paperweight had disappeared. Surely he hadn't taken it with him? He laid great store by that paperweight, his late wife had brought it back as a present from a visit to her relatives in Messina. You would think that it was made of gold. On one occasion he had made Maria go downstairs and empty all the rubbish sacks looking for it before discovering it where he had put it the previous day, in one of his desk drawers.

Bessani arrived at the police station fifteen minutes after the police car carrying Luigi got there and found the capo sitting explosively in an interview room. He judged, correctly, that the police were giving him time to stew in his own juice. It emerged that he had made a considerable scene in refusing to have his fingerprints taken on the grounds that he wasn't a felon, he hadn't been charged with any crime. Bessani asked Luigi if he had been told why he had been brought to the police station. This provoked another outburst.

Detective Inspector Donovan and Detective Sergeant Tyler entered the room and introduced themselves. They seated themselves across the table and the sergeant switched on the recording machine and made the required statement of the date, time and who was present.

The solicitor got in first.

"Perhaps you would tell us why my client has been brought here against his will, Inspector?"

"Certainly," said Donovan. "We would like him to answer some questions concerning some documents that have come into our hands."

"What would be the nature of those documents?"

"Three passports in different names, some travel information and a large sum of money."

"And what relevance do the police think this has to my client?"

"All the passports feature his photograph."

Donovan placed the three passports side by side on the table, opened to show the photographs, and turned his attention to Luigi Coroneli "What explanation do you have, Sir?"

"I don't know what you're talking about, I've never seen them before in my life. Someone has stolen my identity."

"So the passports aren't yours?"

"No," said Luigi.

"And the fingerprints on them won't turn out to be yours?"

"No."

"Nor the £50, 000 pounds odd of money?"

There was a pause before he said, "No, not as far as I know. Perhaps somebody stole it from me?"

"Surely you or your accountant would have missed such a sum had it gone missing?"

Bessani decided that he'd better try and change the subject. He said,

"Clearly my client has no recollection of that money. Tell me Inspector Donovan, are we permitted to know where were these items found?"

"Certainly, they were found in compartments hidden in the doors of a car in a lock-up garage in Welbeck Mews Lane."

"Never heard of the place," said Luigi.

Bessani wished that he'd keep quiet.

"What evidence do the authorities have to connect my client with the car?"

"We think that he owns it."

Bessani leapt on that,

"But you don't positively know that he owns it?"

"At this precise moment, no, but we know for a fact that he owns the garage."

It took a few moments for this to sink in. A WPC took advantage of the moment to come in and hand a note and an object to the Sergeant. Tyler put the object in his pocket and passed the note to Donovan who glanced at it, grinned to the sergeant and stuffed the brief note into his pocket.

The solicitor turned to his client and asked,

"Do you own a garage in," he consulted his notes, "Welbeck Mews Lane?"

"Of course not," said Luigi.

"My client denies all knowledge of the lock-up garage and he doesn't own it."

"According to the records of the Land Registry, a Mr Luigi Coroneli is the registered owner of the garage and the title deeds were forwarded to his address on completion of the registration. And while we are about it, the Land Registry also tell us that Mr Coroneli is also the owner of the houses in Clarges Street and Half Moon Street that were burnt the other night."

A considerable part of the solicitor's business was concerned with the sale, purchase and transfer of residential and business property and he had a healthy respect for the thoroughness of the work of the Land Registry. Loyally, he tried,

"Did you bring my client here to discuss the fires, Inspector?"

"No, not this morning. As you know we already have four men in custody. Today we're concerned with the lock-up garage owned by Mr Coroneli."

"I'm sure that there must be some sort of a mistake."

"There has been no mistake," said Donovan. "Mr Coroneli owns the lock-up garage and, perhaps for the purpose of concealing that ownership, he employs an accommodation agency called Crown Holdings to deal with the correspondence and pay the bills."

"Never heard of them," said Luigi.

The solicitor made a gesture to shut his client up. He said,

"I would suggest to you, Inspector, that ownership of the garage is not the sole reason that you made my client come here this morning."

"True, Mr Bessani."

"Then what would be the nature of the offence that you think, misguidedly of course, my client is guilty of?"

"Possession of forged passports."

The solicitor raised his eyebrows and the Inspector said,

"Yes, they're forgeries, good ones, but forgeries none the less. One of them purports to have been issued to an Italian in Italy, in Rome actually."

"Forgeries that were concealed in a car that my client doesn't own," said the solicitor, "who, may I ask, is the registered owner?"

"According to the vehicle registration authorities, the keeper is the same person who the local council think owns the garage."

151

"Really, Inspector, this gets more ridiculous with every admission that you make. It's not my client that you should be questioning but this person from…" he looked at his notes again, "Crown Holdings."

"Believe me Sir, we have."

"Well then, there's your answer, the fellow is obviously up to no good and I protest most strongly on behalf of both Mr Coroneli and myself, at being made to come here this morning."

He stood up and Luigi also made to get up. Donovan waved his hand and gestured to the solicitor to sit down.

"We're not finished with your client. There's one big snag in your argument that this Mr Julius Carpenter who signs the documents for both the garage and the car, is the owner of the forged passports."

"And what might that be?" said the solicitor dismissively.

"He's black"

It took some more moments for the solicitor to evaluate the import of this. He tried,

"And what difference does that make?"

"Why should a black man have three forged passports made, each with a photo of your client in it?"

"It's not my responsibility to solve your problems, Inspector, but simply to demonstrate that his alleged guilt cannot be proved beyond reasonable doubt."

"Oh, but we believe that it can," said Donovan.

"I'd be interested to learn how."

Donovan said, "that will come later. For the present I must ask you to allow your client to answer my questions. You may, of course advise him not to answer, in which case we will draw our own conclusions, is that clear?"

"Yes, I understand," said the solicitor.

Donovan looked at Luigi and said,

"Do you still deny all knowledge of the car that was found in the garage at Welbeck Mews Lane?"

"I said so, didn't I?" said Luigi.

"Please answer the question, do you deny all knowledge of the car."

"Yes."

"Then how do you account for the fact that your fingerprints, and only your fingerprints, are everywhere on the car, on the steering wheel, on the gear shift lever, on the light switches, the door handles, everywhere, in fact, that a person would touch in driving the car?"

There was a moment of profound silence as both client and solicitor considered what this might mean. Then Luigi said,

"I didn't let you take my fingerprints."

"Yes you did," said Donovan, "give the gentleman back his paper weight, Sergeant."

Tyler took the paperweight out of his pocket and slid it across the table.

"How did you get that?" cried Luigi.

"Well, you seemed to be so fond of it so our PC thought that you'd like to have it with you when he brought you in this morning."

"I'll have the law on you," screamed Luigi.

"We are the law," said Donovan. "Next time we'll talk about the bloodstains. Come on sergeant we're through here for the present."

He and the sergeant stood up. Tyler made the closing announcement and switched off the machine.

"What do you mean by that?" said the solicitor.

"Ask your client," said Donovan. "You're free to go, but your client mustn't leave the country. We will hold you responsible to see that he doesn't."

With which he and Sergeant Tyler walked out of the room, leaving the WPC to see the visitors off the premises.

When they were in the inspector's room, Tyler said,

"Where do we go from here, Don When do you intend to charge him with possession?"

"We let them worry about it for a week or so and meanwhile we put the fear of God up Mr Julius Carpenter and his colleagues and complete our forged passports case. Then we arrest him."

"And the murder of his son-in-law?"

"Unless we have the most amazing slice of luck we're unlikely to be able to convince the CPS that he has a case to answer."

"What about the spots of blood in the car boot?"

"His lawyer will argue that his son-in-law cut himself one day."

Chapter Eighteen

IN BOURNEMOUTH, Sergeant Clare Thornton walked along the pier. She had decided not to bring her car and go to all the bother of seeking permission to bring it beyond the barrier, relishing the idea of a walk instead. It was a pleasant place to be, sauntering seawards towards the fortune teller's kiosk. She didn't anticipate any trouble, she'd simply come to ask an elderly woman and her son some questions. Alice Timpson would have bridled at being described as elderly, she thought of herself as middle-aged but to a young police-person on a sunny morning like this, anyone over fifty was over the hump.

She was spotted by the fortune teller's son as she approached. His role was to persuade passers-by that they should enter the kiosk and have their fortunes told. In performing this task he always had a distant eye for a pair of well shaped legs and if, as she got closer, the owner of those shapely legs turned out to be pretty as well, he oozed extra charm to get her to enter the kiosk. As Clare got near he advanced to meet her and fell into step beside her, demanding her attention as he went into his sales pitch. He felt that he wouldn't mind strolling right up to the end of the pier in the winter sunshine with a girl like this. Clare had returned his smile and given him a cheerful good morning, but he expected her to walk past and was surprised when she stopped and made to enter the kiosk. He said,

"Come to see if Madame Destie can tell your fortune?"

She grinned at him and produced her identity card and said,

"No, I'm a detective."

"Then you'll want her to tell you where the next bank raid will be," grinned the son.

"That'll be the day. I'd like a word with you and your mother."

He moved ahead of Clare and opened the door so that she had to squeeze past him to get in. He said over her shoulder,

"Here's a police detective who wants to ask you some questions."

"You too, buster," said Clare, turning.

He came in and walked round the table to stand beside his mother who was seated at the table in her 'fortune-telling' attire and attitude.

"I'm always ready to help the police," said Madame Destie. "How can I help?"

"We understand that you aren't only a fortune-teller but a medium as well."

"Yes, but I don't advertise the fact, there are some funny people about."

"But you do hold séances at your home."

"Yes," said the fortune-teller, slowly, "Occasionally."

"You claim to have special powers."

"There's no law against being a spiritualist, there are spiritualists all over the country." She thought for a moment and said, "In America, too, the President's wife, Nancy, regularly consulted a medium."

"We're not interested in your being a medium," said Clare, "only in what you claim to be able to do."

"All that I do is to summon my control and he does the rest. No human being can make anything happen," her voice dropped, "on the other side."

"I'm sure that's true" said Clare. "Then why do you claim to be able to do so?"

"You're not listening," said Madame Destie. "It's Passing Cloud, my control who does."

"Does what?" asked Clare, momentarily lost. She hoped that the recorder in the handbag that she had placed on the table, was getting all this.

"Brings me messages from the other side."

"What other side," asked Clare, deliberately playing dumb.

"THE Other Side, from purgatory, from limbo, call it what you will, the place where the poor tortured souls who are denied entry into heaven are forced to wait, sometimes for all eternity."

"And you claim that this, what-did-you-call-it, this control, enables you to speak to such people?"

"Only in a way, he carries messages."

"Then you don't actually speak to dead people?"

"No, as I said already, Passing Cloud does, he carries messages."

"Can he carry anything else?"

Clare had had one eye on the son and she saw him stiffen and touch his mother on the shoulder. Madame Destie clearly had no need of his reminder to be cautious, she had been getting more wary as the questioning persisted. She said,

"I'm sorry but I've wasted enough time answering your questions, I've got my living, such as it is, to earn."

Rather foolishly, Clare remarked,

"I haven't noticed anyone trying to get in."

"That's because we've got the door shut and he's not out there bringing them in," she snapped.

"I've no objection to your son going out there," said Clare.

"You're good at telling other people what to do, aren't you? Some of you people ought to be made to do a real job of work instead of riding round in fancy cars bothering us honest taxpayers."

"Just one more question, then, and it's the one I've already asked, Do you claim that you can get your control to carry objects into purgatory?"

"I've made no such claim."

"We have evidence that you have promised at least two people that you have a special gift of being able to pass money through to what you call the other side."

"I gave no such promises. If people force money on me to make themselves feel better it's not my fault."

"So you didn't ask for money, it was forced upon you?" persisted Clare.

"I've said all that I'm going to say and I must ask you to leave."

With which she turned her back on Clare.

Clare took up her handbag and was out of the door before the son could get there. She walked back to the police station well pleased with the way things had gone.

That afternoon she played the tape back to Inspector Wyatt and made a typed version.

Silvestro Bessani insisted that Luigi Coroneli accompany him back to his office. In the taxi each was deep in his own thoughts, Luigi with rage that the police had found out so much and the solicitor wondering why the capo seemed prepared to lose £ 50,000 by denying that the passports were his, a crime for which, Silvestro thought, he could get him off with a fine. There must be something more about the car that the capo was hiding and that brought him back to the last thing that the policeman had mentioned, some bloodstains.

When they were in his office and supplied with a cup of coffee, the solicitor went over the recent interview with the policemen, saying that he thought that it had sounded that the police had an open and shut case that the car was Luigi's and that he would be wise to admit ownership of the car and the £50,000.

"What about the passports?" said Luigi with a pretence of innocence, "they said that they're forgeries."

"I would plead that you went in fear for your life as evidenced by the burning of your two houses in Mayfair and that having the garage, car and passports in different names was part of your precautions. I'm sure that you would only be fined for possessing the false passports and the fine would be much, much less than the money that you had hidden in the car."

"I'll admit nothing," said the capo. "Their evidence won't hold up in court and I'm not going to go back on what I said at the station, that car isn't mine."

"But they'll produce witnesses from the accommodation company that pay your bills."

"They won't want to give evidence, you'll see."

"And you'll lose the £ 50,000," said Silvestro, to whom the idea bordered on the unthinkable.

"I'll get it back, one way or another. If that's all you can offer, I'm off."

"Before you go, do you have any idea what the Inspector might be referring to when he mentioned bloodstains?"

Luigi flared up. "I pay you for legal advice. You've given me your advice and that's an end to it. I'll let you know if the police bother me again, that's all."

Silvestro was certain that the police would be bothering the capo again and that next time they might keep him in but he didn't say so, he had no intention of finishing up in a back alley with a dagger through the heart so he didn't persist; all that he could do was advise, it was up to the other party to accept or reject that advice.

Luigi arrived back at his office in a filthy temper. The police had been bad enough and then to be questioned by his solicitor, going on and on about the passports, the money, the car, the garage and, most of all, about bloodstains, was more than a good capo should be expected to accept. Perhaps the solicitor should be reminded of who ruled the roost round here. On the other hand, he had to have a lawyer and better the evil you know than a stranger. Leonardo and Salvatori didn't know that he had the car prepared for flight and he wanted to keep it that way.

With this and similar thoughts storming through his mind he swept through Marie's office like a typhoon without a glance in her direction and slammed his office door behind him. Without taking off his overcoat, he opened his safe and took out the package of deeds. The garage was the fourth folder down and sure enough the Land Registry certificate recorded his ownership. He had a thing about property, unlike some capo's, he wouldn't vest their ownership in third parties. He was happy to set up front men as the occupiers but he always retained the ownership. He'd forgotten the Land Registry. He had a passing thought, he wondered if the four houses in the Richmond, Sutton, Croydon and Bromley areas were registered in Alfredo's name?

Maria was in a dilemma, should she tell him that his favourite paperweight was missing? She opened the communicating door and said,

"Would you like a cup of coffee, Mr Coroneli?"

"No. I've had one."

"When you had gone I noticed that….Oh, it's there."

"What's there?"

"Your paperweight, it was missing."

"Those police stole it but I got it back."

Maria thought that an unlikely tale but was pleased that she hadn't been blamed. She turned to leave the room when he barked,

"You told them about my garage, didn't you?"

"What garage?"

"The one in Welbeck Mews Lane."

"I didn't know that you had a garage and anyway I never discuss your business with anyone. I didn't even do it with your son-in-law when he tried it on, saying that you'd told him to ask me."

There, she thought, think about that one.

Luigi was diverted, "He tried it on, did he?"

"Yes Mr Coroneli."

"Did he ever try to get you to, er, let him touch your body?"

"Yes."

"And did you let him?"

"Certainly not, Mr Coroneli. No one does that, except you."

"If you know what's good for you, you'll keep it that way."

"Yes, Mr Coroneli."

She departed to make a cup of coffee for herself, glad to have diverted his anger and thinking what an odious man her boss was. She would include the day's events in her journal.

Jill Jones popped into the Southern Enquiries office and gave Paula a tape of Will's previous night's broadcast, saying that she might find one of the calls interesting.

"You beat me to it, Jill," said Paula. "I always listen to Will and I was going to come over and ask for a copy when I'd finished reading this mornings mail."

"So you heard the old dear who had followed the fortune teller's advice?"

"Yes, and she called the fortune teller Alice, ten to one that's the woman on the pier. Can you let me have the caller's phone number?"

"I've written it on the box. Remember to ask her permission to break the anonymity that we promise all our callers, won't you?"

"Of course. Thanks Jill."

An hour later Paula called the number that Jill had given her. The phone at the other end was picked up on the ninth ring and a small voice said,

"Hello?"

"Good morning," said Paula brightly, "is that Miriam?"

"Yes, Miriam Outhwaite speaking."

"I heard you speaking on the radio last night, Mrs Outhwaite."

"I've never done that before. Could you hear me alright?"

"Yes, you were fine. I'd like to talk with you some more, could I come and see you?"

"Only you see, the radio lady wouldn't let me listen to myself while I was doing it."

"I know," said Paula, "it's something called feed-back or something technical like that."

"That's what she said. You're not one of those awful reporters, are you?"

"No," said Paula.

"Only the lady at the radio promised me that nobody would ever know that it was me."

"Nor they won't, Mrs Outhwaite. Look my name's Paula and I'm going to call you Miriam, may I come and see you?"

"What for?"

"I'd like to know some more about the advice that your friend Alice gave you."

"Ooh, I don't know, she told me that if I told anyone it would spoil everything and I wouldn't get any more interest."

"I wouldn't tell anyone," fibbed Paula, "unless you told me to. Do you have share certificates?"

"Oh no, if I did I'd have to pay income tax, wouldn't I?"

"I see," said Paula, "you know, you really should let me come and talk with you, where do you live?"

"I live in Poole now. When my Cedric was alive we lived in Bournemouth. I quite like it here but all my friends are on the other side of Bournemouth."

"I've got a friend who works for the harbourmaster at Poole, can I come and see you this afternoon at, say, two o'clock?"

"Only if you don't tell anyone."

She gave Paula her address.

Paula followed Fred to Poole harbour that lunch time. They parked their cars by the harbourmaster's building and climbed the iron stairs to Angela's office, a long room with a window the entire length on the seaward side with a long chart table beneath it. Paula wondered how Angela ever managed to drag herself away from the view to do any work. When she came here they always perched on two stools and gazed out of the window as they talked; there was always something happening outside. Angela's desk and the filing cabinets were against the other, landward, wall and at the far end was a door leading into the Harbourmaster's office that was identical to hers. The whole arrangement resembled a ships bridge and to cap it, the toilet and storerooms at ground level were known as the Lower Deck. To Angela, the daughter of a retired sea captain, it was home from home.

The three of them lunched in the Harbour Tavern where, some years earlier, Fred and Angela's romance had blossomed.

Paula was at Miriam Outhwaite's apartment door at precisely two p.m. She knocked and a timid voice said, "Who's there?"

"Paula, Miriam, we agreed that I could come at two."

"Oh yes."

The door opened on a chain and an anxious face looked at Paula. Paula smiled, the door was pushed to and there was fumbling with the chain, then the door opened fully and the old lady said,

"Please come in, my dear."

Paula judged the old lady to be in her mid-seventies, straight upright, sparingly built with a mop of grey hair and blue eyes that regarded the world through gold rimmed spectacles.

160

The door opened directly into a neat but poorly furnished sitting room . Miriam indicated the chair that Paula should sit in and then seated herself opposite and asked

"What exactly is it that you want to know?"

"I'd like you to tell me all about the investment that your friend Alice made for you."

Paula noticed that the old lady had leant forward and turned her head slightly to hear better.

"She said that if I told anyone it would spoil everything and my investment would become valueless and I can't afford for that to happen."

"How much did you invest?" said Paula more loudly

"Twenty thousand pounds."

"When was this?"

"Last year, I've had two dividends, one was five hundred and two pounds and the one last month was four hundred and eighty, Alice said that the stock market was down, whatever that is."

Paula did a rapid calculation, a return of nine hundred and eighty two pounds was just under five percent gross, a satisfactory but not remarkable return for a non-tax payer.

"Do you know what your money is invested in, Miriam?"

"Alice does all the paper work, she's ever so good."

"How is the interest paid?"

"Alice gives me the cheque."

"What is the name of the company that's written on the cheque?"

"Why are you asking me all these questions, there's nothing wrong, is there?"

"Honestly, I don't know, Miriam. What's the name on the cheque?"

"Alice Timpson."

"You mean that it's a personal cheque from your friend?"

"Yes, she said that it's to keep it secret from the Income Tax people. You won't tell, will you?"

"Is Alice Timpson the Madame Destie who tells fortunes on the pier?"

"Yes, that's how I met her. I went and consulted her when my dear Cedric died. She told me that he was safe in heaven but was worried if I'd have enough to live on. I thought how clever she was to know that it was becoming a bit of a struggle."

"So she advised you?"

"Yes, she was ever so good. On my third visit she said that I should get some money by selling our house and investing the money, so that's what I did. You won't tell anyone, will you?"

"No, Miriam, I won't let you down," replied Paula obliquely.

She left soon afterwards after declining a cup of tea.

Back in their office she described the Miriam Outhwaite case to Fred. He pointed out that they weren't in the charity business, she wasn't their case, she hadn't contracted them to investigate anything on her behalf, and she wouldn't generate income for them. He agreed, however that, when the police had charged Alice Timpson with obtaining money by false pretences, they might lean on her and try to get her to make restitution in order to present herself at her trial in the best possible light.

Chapter Nineteen

THE operation was considered to be of such importance that Salvatori attended the briefing of the soldiers in person. It had been agreed at the discussion with Luigi and Leonardo that morning that they would teach the upstart Alfredo an expensive lesson that very night, they would return the compliment by fire-bombing his houses in the more affluent suburbs. They had discussed the when, the how they knew about.

Luigi wanted to cause the maximum possible chaos and confusion, to hit them at their busiest time, in fact. The problem was they didn't know when that was. Trade in the Mayfair houses started at business-going-home time and was fairly busy until eleven. Would the pattern be different in the suburbs? Would there be a surge in clients as the commuter trains discharged their sophisticated cargo and would males come out in the later evening hours? There was an underlying assumption that the bulk of the clients would be married men. Leonardo thought that a sociologist could well earn a PhD on the subject. If a male he might well enjoy the research. Then he thought of Greta and decided that a female researcher might do the same.

Leonardo was opposed to the whole scheme, he favoured quietly moving into the Corleone rackets using the superior Coroneli manpower and money but the other two were determined on an eye for an eye approach. It was Leonardo who suggested that it didn't matter what time they struck, the important thing was to do it when it best suited the attackers, to ensure that no harm befell their soldiers, to do it when the traffic wasn't too heavy and ensure that all would be back in their north London haunts when the police came looking.

They decided on eight-thirty. Four two-man teams.

All four target houses had been chosen by Alfredo to make a client's entry and exit as discreet as possible. They were detached, set back from the road and had trees at the front and sides. Reconnaissance had established that the front doors of the houses were closed. Private houses in the suburbs always have their front door closed. A client would knock on the door which would be opened by a young man who presumably made a rapid assessment of the trouble-making potential or wealth of the visitor, opened the door wide and allowed the man in.

One of the tabloids carried the most comprehensive report the next morning. It boasted, the way newspapers do, that it was fortunate to have had one of its reporters nearby when the attack on the house in Bromley took place and he had phoned the story in. He had, in fact, been upstairs in bed with a shapely brunette. The other papers merely reported that a terrorist outrage had taken place the previous evening when four occupiers of private houses had been stabbed and their houses, in Richmond, Sutton, Croydon and Bromley, set on fire.

In a way they were all scooped by the Hawkridge Media newsroom which carried the story on it's ten o'clock news the night that it happened, thanks to the fact that the network's production manager, Sid Durand, and his wife, Penny, who happened to be Timmy Hawkridge's personal secretary, lived in the house in the next avenue who's garden practically backed on to the brothel. Nothing ever escaped Penny's eye and they had long known what went on at the house. In the summer they would see the girls sunbathing in the garden and at night they saw sufficient to know that the girls weren't Sunday school teachers. Their approach (Penny's approach, actually and Sid knew better than to argue) was to thank God that she wasn't one of them and it wasn't any of their business. Good luck to them.

That night they had been watching the TV when they heard a commotion at the back and found that the ground floor of 'that' house was on fire and that a lot of men and girls in various stages of attire were milling around in the garden. Closer inspection showed that one of the men was lying on the ground and others were tending him. The men were fast disappearing round the side of the house and soon it was just the girls and the man on the ground.

Penny spoke with some of the girls over the garden fence. From their lurid accounts of their personal experiences and what the injured man had said, it appeared that a man had knocked at the door, he looked OK so the guard had opened it to let him in whereupon the man had produced a knife and stabbed him while a second man had appeared, lit a Molotov cocktail and thrown it into the foyer. They had no idea who had done such a terrible thing.

Sid had phoned the story in and was thanked. Some crank I expect was the comment. While the news-room were putting the ten o'clock bulletin together, reports of three other attacks were coming in on the wire, so the editors took another look at what Sid had reported, put two and two together and broadcast that all four arson attacks had taken place at the same time which was evidence of the sort of planning done by terrorist groups.

It was not until the next morning that the true enormity of what had taken place emerged. Four large detached houses had been attacked. Three had suffered extensive fire damage to the ground floor and staircase and smoke damage through the upper floors and the fourth house had been totally burned, only the shell remaining. In this house one of the girl residents who had been in bed upstairs, had been burnt to death. In all four houses a man had been stabbed, two were seriously ill in hospital and two had been pronounced dead on arrival there.

By mid-day the media were in full cry, was this another terrorist attack? The more sober element noted the similarity of the attacks to what had occurred in Mayfair, in each case the houses had been occupied by young ladies in, what they coyly described as, the entertainment business. The Times stated bluntly that London was witnessing a war between gangs and wondered if it was the old style mafia resisting an attempt by the East European gangs to move in on one of their most profitable fields, prostitution.

At Canary Wharf Penny gave Timmy a lurid account of what had happened at Croydon and repeated it to Helene when she came along to his room to share their usual coffee and sandwiches lunch.

Luigi was beside himself with satisfaction, he arrived at the office wearing the smug smile that always appeared when he had concluded a deal to his advantage. Maria ventured to say that the dreadful fires in the Home Counties were just like the ones that had burnt his houses in Mayfair and her boss had snorted, laughed outright and mumbled "Serves them right."

Leonardo and Salvatori arrived at the office soon after Luigi. Maria could hear them laughing and congratulating themselves in Italian on the night's events. She listened intently, she could understand most of it. It seemed that her boss was responsible for what had happened and that Salvatori and his soldiers had delivered what they hoped would be a knock-out blow to the upstart Alfredo. With property prices as high as they were in the select suburbs, the night had cost him more than the million pounds that Luigi had stipulated as the price of peace. Added to which, pointed out Salvatori, Alfredo had lost two more men permanently and two more were in hospital, making a total of four dead and six out of action. Not forgetting that one of his girls had perished. How Alfredo must regret the mad impulse that led to the Mayfair bombing. His soldiers and girls must be wondering where the next attack would be.

Leonardo had remarked that perhaps the attacks had been too successful and that they should now be more concerned with the police than with Alfredo. Luigi and Salvatori had scoffed at the thought, there was nothing to connect them with the crimes. Leonardo had pointed out that the police would be looking for witnesses who might have seen the raiders arrive. They would also be looking at the thousands of images caught by the CCTV cameras in Richmond, Sutton, Croydon and Bromley. Let them look, had been the response.

Maria noted that Luigi didn't tell his aide's about the police interest in his garage and car. She assumed, correctly, that they were ignorant of their existence.

At about the same time as Luigi and Salvatori were congratulating each other, Paula was phoning Detective Sergeant Clare Thornton and telling her about Miriam Outhwaite and the fortune teller. Clare said,

"You suspect that she's stolen the old woman's money?"

"Yes," said Paula, "it's the old confidence trick, she's paying her interest out of the capital. Mirium must be in her late seventies and at the present rate of payment she would be close to a hundred before the money ran out. But, of course, her dear friend Alice, the fortune teller, would have invented a financial collapse and stopped paying interest long before then."

"Surely her relatives would ask questions?"

"Old people are secretive and Alice has convinced her that if she lets anyone know the income tax man will get to hear about it and take a chunk of it away."

"Then why did she tell you?" asked Clare.

"Because I promised not to tell anybody, I suppose."

"It's your honest face that does it," grinned Clare. "Are you proposing that we should add her to the charge sheet?"

"Not to start with, that can come later. What we thought of doing was to wait until Madame Destie has been arrested, charged and released on police bail and then Fred would go and lean on her and persuade her that she would get a reduced sentence if she could appear in court as a penitent who had done her best to right the wrongs that she has done."

"You'll be lucky," laughed Clare down the phone.

"Well it's worth a try, remember we've got a client who was persuaded to part with five hundred pounds. The question is, do you know when it's likely that she and her son will be charged?"

"Before the end of the present week. I'll keep you posted."

Scotland Yard discounted the theory that Arab terrorists were responsible for the fires and stabbings in the Home Counties. The similarity of the targets and the fact that known mafia figures had been seen doling out money to the dispossessed girls in Mayfair, suggested that the north London mafia family was exacting some sort of revenge.

Inspector Donovan was told to take the case in cooperation with the county police forces. He sent to each district a message that it was thought that the fire and stabbing that had occurred in their area the previous night was part of a major investigation that the Yard had in hand and asking to be kept informed of developments. He recognised how busy the investigating officers would be at the present time and asked that he be informed as soon as possible who owned each of the houses that had been torched. He hoped to visit them to exchange views on the morrow.

Sergeant Tyler read it and said,

"Your usual diplomatic self I see, Don. What do you intend to do now?"

"I thought that we might pay our friend Luigi Coroneli a visit."

"He'll start screaming harassment."

"Let him. I don't mind if he insists on having his solicitor present, I thought that Senor Bessani looked more than a little uncomfortable last time."

"What line will you take?" asked the sergeant.

"I thought that we might point out the similarity between what happened last night and what happened to his houses some days ago and watch his reaction."

"And then?"

"I thought that we might mention possible guilty parties, did he think that it could be the Russian mafia or the Albanians or even one mafia family making war on another, like his north London mob and Corleone's south London mob?"

"Showing our hand a bit, aren't you?"

"I can see no reason why we shouldn't can you?"

167

"Well, you'll be sticking your neck out, we all know that he's the capo but to date nobody's said so to his face."

"Ah but now we've got something on him, the forged passports and the secret car so let's try and ruffle him up a bit further."

The first that Maria knew was when the man who kept his eye open for visitors on the ground floor hastily phoned her to say that two policemen were on the way up. She had just put down the phone and risen to go and tell her boss when her door opened and that nice Inspector came in, followed by the other one. He said,

"Don't bother, we'll announce ourselves."

With which he walked across the small room, opened the communicating door, and went into Luigi's room. Luigi looked up, startled, and said,

"What do you mean by bursting in here like this. Get out, I've got nothing further to say to you."

"Oh," said Donovan, "that's a shame because we've got a lot to say to you."

"I don't want to know," shouted Luigi, then to Maria who was standing helpless in the doorway. "Get Bessani, tell him to come here now."

Maria went back to her desk and passed the message to the solicitor's secretary who said that her boss was busy with an important client and she'd tell him when he was free.

"Mr Coroneli won't like that," said Maria.

"Then he'll have to lump it, won't he?" said the girl and put the phone down. Maria went back into Luigi's room. He looked up and barked,

"Well, did you get him?"

"He's busy with a client...."

"Can't you ever get anything right," He picked up the phone and pushed it at Maria, shouting "Get me the number."

She dialled the number and when the secretary answered, passed the handset to Luigi.

"Hello," he shouted, "when I tell your boss that I want him I mean now, not in ten minutes time."

The listeners could hear a voice and then Luigi shouted,

"I don't care how important his client might think he is, if Bessani knows what's good for him he'll come on the line now."

There was a click and Luigi looked at the phone in disbelief, saying,

"She put the phone down on me. I'll kill the bitch."

"You seem to have forgotten that we're police officers," said Donovan. "I should warn you, Sir, that we've just heard you threaten the life of another person."

"People don't do that to Luigi Coroneli," said the capo, beside himself with rage.

"Nevertheless you don't utter threats, this isn't Sicily."

"What do you mean by that. Anyway, what do you want?"

"We want to ask you some questions about last nights fires and murders in south London."

"What about them?" Luigi couldn't prevent a hint of pleasure creeping into his voice.

"They were very similar to what happened to your two brothels in Mayfair, weren't they?"

"I don't know what you're talking about, I was here all the evening, wasn't I Maria?"

Maria hesitated, blushed and said, "Er, yes Mr Coroneli"

Donovan noted the slight hesitation

"And what time did you leave?"

"After midnight," said Luigi with a smirk.

Donovan looked at Maria and she dropped her eyes in confusion. He decided that she should be questioned when her boss wasn't present. He continued,

"You know as well as I do that the houses were brothels owned by your opposite number Alfredo Corleone".

"He's out of his depth. He should have stuck to fighting gangs of West Indians," said Luigi, dismissively.

"That's as maybe," said the inspector, " but last night's raids look very much like tit for tat, only more so."

"Why should that concern me?"

"I would remind you that we have four of his mafia family in custody for setting fire to two of your brothels, so we know quite a bit about your rivalry. Most law abiding people and a good number of policemen don't give a hoot if gangsters set fire to each other's property and occasionally injure each other but this time two men were killed and a girl was burned to death. That makes it several times more serious and naturally we think that you have some questions to answer about those events and the stabbing of the two Corleone men in Mayfair some days ago."

Maria was feeling guilty. Yesterday morning she had overheard Luigi and his henchmen plotting last night's raids but she hadn't dreamed that anyone might get hurt. She should have gone to the police yesterday. And, by the sound of it, she thought, if she did so she would be signing her own death warrant.

"I told you, I was here," said Luigi.

"Oh, we're sure that you wouldn't have got your hands dirty doing your own dirty work, you capo's make other people do it for you, don't you?" said Donovan, then added on the spur of the moment, "Except when it's a member of your own family, of course."

"What do you mean by that?" said Luigi in a loud voice, looking up.

"You know very well what I mean," said the inspector, "we police can learn a lot from a few spots of blood and what a witness saw." He turned conversationally to Maria and said, "Did you know Michael Bernoulli?"

Maria looked lost and mumbled "Yes, he was married to Mr Coroneli's daughter."

"Did it occur to you that it was a remarkable coincidence, some would say a happy coincidence and others might say a very convenient coincidence, that he was murdered just before we could arrest him for murder?"

Maria looked helplessly at her boss.

"I've had enough of this," said Luigi, standing up. "Get out of this building. You'll regret coming here today, Mr clever policeman, you won't feel so clever when Bessani's had a word with your superiors."

"That's alright, Mr Coroneli, I've said what I came here to say," said Donovan. "Don't think of leaving the country, will you because you'll be hearing from us again in the very near future."

Donovan and Tyler left. In any case Donovan had run out of things to say and Tyler thought that he had said too much.

It was time to go home, anyway.

Maria remained in Luigi's room and said,

"You weren't here last night, Mr Coroneli, why did you say that you were?"

"That's my business. It doesn't do to be too open with those people.

You'll do as your told and keep quiet if you know what's good for you."

"But now you've made me as guilty as you are by making me lie to the police."

"What do you mean you stupid girl. You'd better watch your tongue."

Maria was angry, without thinking she said,"I've heard you plotting crimes with Salvatori and Leonardo in here."

"Get out and hold your tongue."

Maria left the room. Luigi gazed at her departing back, thinking that he'd better do something about her. For her part, Maria realised that she had given the game away, they did all their plotting in Italian, a language she professed not to understand.

Chapter Twenty

ALICE TIMPSON, aka Madame Destie, and her son were taken to the police station the next morning and questioned by Inspector John Wyatt and Sergeant Clare Thornton. The fortuneteller got her protest in first.

"What do you mean by sending policemen to make us come here like common criminals?"

"To ask you some questions," said Wyatt.

"We've got nothing to say to you. I'll write to my Member of Parliament."

They all say that, thought Clare. I wonder if she knows who he or she is?"

"That's your privilege," said Wyatt. "Meanwhile perhaps you'd explain some of the claims that you make."

"Such as?" said the woman.

"Well, for starters, being able to tell people's fortunes."

"Second sight's a gift that I was born with. You wouldn't know."

"Oh but we do," said the inspector, "we police have it too, we use it to look behind the lies that people tell us."

Madame Destie took a moment to think about that, then said,

"Lies indeed. I don't expect people like you to understand the occult."

"The punters don't take it seriously," said her son.

"Hold your tongue," snapped his mother.

"Aw, Mum, they know that it's just a piece of seaside fun, like what the butler saw."

"That's enough of that," said Madame Destie.

"We also understand that you claim to be a medium and hold séances at your house," said Inspector Wyatt.

"So what, there's no law against that."

"That depends on the claims that you make."

"I don't make claims, the spirits guide me, it's the spirits that bring comfort to the bereaved by bringing messages from beyond the grave."

"Passing Cloud," muttered Clare, remembering what Paula had told her.

"Yes," said Madame Destie, automatically lowering her voice, "My spirit guide on the other side is called Passing Cloud."

She was beginning to feel more confident, thinking that if the police had anything to charge her with they would have shown their hand by now.

"We understand that you are assisted in this by your son and by a Mr and Mrs Smith and a Mr and Mrs Jones."

"What if I am, my control likes to have an audience"

"We haven't heard the Smiths and Jones's support your claims," said Wyatt.

You cunning blighter, thought Clare, that's true but only because we haven't spoken with them. Madame Destie ignored this and said,

"I ask again, why have we been brought here?"

"To explain why you took the sum of £500 from a Mrs Valerie Sutton."

"She insisted on giving it to me," said the fortune teller.

"You told her that her mother was in limbo because Saint Peter wouldn't let her into heaven until she gave him £500."

"Prove it."

"So she gave you the money in banknotes for you to pass to your control."

"You can't prove a thing," said Madame Destie.

"Ah, but we can in the case of Mrs Simms though, can't we sergeant?"

"Yes Inspector. You remember the young widow, Mrs Paula Simms, don't you Mrs Timpson? If you don't I'm sure that your son does."

"What about her?" said the fortune teller, suddenly wary.

"You promised her that you could pass £10,000 to her recently deceased husband to enable him to right some wrongs that he had done on earth."

"I've never heard such rubbish," said the fortune teller. "Anyway my bank told me this morning that the bitch had stopped the cheque, so it was never credited to my account and so I will argue that I never received it. So you haven't got a case. They'd laugh you out of court."

"Then there's Miriam Outhwaite," muttered Clare.

" I've had enough of this," shouted Madame Destie. "Come on son, we're leaving."

With which she stood up and made for the door, only to be halted by the policeman who beat her to it. Inspector Wyatt stood and said,

"I'm afraid that it's not to be as easy as that. Alice Timpson, I'm placing you under arrest on charges of obtaining money and attempting to obtain money by false pretences and I will be charging your son as an accessory. After processing and the completion of the formal proceedings, you will be released on police bail and notified in due course of the date and time selected for your trial."

Much later that day, a very subdued Alice Timpson and her son were allowed to leave the police station.

Many days later, in London, it was an inspector in the local police station who alerted Detective Inspector Don Donovan. The man had attended the scene of the fatality as a matter of routine and, remembering Scotland Yard's interest in the Coroneli family, rang Don to tell him of the sad accident that had befallen Mr Coroneli's secretary sometime during the previous night.

Sergeant Tyler went to the station to ask questions. It seemed that Maria had been electrocuted while doing her ironing in the small kitchen of her apartment in the building in which she worked. She had fallen down still grasping the iron which had burnt a hole in the linoleum. The police who attended the scene thought the iron to be old and defective and could have given a severe shock to a user at any time. The miracle was that it hadn't happened earlier. The short circuit that had killed Maria had pulled off the relay and hence although the linoleum had been burned and the wooden floor beneath charred by the residual heat of the iron, there had been no more serious fire.

The girl's employer Mr Coroneli had discovered the body that morning. When she hadn't appeared for work he had gone to investigate why and found her lying on the floor beside the ironing board. He had pointed out to the ambulance men that the flat was equipped with a brand new iron that was still in its box in a cabinet in the kitchen. He was said to be distraught.

Tyler had phoned Donovan and then hurried round to the Coroneli building to see for himself. He found two men in the kitchen in the process of taking up the damaged linoleum and replacing it with new and they had no idea where the ironing board had gone, they thought that the police had the iron. Sergeant Tyler thought that the local station had been lax. He would have to get hold of that iron. While he was thinking about this he heard a noise from an adjacent room and went along the short passage. He found a young woman busy emptying the drawers and cupboards and putting the contents into cardboard boxes.

Sergeant Tyler introduced himself. The girl, who was crouched in front of a chest of drawers, turned and looked up. She smiled and said,

"You're the policeman who asked about my husband's accident."

Tyler realised that she was Sophia, Coroneli's daughter. What could be more natural than her helping her father? As if she had read his thoughts she went on,

"Papa asked me to empty out poor Maria's things. I know that it's a bit soon but he'll have to get a new secretary and this flat goes with the job."

"I see," said the sergeant, thinking that the new secretary could hardly appear overnight. Why the hurry? But then Luigi Coroneli was a peculiar sort of man. His daughter seemed OK though.

"What will you do with them?" asked Tyler.

"I'll get one of the men to take them round to her mother."

"Have you found any papers, diaries or so on?"

"No, not a thing, Papa asked me that. She kept a desk diary in the office, of course, but there aren't any personal papers; if anyone wrote to her she didn't keep the letters. Not even birthday cards and things. I do."

Just then there was a noise on the stairs and Luigi Coroneli walked in. When he saw who it was talking with his daughter, he stormed,

"What are you doing here, this is none of your business, get out."

"Now now, Papa, remember your blood pressure. I was just telling the sergeant that Maria didn't have any papers in her flat or in her desk, except for the desk diary and that was filled with the usual things, mainly your appointments, nothing personal."

"Anyway, he shouldn't be here without asking my permission, I know my rights."

"Don't be stuffy, Papa, he's going now, aren't you sergeant?"

"Yes, thank you for your courtesy, Mrs Bernoulli," said the sergeant.

He walked past her father without a word and made his way back to Scotland Yard.

He described what had happened to Inspector Donovan, who said,

"So she was electrocuted the previous night and Luigi Coroneli appears to be hell-bent on removing all traces of her?"

"That's how it looks. The daughter seemed to be alright, she said that he wanted to get it ready for a new secretary."

"He couldn't possibly find a new girl that quickly," said Donovan, "unless he had one in waiting."

"I thought that the total absence of any personal papers seemed to be odd. According to the daughter there were absolutely none, no diary, no letters, no nothing."

"You've got one of your feelings, haven't you, Sid?"

"Well," said the sergeant, "I don't know what the people upstairs or in the local station will say, but it might be useful to make a few deeper enquiries."

"Starting where, with Luigi?"

"God forbid, he'd scream harassment. No, what I had in mind was that we might take a closer look at the body to start with."

"OK," said Donovan, "fix it with the local station and the pathologist."

Sergeant Tyler did some telephoning and that afternoon found him closeted with the young doctor who had completed the initial examination of Maria's body.

"Just what is it that you're interested in, Sergeant?" asked Doctor Cole.

"We don't know, it's simply that she worked for a man who we have had reason to question concerning several violent deaths recently and this is another one, that's all."

"You mean that you suspect that he's going round bumping people off?" asked the doctor incredulously.

"Nothing so crude as that, it's simply that people have been killed in activities that we know that he has an interest in, I can't say more."

"Very well, then what am I looking for?"

"I don't know," said the sergeant, "anything unusual, I suppose."

"I see," said Doctor Cole. "Well, I wouldn't say that it's unusual these days but she had sexual intercourse shortly before she was killed."

"Did she now," said Tyler, "have you taken samples for DNA?"

"No, do you think that we should?"

"Yes most certainly."

"There is one other small thing," said the doctor, "there's a recent bruise on the back of her head, hidden in the hair."

"I know that it's difficult to judge these things but could whatever caused the bruise have made her unconscious?"

The young doctor thought about that and eventually said,

"I wouldn't say that it couldn't have done."

"Could the bruise have been caused by her fall after the shock?"

This time there was no hesitation,

"No, the bruise is much too low on her head."

"OK,"said the sergeant,"now tell me, did the electric shock that killed her leave any signs on the skin of her hands?"

"Now that's something that did puzzle me," said Doctor Cole. "The paramedics who brought her in reported that she was wearing only a nightdress. She had been found by her boss with an old electric iron grasped in her right hand. He'd removed the iron and tried to revive her before they arrived although he should have known that she had been dead for some hours. But the marks are more on the back of her hand than on the palm."

"What marks?"

"I assumed that they had something to do with the electric shock and that she had been ironing with the iron and somehow managed to put the back of her hand on the electric cable or something, but now that I say it, it does sound a bit improbable."

"It does seem odd," said the sergeant. "She has a bruise on the back of her head, burn marks more on the back of her hand than the front, manages to keep hold of the hot iron in her death throes without burning herself, drops to the floor, again managing to keep the iron away from herself or anything inflammable and the iron then does a neat burn-through of the non-inflammable floor covering. Where is the iron and it's electric lead?"

"I assume that the local police have it," said Doctor Cole.

"I'll ask them," said Sergeant Tyler, "thanks for your help. Don't forget about the DNA samples and I'd have another look at the bruise and the burn marks if I was you."

"Sounds as if I'd better, doesn't it?"

"Oh and one other thing, let's keep what we've been discussing between ourselves for the present."

Fred Smart walked along the pier. His approach didn't interest the fortune teller's son, he was of the wrong gender and men didn't often have their fortunes told. The son was in any case, subdued, oppressed at being arrested and at the thought of the forthcoming trial. On the way back from the police station he'd argued with his mother that they should give up, perhaps even get on one of the ferry steamers that plied from Poole harbour and go to France. His mother had laughed in his face, told him not to be yellow livered like his father and called him a chip off the old block. They'd face the charges, pay the fine (in instalments, of course) and carry on as before –English people have short memories, you'll see. Perhaps they'd move to Torquay.

The son was therefore surprised when, instead of walking straight past, the man turned into his mother's kiosk.

Madame Destie was seated as usual on the far side of the table attired in her usual dark clothes.

"Come on in, dear, what do you want, the quick one or the longer ten pound reading?"

"Neither," said Fred, "I've come to talk about Miriam Outhwaite."

"Who's Miriam Outhwaite when she's at home?"

"She's the old woman who you persuaded to give you £20,000 to invest."

"I'm not here to discuss my business dealings with you," snapped Madame Destie. "Anyway she's got nothing to complain about, she's had two good dividends. Now get out of here and let me get on with earning my living."

Fred sat tight. The son put a hand on his shoulder and Fred turned and twisted his arm. The son stepped back, after all, this man was bigger than he was.

"I'll call the police," said the fortuneteller.

"OK," said Fred, "do that, then I can tell them how you tricked an old woman out of £20,000. I don't think that they know about Miriam Outhwaite yet and it will make sure that you go to prison and don't just get fined."

"They wouldn't dare to send me to prison," said Madame Destie.

"Don't fool yourself, as things stand at the moment, both you and your son will go down for several years," said Fred.

"Rubbish, get out of my kiosk, I've nothing further to say."

"You'll regret it," said Fred. "I'd come to offer you the chance of getting away with a fine."

"Why don't you listen to what the man's got to say, Mum?" said the son.

"Who are you, anyway, coming in here and making accusations?" said the fortuneteller.

"My name is Fred Smart, I'm a private investigator from Southern Enquiries."

"And she's hired you to get her money back?"

"No," said Fred, "she has no idea that we're interested in her case, we're doing it because we're good citizens."

"That's a joke, I bet that you're after her money."

"The reason that I came here this morning was to point out to you that it would make a very favourable impression on the court, if your lawyer could point out that you had given the old lady her money back."

"But I've given her nigh on a thousand pounds back already."

"Nine hundred and eighty two pounds to be precise," said Fred.

"That's right, that's her dividend for investing in my fortune telling business, paid on the dot every six months."

Fred hadn't expected this. On the face of it, it was a plausible argument, that Miriam Outhwaite had simply lent the fortuneteller the sum of £20,000, repayable with interest in six monthly instalments. He said,

"Mrs Outhwaite claims that you offered to invest her money to give a good dividend and promised her that she would be able to get her investment back when she asked for it."

"Has she got any documents or witnesses to prove what she says?"

"Not that I'm aware of," said Fred.

"There you are then, you haven't got a leg to stand on," said the fortune teller.

Fred had got his ideas back on track.

"Whether the money was for you to invest in other companies or a loan to yourself isn't relevant, she wants her money back now and I'm putting it to you that there would be no need to mention to the police that you took £20,000 from a trusting old woman, if you gave her the money back."

"If I did it would be less the money that I've already repaid." She thought a little and said, "and my expenses."

Although it seemed that Madame Destie might be coming round to the idea, Fred daren't let this pass.

"What expenses and how much?"

"All the bother of putting her money in my bank and drawing checks and things and my time, say at least £500."

"Alright," said Fred, "you give her £18,500 back and we don't mention the matter to the police."

"I couldn't possibly give it back to her all at once, for one thing I

179

don't have £18,500 pounds in the bank even if you do, fortune telling isn't the most profitable business to be in these days."

"So what you're offering is to repay the money as and if you can? And in return for that offer I make no mention to the police of the £20,000 which might make the difference between a fine and a prison sentence?"

"That's about it," said Madame Destie, not unpleased at the way the conversation appeared to be going.

"I don't think that's good enough," said Fred.

"I don't care what you think, mister. Think about it. If I have to pay a fine, I shall plead poverty and the court will have to let me pay by instalments and if I go to jail I'll consider that it wipes out all my debts, so either way the old woman won't get any more money from me."

"Aw Mum, I don't want to go to prison," said her son.

"You won't, my boy, I'll see to that, I'll tell them that you knew nothing about any of this and you'll be let off."

"But I don't want you to go to prison either, it was horrible the last time."

"Be quiet, it'll be alright, I'll get away with a fine." She turned to Fred. "I don't care if you tell the police about old mother Outhwaite, get it over with, I say. And now get out of my kiosk, I've got a living to earn, such as it is."

Fred came away, somewhat chastened, he hadn't expected such a categorical rejection. But at least he'd been able to grope under the table and remove the bug that Paula had put there some weeks earlier.

Chapter Twenty-One

Donovan and Tyler were once more in conference.

"So you are convinced that there is something fishy about her death?" said the inspector.

"Yes, somehow it doesn't add up."

"What have we got?" asked Donovan and then went on to answer his own question.

"We've got a girl in the prime of life who, it seems, doesn't keep a diary or any personal papers, who had just had sex with a person unknown......"

"...but who's DNA we have asked the doctor to determine," put in the sergeant.

Donovan ploughed on, "who gets a knock on the back of her head and electrocutes herself. She falls down without burning herself or her flimsy nightdress and the iron burns through the kitchen linoleum. OK?"

"Yes, don't forget the marks on her hand."

"I was coming to those, I think that we will have to look some more at those, with the help of the experts."

"There's another thing," said Tyler. "What was she doing, doing the ironing after, well, you know."

"Yes, Sid, I know. My wife just wants to go to sleep afterwards."

"So does mine. Then there's the behaviour of the man. He makes love with an attractive girl and leaves before ten o'clock. Most lovers would have hung around longer."

"True," said Donovan, "it's as if she had entertained a paying customer."

"Or someone who had some other sort of claim on her."

"A colleague at work?" asked Donovan. "We haven't paid much attention to the other people who work in that building, have we?"

"Of course we haven't any proof that she had the sex in her flat, she could have been out."

"It would have helped if we had been able to sniff around her flat before Luigi and Co rushed in to clean it up," said the inspector, "we might have found some evidence that a man had been in her bedroom."

"Such as?" prompted the sergeant.

"Oh, I don't know, hair that wasn't Maria's on the pillow, that sort of thing."

"What would that have shown. We know that she'd had sex and the DNA will help identify with whom when we sort out the likely candidates. Why do we need more?"

"Because evidence of the same person in her flat will indicate not only that they made love there but also a degree of familiarity. It wasn't a one-night stand."

"I see," said the sergeant, thinking it over and thinking it a bit tenuous. "How about a comb or hairbrush?"

"Those might do, why do you ask?"

"Well, when I was there Luigi's daughter was busy packing all of Maria's belongings ready to send to her mother. I very much doubt that she cleaned them first."

"It's worth a try, Sid, see what you can do. The other thing that I think we should do is lean on Crown Holdings a bit. I'll handle that."

Inspector Donovan asked uniformed officers to go to Crown Holdings and bring in a Mr Julius Carpenter. Mr Carpenter arrived, protesting that he'd done no wrong and couldn't see why the filth were wasting his time. He was taken to an interview room. He was shortly joined by Detective Inspector Donovan and a Detective Constable who switched on the recorder and made the opening announcement.

Julius Carpenter launched into his protest. Donovan sat placidly and let him talk himself out. Eventually he said,

"Finished? I assume that all that was asking why you had been brought here today. I'll tell you, and after I've told you, you may want to have your solicitor present."

"I don't want no brief," interrupted Julius. "I'm clean, I ain't done nothing, not since I got married."

"You may want your solicitor," continued Donovan, "because we believe that you killed Michael Bernoulli on the night of September 23rd of this year."

"You believe what?" cried Julius, nearly falling as he started up from his chair.

"We believe that you murdered Mr Luigi Coroneli's son-in-law," said Donovan.

"You're out of your mind. We afro's wouldn't do anything to get mixed up with the Coroneli mob."

"We have conclusive evidence that the car that you claim that you own and keep in a garage at Welbeck Mews Lane was the vehicle used in the murder. Since you are the only person who admits to having access to the garage and to the car, it must have been you."

"You know that's not true, man," said Julius, indignantly. "One of your people came round a week or more ago and showed us some photo's of the guy who pays the bills, he's the one who should be answering your questions, not me."

"But you could have taken the car out, couldn't you, you've got the keys?"

"We probably have, somewhere in the office but I didn't use them."

"Did you tell the man in the picture, the man who you say pays the bills, that the police had been to your office asking questions about him?"

"Roger Judd left a message on his answer-phone. I remember because Rog was pleased that the geyser wasn't in and he hadn't had to speak to him in person."

"How did he know how to get in touch with the man?"

"We had a number to ring in an emergency. Rog reckoned that the fil," he corrected himself, "the police, asking questions about his picture might be an emergency."

"Did he get in touch?" asked Donovan.

"Not a dicky bird," said Julius, feeling that the pressure was off. Then,

"Don't get the impression that you're off the hook, Mr Carpenter, we'll want to know how many other crooks Crown Holdings is fronting for."

"You can't run us in for representing people," said Julius indignantly, "it's our business and we don't put our noses into other people's, we wouldn't last long if we did. Can I go now?"

"Yes," said Donovan, "but watch your step in future."

Julius stood up and started to turn towards the door, then turned back with a puzzled look. He said,

"What was that date you mentioned at the beginning?"

"23rd September."

Julius's face lit up. "I was in Jamaica, that's the day we buried my wife's mother. Lovely ceremony and a big party afterwards, the old woman would have loved it. So you see, the only thing I murdered that day was a big bottle of rum."

"We can check that," said Donovan.

"Check away, man. We went on the 21st and came back a week later. And we didn't bring no drugs either, we've got no time for that stuff."

Donovan knew that this was undoubtedly true.

With more due cautions to watch his step in future, which Donovan knew were like water off a duck's back, Julius Carpenter was allowed to depart, protesting because the police would not provide transport back to his office after wasting the best part of the morning.

Inspector Donovan agreed with the latter.

That afternoon, accompanied by a policewoman, he journeyed out to Highgate, to Lime Gardens to be exact. They walked up the drive and rang the bell. After a minute or so Sophia Bernoulli opened the door on a chain while wiping her hands with a towel. The police pair showed her their identity and Donovan asked if they might have a word with her.

"What about?" asked Sophia.

"Your husband's death," said Donovan.

"Oh dear, I thought all that was finished with. Poor Michael, can't you let him rest in peace?"

"I only wish that we could but something else has come up."

"Then you'd better come in."

She led them into the same tastefully furnished sitting room as before and saw that they were seated before herself sitting down opposite to the inspector and saying,

"Now, what's this something that has come up?"

"It's about the car in Welbeck Mews Lane."

She looked at him dumbly and said, as he expected.

"Where on earth is Welbeck Mews Lane and what car are you talking about?"

"Welbeck Mews Lane is less than a mile away from here as the crow flies and the car belongs to your father. When did you drive it last?"

"My dear inspector, I haven't the foggiest idea what you are talking about. I know nothing about any garage or car and obviously I've never driven it. Furthermore I don't believe that my father has such a car."

"As regards your father, believe me, there is absolutely no doubt that he has driven the car."

"Then you should be speaking with him, shouldn't you?" said Sophia, smiling.

"We have spoken with your father and doubtless we will again," said Donovan, "but in a murder investigation the police have a duty to question everyone who had an opportunity, however remote, to have played a part."

"A murder investigation," cried the girl, shocked. "Michael was killed by a hit and run driver."

"No he wasn't, he was murdered, almost outside your front entrance."

She sat there, hand to her mouth, staring at the inspector.

"But I thought…" she started.

"I'm afraid that was what we were supposed to think, but your husband wasn't hit by a passing vehicle but by a blunt implement. Pity really because we were looking for him to charge him with murder. Two murders, actually," said the inspector conversationally adding, "and rape."

Sophia looked at him dumbfounded. After more than a minute she said in a small voice,

"I don't believe it. You're making it up."

"I'm sorry but I'm not. It would cost me my job if I made things up. Your husband would have been arrested and taken to Bournemouth where the offences were committed and he would assuredly have been found guilty on all three counts and sent to prison for life."

"I don't believe it," but her voice was much less certain.

"So you see why I have to ask you these questions," said Donovan.

"Because if I had known about the things that you allege, I might have had it out with him?"

"Something like that."

"You mean that I could have killed my husband," said the girl, suddenly regaining her poise but still with her hand to her mouth.

"It's possible," said Donovan, "the majority of killings are done by a close relative."

"Don't be ridiculous, the only close relatives Michael had were me and Papa."

Donovan noticed that there was a slight hesitation and change of tone as she said Papa. She went on "Does Papa know that you're here asking me all these questions?"

"I shouldn't think so. I didn't tell him that we were coming."

"He'll be mad, probably lodge a complaint with your Commissioner or something," said the girl.

"There's nothing that I can do about that," said Donovan, "but in law, as a married woman, you are your own person and your father has no authority over you or responsibility for you. I would also remind you that you invited us into your home and what perhaps I should have told you earlier, the whole of this discussion has been recorded." He looked at the WPC and she nodded. He went on "We will give you a transcription of it or a copy of the tape if you wish."

"I'm not married any more, I'm a widow."

"But your marriage to Michael still makes you a separate entity in law."

"Papa is all that I've got," said the girl, "he does everything for me."

"Of course he does, I was simply explaining why there was no reason that I should tell your father that we were coming here today." He changed the subject; "It is sad about Maria, isn't it?"

She took a moment to adjust, then said, "Yes, she was a nice person, what an awful way to die, all alone like that. Papa relied on her a lot."

"I'm sure that he did," said Donovan, "she was always there."

"Yes, that's why Papa insisted that his secretary should live in the flat. Mama didn't think that she should, I used to hear her going on about it."

"It won't be easy to find a replacement," tried Donovan.

"I know. I'm a self-taught typist and I suggested to Papa that I should become his secretary but he wouldn't hear of it. Said that it would spoil our relationship."

"I think that he is probably right," said the inspector.

They left soon after, thanking her for her help.

Sergeant Tyler told another WPC that he wanted her to come with him to visit Maria's mother. The first task that he gave to the detective constable was discovering where she lived,. He gave the girl strict instructions, she must not ask Luigi or any of his cohorts, he didn't want another death on his hands. Detective Constable Leonora Houston was a resourceful young woman, she put herself in Maria's place. Who, outside the Coroneli office, might know her, what routine things would she do and in which of those might she have chatted about her affairs?

The answer was plain, her hairdresser. Leonora visited two before she entered the Salon Delores. She'd had a light trim in the first salon,

186

a wash and set at the second and from Delores she was reduced to asking about cosmetics at the counter just inside the door, in the course of which she remarked,

"Sad about Maria's accident, wasn't it?"

"Accident," scoffed Delores, "Accident my foot, she no more had an accident than fly to the moon."

"Oh," said Leonora. "What do you think happened then?"

"That's for the police to find out but you can bet that oily sod Coroneli had something to do with it."

"That's the man she worked for, isn't it?"

"Yes. I feel guilty because I told her to apply for the job as his secretary. It looked very good on paper. She was a total innocent, I didn't realise at the time, how innocent. She was so pleased to have such a good job, not only a salary but a flat to go with it. Next month she was round here horrified, her boss Luigi Coroneli was making her have sex with him or else she'd lose the job, flat and her good looks. And her a virgin. I got her put on the pill."

"He doesn't sound a very nice man," said Leonora.

"He's not," said Delores. She dropped her voice. "They say that he's the boss man of the local mafia and is responsible for half the vice in London. I don't know but my sister's husband, who has an Italian mother, says so and he should know."

Leonora wondered how the hairdresser's sister's husband – the one who's mother came from Italy – would know such a thing, so she said,

"He'd know, would he?"

"Yes, he works for another of them down in Croydon. He says that his one and Coroneli are daggers drawn, setting fire to each other's houses. You know what I mean, dear, don't you? houses with girls in them."

"Oooh," said Leonora. "I can see why you think that there might be something fishy about Maria's accident."

"You mark my word, truth will out."

"I expect that her family are upset," tried Leonora.

"Oh yes, she was an only child and now her old mother is all alone."

This is it, thought the detective and said,

"Does she live near here?"

"Fairly near, she lives in a council flat the other side of the park, Bauer's Building it's called, I've been meaning to go and see the old woman but haven't had the time."

"I think that lady under the hair dryer wants you," said Leonora.

"Coming dear," shouted Delores, moving into the depths of the salon.

"Thanks," said Leonora turning towards the door.

Delores removed the dryer from her customer and as she combed out the hair, remarked in passing as it were,

"Fancy that, she kept me chatting for all that time and then went off without buying anything. Youngsters these days have a cheek, don't they?"

Leonora made her way across the park and eventually found Bauer's Building, a grim looking reinforced concrete edifice, built by a council more concerned with maximising the number of accommodation units than architectural beauty. It had occurred to her half way that she could probably have found the information that she wanted in the Electoral Register or in the Council Housing list, provided that she had time to search the lists of all the London boroughs and that the mother was registered in one or other or both. On reflection, hers was the better way, it would lead her to the right Mrs Harkness.

According to the mailbox beside a lift that sported a large Out-of-Order notice, the apartment that she wanted was number 24. She walked up the stairs to the second floor and rang the bell; thankful that the mother didn't live in Flat No 74. There were sounds behind the door and the noise of bolts being pulled back. Eventually the door was opened a few inches on a chain to reveal the face of a grey haired woman much older than Leonora had expected. Clearly Maria was the offspring of elderly parents.

"What do you want," the face demanded.

Leonora showed her police identity and said,

"I'm DC Leonora Houston and I'm looking for the mother of Maria Harkness."

"I'm Mrs Harkness, her mother. What do you want?"

"I'd like a brief word with you if I may, Mrs Harkness."

"You'd better come inside then, don't want all the neighbours to know, do we?"

She opened the door and admitted Leonora into a room in which everything shone with polish. She gestured to a straight back chair and perched on the one opposite, saying,

"Now tell me want you want. It's about my Maria, you say?"

"Yes Mrs Harkness, it's about Maria. We are taking another look at the circumstances surrounding her death."

"I'll never believe that she was accidentally electrocuted, my Maria was a careful girl."

"That's why we're having another look. We think that there may have been someone else in her flat that evening and we're looking for evidence. That's why I'm here."

"Well, I wouldn't know, would I? But I do know that that awful man she worked for used to pop in from time to time when he was least expected. Maria didn't like him."

"We understand that they brought Maria's clothes and things home to you. Could I look at them, please?"

"They're in her bedroom. I can't tell you where anything is because I haven't had the heart to open any of the boxes, her not being buried yet."

"I know how distressing this must be for you. Do you mind if I take a look?"

"You'll have to do it on your own," said the mother, nearly in tears.

"That's alright, if you'll show me the way."

Mrs Harkness indicated a room on the other side of the passage. Leonora went in. The room contained a single bed, a wardrobe and a chest of drawers that also served as a bedside table. The rest of the space within the room was filled with cardboard boxes and plastic dress covers, they were piled on the bed and occupied the whole of the available floor space. The problem was where could she put the things she took out of a box while she delved towards the things at its bottom and where on earth should she begin? There was only one place and that was in the area kept clear to allow the door to open. She warned Mrs Harkness of the situation and borrowed a knife to cut the tape sealing the top of each box.

Leonora reasoned that all the toilet articles were likely to be in the same box or boxes and decided to start by opening the top of each in turn to see the nature of the contents.

She had looked into four from the floor – which were now stacked behind her – and two from the bed when she found toilet articles in box number seven. She carefully removed the contents, placing them on the pile behind her but there were no combs or hairbrushes. There must be another box with toilet things. She re-packed the box.

One by one she slit open the sealing tape on the top of the next four boxes taken from the floor; no toilet articles. Leonora had long decided that looking was the easy bit, the difficult bit was lifting the heavy boxes and shuffling round to put them on the floor behind her. She now had eight boxes obstructing the door.

What she was looking for was in the first of the second pair on the bed, two hairbrushes and three combs. She put them separately in plastic bags taken from her shoulder bag and arranged the box in which she had found them to be on the end of the bed closest to the door. She then set about putting the eight boxes back where they had come from so that she could get out of the room. She was pleased at how light the boxes now seemed to be as she pirouetted between them to put them on the floor from whence she had taken them, her task successfully completed.

She showed Mrs Harkness the items that she wished to take away for examination and gave her a receipt, assuring her that they would be returned in due course.

"Wait a minute, dear, I must make a note of it in my diary," said Mrs Harkness. She hurried upstairs and came down clutching a small red book in which she proceeded to write something. Leonora said idly,

"I see that you're left handed."

"Yes, it runs in the family, my mother was and so was my grandmother, that was in Italy."

"What happens when you marry a right handed man?"

"Makes no difference, the children are left handed."

"So Maria was left handed then?"

"Yes and didn't it cause a lot of bother."

"How was that?" asked Leonora, still humouring the woman.

"Well, we paid for her to go to a church school and the Holy Mother wouldn't let her write with her left hand. She said that the Lord was right handed and that all of his children had to be right handed and if we didn't like it we would have to take her to another school."

"So she learnt to write with her right hand?"

"Yes, in the end she could write equally well with either hand but she did everything else with her left hand."

Leonora's interest suddenly quickened.

"Which hand did she use to do the ironing ?"

"The left, of course."

"I don't think that I've ever seen anyone doing the ironing with their left hand"

"Maria did and so do I."

Leonora thanked her for her help and returned to headquarters, well pleased.

Chapter Twenty-Two

INSPECTOR DONOVAN'S superiors sent for him to discuss the progress, or rather what appeared to them to be, the lack of progress, in the two arson cases. Donovan took Sergeant Tyler with him and was minded to remind them that officers from other forces were also involved with the cases. When they entered the room he took one look at his Chief's Inspector's face and didn't.

"You don't seem to have made much progress with the mafia arson enquiry, Donovan," was the opening gambit.

"The investigation is progressing Chief Superintendent," said Donovan. "The four responsible for the Mayfair fires are in custody and we're following up on the ones in the Home Counties."

"You haven't made any arrests for the latter," said the Chief Inspector.

"My spies tell me that you've been messing about with a car that you found in a garage out Highgate way," said the Chief Super.

Donovan gave him an old-fashioned look, grinned and said,

"All part of the same enquiry, Chief."

The Chief Superintendent had been the first inspector that Donovan had worked under when he had joined the police. He knew that Donovan had an uncanny ability to sniff out criminals and was aware of his habit of keeping all of his cards close to his chest until he had a case all wrapped up. What was more, he knew that Donovan got results. He relaxed and grinned at Donovan and said,

"Stop horsing about Don, what are you up to?"

Donovan grinned back and his immediate boss breathed a sigh of relief.

"It's all part of the same picture, Chief. I'm after Luigi Coroneli. We all know that he's the capo of the biggest mafi mob in London and into every sort of vice. To date, try as we may, we haven't been able to nail him personally for any crime, some poor underling has always come forward to take the blame. This time we may have a lead that he won't be able to wriggle out of."

"How do the fires in the Home Counties come into it?"

"It's a long story," tried Donovan.

The Chief Superintendent leant forward, put his elbows on his desk and rested his chin on his steepled hands, saying,

"I'll tell you if I find it boring."

"Well, Chief. The Dorset police had a case in which Southampton's star player was pushed into a river in his car at a village near to Bournemouth and killed."

"I remember that. They found the vehicle that did the ramming and identified a partial fingerprint and you made an arrest."

"That's right, he should be coming up for trial soon, name of Carlo Johnson who we believe is one of the Coroneli mob. Then we had the two fires in brothels in Mayfair. Land Registry records show that the properties are owned by Luigi Coroneli."

"That doesn't necessarily mean that he ran the brothels, it might be a tenant."

"No Chief but we have pictorial evidence that on the night of the fires, Coroneli's number one money-man called Leonardo Bianci was at the scene giving wads of money to the two madams to get hotel rooms for the girls."

"Go on."

"The next day the girls helped us prepare photo-fit pictures of the customers who we think planted the incendiary devices in their rooms and we gave them national coverage in the media the next morning. Lo and behold the same four men turned up in the Four Oaks Club in Mayfair and started wrecking the owner's office. The owners are Italian and are known to us, one of them seems to have innocently started the chain of events that led to two murders and a rape in Bournemouth."

"Was that the thing where the Chancellor of the Exchequer waded into the river to recover the girl's body?"

"Yes, that's it Chief and it started our present enquiry because we identified the murderer as a Michael Bernoulli who we later discovered was Luigi Coroneli's son-in-law. We didn't know that he was married to the Coroneli girl until after his body was found outside their house in Highgate, the apparent victim of a hit-and-run accident."

"Apparent victim?"

"I know that the local station have closed the case but I wasn't satisfied, he was struck on the back of the head, just above the neck, in my view too low for a lorry and too high for a car and anyway, if he was going out to meet someone, why didn't he take his own car?"

"You think that someone was going to pick him up and ran into him instead."

"No chief, I think that he went to meet someone and they hit him on the back of the head with the proverbial blunt instrument and I think that the someone was Luigi Coroneli."

"Why?"

"There are two answers to that question, Chief, Why do I think that it was him and why did he do it? That morning I had had the proprietor of the Four Oaks Club in to grill him about who was the debt collector who he had sent to Bournemouth? He was too scared to say but I said that we knew that it was a small-time crook called Michael Bernoulli who we were now looking for to charge with a double murder and rape. He had his solicitor with him, a man of Italian extraction called," he consulted his file, "Silvestro Bessani, and he's also Luigi Coroneli's solicitor and he must have known that the man who we were looking for was his client's daughter's husband. My guess is that he tipped Luigi off."

"Sounds reasonable. Why did he do it?"

"We think to protect his daughter He probably knew by now that the fellow was an out-and-out rotter who should never have been permitted to marry his daughter and this could have been the last straw, so he killed him to avoid the publicity and the emotional disturbance for his daughter of seeing her husband tried for rape and murder. And, of course, a conviction would reflect badly on the Coroneli mafia 'family.' "

"So you set out to try to nail him personally. Is this where the garage out Highgate way comes in?"

"Yes Chief. We had a slice of luck. We interviewed the four arsonists. They wouldn't admit it but they are all soldiers of the Corleone mafia family operating in South London. The degree of obduracy varied and we learnt something. For instance, one of them confirmed that the man Carlo Johnson who pushed the footballer's car – and incidentally his girl-friend – into the river, is a member of the North London mafia and that it was intended to be a not-so-gentle reminder to the football club to pay-up or else."

"It was part of the attempt to blackmail the football club?"

"Yes, Chief only it went horribly wrong. It seems that the South London mob didn't like the North London mob attempting to blackmail a South of London football club so they took their revenge by setting fire to the houses in Mayfair to which the North London mob replied in kind, burning four houses and killing three people in the Home Counties plus two stabbed in Soho."

"About the garage…?" prompted the Chief Superintendent.

"Ah yes, the garage," said Donovan. "It was just as we were finishing interviewing the last of the four men responsible for the Mayfair fires. We'd got him talking, by speaking about the other mob. He confirmed that the southern lot didn't like the northern lot trying to blackmail a southern football club. He thought that it wouldn't matter if he landed the other mob in it. As regards a lorry killing Michael Bernoulli, he said that we'd be fools if we were taken-in by a coincidence like that and added that he'd heard someone mention Welbeck Mews. That's literally all that was said. So Sergeant Tyler did a great search of the area and came up with a row of ten lock-up garages in Welbeck Mews Lane. We asked the Fire Brigade to be good chaps and see if any of them contained inflammable or dangerous substances. They found a hundred stolen lap-tops in one and Coroneli's secret car in another."

"How did you know that it was his?"

"The sergeant listed all the registration numbers, identified the keepers names and addresses on the DVLA computer and then checked with the keepers. One turned out to be registered in the name of a black gentleman called," he paused and Sergeant Tyler said,

"Julius Carpenter."

"That's it, Julius Carpenter. He and two others run an accommodation address business called Crown Holdings. Carpenter informed the DVLR and the local council that he was the keeper and paid the bills. He recognised a picture of Luigi as the man who visited them every six months and gave them the cash to pay the bills. Meanwhile the Land Registry told us that the real owner of the garage property is Luigi Coroneli."

"What about the car?" asked the Chief Superintendent.

"We asked forensic to examine it. They found a secret compartment in each front door containing three passports and a large sum of money in US dollars and Euro's. One of the passports is Italian. All have Luigi Coroneli's picture and all are forgeries. But what may be the most important of their finds was minute blood spots just inside the boot."

"As if a body was carried in it?"

"No, Chief, just a few minute spots."

"It wouldn't be you, Don, if you didn't have a theory, would it? Come on, out with it."

"It's all down to the sergeant really," said Donovan while Tyler made dismissive gestures. "He found a witness."

"But the local police accepted the accident theory."

"Yes Chief but they're run off their feet and they didn't look beyond the obvious."

"Who's this witness?"

"An elderly lady who lives opposite, she went upstairs to pull the curtains and saw a car with the boot open, stopped right where the body was found with two figures moving across and obscuring the rear lights. She even noticed that there was a red warning light when the driver shut the boot and opened the offside front door to get in and drive off. Because all of the houses are detached and surrounded with trees, we went and stood in her window and checked that she could have seen the spot. It was as she said so we took pictures. She had also noted the event in her diary."

"The experts tell us that DNA tests tell us that the blood spots came from Michael Bernoulli," said Sergeant Tyler.

"We had Luigi Coroneli in and questioned him, he denied knowing where Welbeck Mews Lane is, he denied owning the car and he denied all knowledge of the passports.. He went a bit quiet when we asked him if the money was his. It was clearly a wrench to deny title to £50,000."

"Where do you go from here?" asked the Chief Superintendent, un-steepling his hands.

"Oh, but I'm not finished yet," said Donovan, thinking you asked for the whole story. So sit down and listen.

"You mean that there's more?" grinned the Chief Inspector who knew what was coming.

"Two mornings ago officers were called to the building in which Luigi Coroneli has offices and in which his secretary has a small flat. It seems that his secretary, Maria Harkness, hadn't arrived for work and he had gone looking for her. He found her in her nightdress, dead on the kitchen floor with an electric iron clutched in her hand."

"Was the iron defective?"

"We'll never know. When the local officers questioned him, Coroneli said that he'd never seen it before and that she had a brand new one that went with the flat in a box in the kitchen cupboard. When the police went back for the old iron, they found that he had thrown it away."

"They should have made him recover it, after all it must have been barely an hour since he'd found the body," said the Chief Inspector. "Would you be content with a verdict of accidental death, Don?"

"By no means, there are other things that require an explanation."

"Such as?"

"The pathologists discovered that she had been intimate with someone that evening. The doctor guessed that she'd died between ten and eleven. What was she doing, ironing, dressed only in her nightdress."

"You find that odd?"

"Yes Chief, most women like to snuggle down after, well, you know, afterwards and most lovers wouldn't be keen to get away so early."

"Unless they had a wife waiting at home," said the Chief Inspector.

"There is that, of course, that's why we are trying to get hold of one of her hair brushes or combs," said Donovan.

"Why?"

"I think that it's important to establish whether she went out and had sex or whether the man came to her flat. If they'd had sex in the bed it's possible that he would have brushed or combed his hair afterwards. The latter would suggest to me that we should look close to home."

"But why is it important who was there? She was electrocuted."

"Sorry, Chief, I should have said, there was a small bruise on the back of her head, hidden by hair and two small burn marks on her right hand. It is difficult to see how an iron could have caused them and the pathologist assures me that the bruise could not have been caused by her falling down after receiving the electric shock."

"Even if you find that the DNA of the semen and the hair are the same, it won't tell you who the man is, will it? Nor whether he killed her," said the Chief Superintendent.

"We're working on that," said Donovan.

"You're sure that you're not building this up into more than an unfortunate accident just because it concerns the hated Coroneli, Don?" asked the Chief Super.

"Oh yes Chief, its all too neat, she has an electric shock, she falls down but the iron remains in her hand, it doesn't touch her body or her clothes and it melts a neat hole in the linoleum. In the real world she would probably have dropped it and the chances are that it would have burnt her flimsy nightdress and her body or legs on the way down and finished up by setting fire either to her or to the things in the clothes basket."

"Well, you seem to have drawn a number of crimes together fairly convincingly. See what you can do about those deaths and fires in the Home Counties that the media keep on about."

"OK Chief," said Donovan, smiling, "I'll keep you posted on developments."

"That'll be the day," said the Chief Superintendent.

As they walked down the stairs, Sergeant Tyler grinned wryly. The Chief Super and his Inspector made a good pair.

Upon her return to the office, Leonora got hold of the files on the death of Maria and read through them. She had been sure that she was right and there it was in Sergeant Tyler's report, Maria had been found with an old electric iron clutched in her right hand. Something was wrong somewhere. She carried on reading, Sergeant Tyler had been suspicious of the small marks on the back of her hand –again the right hand – and had asked the doctor, Dr Cole, to have a closer look at them and at the bruise on the back of her head. She went to the latest entries, there was nothing more recent from the doctor. He ought to be hastened. Better still, she'd volunteer to see him, she believed that the personal approach produced the best results. Whether it would be the same if she was fat and forty she didn't know but it worked for a slender twenty-four year old brunette.

She had been told to use her initiative. The annual personnel fitness reports had a heading that discussed an officer's initiative, so she'd show them. She took the hairbrushes and combs to the forensic people and explained what was wanted and then phoned the doctor and arranged to see him on his own ground in the morning.

Sergeant Tyler had explained to her why they required some evidence that a man had been in the apartment that evening. Presumably it would show that the same person had intercourse with Maria that evening. But it wouldn't identify the man unless his DNA was already on record. Leonora thought about that. If she was the Prime Minister she'd pass a law saying that all babies had to have their

DNA taken at birth. Then she wondered if it took a few years to develop, like teeth. That made her think about taking babies fingerprints and then what the civil liberties people would find to object to in that and she gave up.

When they got back from briefing the Chiefs, she reported what she had found out and done that afternoon to the Inspector and the Sergeant.

"You're sure of that, Leonora, she wrote with her right hand but was left-handed in everything else?"

"Yes Gov, she always held the iron in her left hand, like her mother."

"Let's take this slowly," said Donovan, "she writes with her right hand so anyone seeing her in her office would assume that she was right handed like most people. But she would hold an iron in her left hand. Yet she's found lying neatly on the floor with an old iron grasped in her right hand and she'd got there without burning herself or her nightdress."

"And she had a bruise on the back of her head and two small marks on her right hand," said the sergeant.

"I've arranged to go and talk to the doctor tomorrow morning," said Leonora.

"Good for you," said Donovan absently, still thinking about the body on the floor. Then he said,

"What we want is Luigi Coroneli's DNA. How can we get that?"

"We bring him to the station and take a swab from his mouth," said the sergeant.

"We can't force him to give it and he's bound to have that lawyer with him," said Donovan.

"If we could get into his house we should be able to find something like a tissue in the waste paper basket or hair inside the brim of his hat," said the WPC. "It might be sufficient to enable us to get a warrant for his arrest and when he's a prisoner we ought to be able to do the thing properly."

"We might find something like that in his office," said the sergeant.

"If he was at the flat that night he must have come by car," said Donovan, "and there might be something in his car, his proper car, the one that we're allowed to know about."

"Pity that he doesn't smoke, isn't it?"

"Surely all that we've got to do is to wait until he goes to the barbers?" said Leonora.

"That would mean keeping him under observation for all the shop hours for anything up to a month or more," said Donovan.

"Not necessarily," said the WPC. "If she was an efficient secretary, Maria's office desk diary has probably got a note of who his Doctor, Dentist, Solicitor and Hairdresser are and a note of his appointments. This should show when he went to the hairdressers and we ought to be able to get an idea of when his next visit is due. There may even be a note in Maria's personal diary."

"It's worth a try, Gov," said Tyler.

"OK," said Donovan, grinning at her "you've got yourself a job, Leonora, see what you can find out."

Chapter Twenty-Three

THE following morning Donovan and Tyler journeyed to Croydon and consulted the inspector in charge of the investigation into the murders that had accompanied the fires. He raised no objection to Donovan's suggestion that he would like to interview Alfredo Corleone in connection with the fires in Mayfair although his manner indicated that he feared that it would be a waste of time.

When they were once more in their car the sergeant said,

"You didn't mention us going to see the widows?"

"No," said Donovan, "If we visit them I thought that I'd let him think that they're an outcome of our talk with the capo."

They parked and walked into the Corleone offices. Two young men in well fitting suits moved to block their way; Tyler noticed that their right hands had instinctively moved towards their lapels. The police officers showed their credentials and the right hands were once more down at the young men's sides.

Donovan explained that they were from Scotland Yard and wished to speak with Mr Corleone about the fires.

The elder of the two said, "Mr Corleone isn't available."

"Do you mean that he's not here, not free or are you simply being difficult?"

"Mr Corleone doesn't see anyone unless they make an appointment in advance."

"Very well," said Donovan. "I'm making an appointment in advance. The police wish to see your capo in five minutes time. If he doesn't see us I'll send uniformed officers to bring him in to the station, got that, sonny? Now go and tell him."

The elder of the two turned on his heel and disappeared. The other stood his ground. After a few minutes the first man returned and said,

"Mr Corleone will try to fit you in if you'd come this way."

He led the way up a flight of stairs, through a secretary's office and into the capo's room. Corleone stood up behind his large desk, smiling expansively and said,

"Come in gentlemen, I understand that you want to talk about those dreadful fires. Please sit down."

"Yes," said Donovan as he and the sergeant seated themselves in the two chairs in front of the desk while the bodyguard positioned himself in front of the door. Tyler wondered why he didn't come and stand behind his capo like they do in the gangster movies.

"Dreadful, dreadful," said Corleone, "are you any closer to finding out those responsible?"

"Oh yes," said Donovan "We've got four men under arrest."

"Good, good, have you found out which ones were responsible for the murders?"

"There weren't any murders, only the fires."

"You're mistaken, Inspector, two of my, er ,two men were stabbed and an unfortunate girl died from the smoke."

"Oh," said Donovan, "you're talking about the fires south of the river, we've come to talk about the fires north of the river, the fires that you were responsible for."

It took a moment for this to sink in.

"What do you mean? I don't know what you're talking about."

"Perhaps you will when I mention your friend Luigi Coroneli's attempt to blackmail the Southampton football club that led to a murder. You'll be pleased to know that we've got the man – or should I call him the soldier – who did that, in custody."

"I don't know what any of this has got to do with me."

"Oh, come on Alfredo, we're all grown up, we know that you were so fired up because your friend Coroneli had done something south of the river that you sent four of your soldiers to set fire to his houses. The really stupid thing that you did was to send them into the West End a day or so later, didn't you realise that by then the sergeant here – he indicated Tyler – would have had the girls make photofit pictures of them?"

Corleone mumbled something in Italian. Donovan went on,

"Then you stupidly sent two more into Soho to sound-out the drug trade and they were killed. This brought the Coroneli mob south of the river, thirsting for revenge and they killed two more. That's four dead and four in prison, it's a wonder that any of your so-called soldiers have any trust in your judgement any more, isn't it?"

"I don't have to listen to this," screamed Corleone. "Get out of my room."

"What, don't you want to hear what we've got on friend Coroneli?"

"Another pack of lies, I expect?"

"Oh no, Alfredo, as it stands at present all that you'll be going down for is conspiracy, arson, living on immoral earnings, running a protection racket and trafficking in drugs. Luigi will go down for all of that plus two cases of premeditated murder. That should cheer you up."

"You haven't got any proof for these wild accusations. I've got a witness. I'll have my lawyers protest to your Commissioner, that's what I'll do."

"I'm sure that he'll be pleased to hear from you. Did you see that we arrested the man in Catford who made the electronics for the things that your soldiers put under the girl's beds? He's not a Mafiosi and he says that he made them for you."

"I'll deny it, there was nothing on paper."

"Well, Alfredo, that's what Scotland Yard wanted to tell you, make the most of the next few weeks."

Donovan stood up followed by a rather bemused Tyler. Don really had gone too far this time and it had all been recorded on the recorder in his pocket. They walked past the bodyguard who quickly turned and regained the lead. As they left the building Donovan said to the one who hadn't been in the room,

"Make him tell you everything that I said to your capo and then, I suggest, look for another job."

They got back in their car. Before he started the engine Sergeant Tyler ventured,

"Don't you think that you went a bit over the top in there, Don?"

"In what way, Sid?"

"Well, you virtually told him all that we have on them."

"Yes, now he knows that we know, but if he's got any sense at all he'll have worked that out already. The audience it was meant for was the man behind us. He's bound to tell the other one and thus the word will get out and make Alfredo's soldiers even more uncertain whether he's the man to be their capo."

"Where to now?" asked Tyler, starting the engine.

"Let's go back to the Yard, the wives can wait. It might pay us to harp on the theme that Alfredo has put them all in it the next time we interview the four prisoners."

Detective Constable Leonora Houston went first to the Path.Lab to see Doctor Cole. He took her into his office, saw that she was comfortably seated and said,

"Now, what can I do for you, young lady?"

"We'd like to know if you have discovered anything more about the cause of death of Maria Harkness."

"The girl who was electrocuted doing her ironing?"

"Yes."

"Well, she certainly suffered a cardiac arrest and the circumstantial evidence is that it was caused by an electric shock."

"What about the bruise on the back of her head and the small marks on her hand?"

"Ah yes, well, the indications are that the bruise occurred before death."

"And the marks on her hand?" persisted Leonora.

"Why are you police so interested in this case? Apparently the unfortunate girl was ironing with a defective iron and got a shock that killed her. It's happening all the time, so why the fuss?"

"Because the iron was in her right hand."

"So?"

"She was left handed and, according to her mother, always ironed with her left hand."

Doctor Cole thought about this and eventually said,

"I see, so you suspect foul play. Why didn't you people tell me this before?"

"Because we only found it out ourselves, yesterday."

"I see, I don't think that it will make any difference to my conclusions but the bruising before death now takes on an added significance, clearly there is the possibility that she was stunned and then the whole grisly electrocution tableau arranged on the floor."

"Which would explain how it was that she didn't burn herself or her nightie when she fell," put in the policewoman.

"Yes, I'll admit that puzzled me, it was too neat. I suppose that this lets off the people she worked with?"

"How so?" asked Leonora.

"They would have known that she was left handed."

"'Fraid not, she was ambidextrous and always wrote with her right hand because the nuns at her school made her."

"But not her ironing?"

"No, she did it her mother's way, she is left handed."

"I'll think some more about it but I don't think that the corpse can tell us any more."

He rose and Leonora picked up her shoulder bag and turned towards the door. At the door she turned like Inspector Columbo and said,

"One last thing, Doctor, it is possible to get a person's DNA from a piece of their hair, isn't it?"

"Yes," smiled the doctor, "but people don't like people creeping up behind them and snipping off pieces of their hair, even pretty WPC's."

She made her way to the Coroneli offices. She had prepared for what she intended to do. She walked into what had been Maria's office. A sallow young man was seated at the desk. He looked up and half smiled, saying, Leonora felt, with relief,

"He's out."

Leonora showed the man her identification and said,

"I didn't come to see Mr Luigi Coroneli, I came for this."

She picked up the desk diary, saying, "I am impounding this in connection with the death of Miss Maria Harkness. It will be returned when we have completed our enquiries. Please stand up."

She walked round to his side of the desk and opened the top drawer. She quickly examined the contents. In the second drawer down she found two small notebooks, on which someone had written Addresses and Telephone Log respectively. She put them in her satchel with the desk diary. The remaining drawers contained nothing of interest for the enquiry.

She added the words Address Book and Telephone Log to the receipt note that she had come prepared with and put it down on the desk.

She had turned on her heel and was out of the door before he said,

"Oy, you can't do that, what will Mr Cor..."

By then she was on her way.

Back in the station she leafed through the three books. Maria was clearly an efficient secretary, it was all there, names addresses, telephone numbers, faxes and e-mail addresses. The telephone log noted every call coming into and out of the office and the diary had all his appointments, including those with his dentist and doctor.

When Donovan and Tyler reappeared after lunch she showed them her spoils

"And he actually let you bring these away?" said the Inspector.

"He wasn't there so I gave the stand-in a receipt and brought them away."

"I wouldn't like to be in his shoes when Luigi got back. We can expect a phone call at any moment now so I suggest that you get the last three months pages of each book photo-copied as quickly as you can."

"OK Gov, but we are entitled to requisition evidence if we consider it to be necessary, aren't we, so why the hurry?"

"Of course we are, this is just to cover all the angles, you did well, just what we wanted."

It came an hour later, not from Luigi Coroneli but from the solicitor, Silvestro Bessani.

"Inspector Donovan, I understand that one of your officers visited the Coroneli offices this morning and removed certain documents."

"Yes, that's right, Maria Harkness's desk diary, Address Book and Telephone Log. My officer gave them a receipt."

"She took advantage of my client's absence, he wouldn't have let them go."

"He wouldn't have been able to object, the documents are required in connection with enquiries into the death of his secretary," said Donovan.

"I didn't know that there was any problem there, the poor girl was accidentally electrocuted."

"There are certain features about her death that require further consideration."

"Am I permitted to know what those features are?"

"No, Mr Bessani, you're not."

"I could ask your superiors or cite the Freedom of Information Act."

"That's your privilege but I can assure you that you will not receive any information until we are further down the road with our enquiries."

"We shall see about that," said the solicitor and rang off.

Donovan's phone rang half an hour later. The Chief Superintendent required his presence, NOW. He walked into the Chief's room to be greeted by a bellow,

"What the hell do you think you're playing at?"

"What's that Chief?"

"I've had two phone calls, one from the Super in Croydon claiming that you were down there this morning raising merry hell in Corleone's place and I've just had a call from a solicitor called," he picked up a scrap of paper on his desk and scowled at it, "Bessani, claiming that one of your officers walked into Luigi Coroneli's offices this morning and requisitioned their desk diary."

"That's about it, Chief," said Donovan, quite unperturbed.

"That's about what?"

"What happened, I went down to Croydon and told Alfredo Corleone that we had the goods on him for sending his chaps to burn Luigi's houses and Detective Constable Houston used her initiative to execute the task I set her."

"And what task was that, may I ask?"

"Oh yes Chief, ask away. I told her to find out where Luigi Coroneli gets his hair cut."

"You did what?" exploded the Chief Superintendent.

"Told her to find out..."

"Yes I heard you the first time," interrupted the Chief. "You risked getting the Met sued for tens of thousands of pounds just to find out where Coroneli gets his hair cut. What on earth for?"

"To get his DNA."

"You mean to tell me that it's part of a scheme to get a piece of his hair for testing?"

"That's right, Chief, we couldn't think of any other way to do it without physically approaching him and you wouldn't have wanted us to do that, would you?"

The Chief Super could feel himself being sucked in to one of Donovan's madcap schemes, just like it had been in the old days, but he couldn't resist it. He said,

"And just how do you intend to secure this sample of cut hair, get a temporary job sweeping up at the barbers?"

"We hadn't quite worked that out, Chief, but I'm sure that Constable Houston will give your suggestion due consideration."

"Stop horsing about, Don. What do I do about this solicitor?"

"Tell him that one of my junior officers got carried away this morning and that we will bring them to his office at ten a.m tomorrow and give them back to him. Then he'll be able to show Coroneli what a powerful fellow he is, he got them back from the dreaded Met. Of course I shall give him a letter at the same time, recording their return to him as Coroneli's legal adviser and warning him that they may be required as evidence in a case and that from then on, he's responsible for their safe custody."

"You really are a devious sod, Don." He grinned at him, "I suppose that your people are busy downstairs taking copies?"

"I had a good teacher, Chief."

"This Bessani said something about the Freedom of Information Act, what was he getting at?"

"He phoned me earlier and protested that we wouldn't have been permitted to bring the items away if Luigi had been there. I became all official and said that we were within our rights in sequestering documents that might be relevant to the investigation into Maria Harkness's death and he asked for the facts that gave us reason to suspect that her death might be other than an unfortunate accident. I declined and he made threats."

"It's coming back to me now. You think that Bessani was the one who tipped off Luigi Coroneli that the police were looking for a crook called Michael Bernoulli to charge him with murder, don't you?"

"And rape," said Donovan.

"I get the point, a capo might overlook a simple double murder but a fond father-in-law might be all bitter and twisted about rape. Where does this leave Bessani?"

"Assuming that we get sufficient evidence to arrest Luigi Coroneli and charge him with the murder of Michael Bernoulli, it would be my recommendation that we charge Bessani with being an accessory or of attempting to frustrate the course of justice or some such thing."

"He'd wriggle out of it," said the Chief.

"I know, but not before we'd plastered his name as a shady lawyer on every TV set and newspaper in the country."

"OK Don, I'll phone him and say that you will return them to his safe custody tomorrow at ten and that if he wishes to write to the Met citing the Freedom of Information thing we'll think about it."

"Fine Chief," said Donovan, rising and turning towards the door. A voice behind him said,

"You'll have to figure out when he goes to get his hair cut and someone will have to follow him in, perhaps looking like a tramp, nobody is surprised at tramps messing about with dirt on the floor."

Donovan continued out of the door, turning his head to say,

"Thanks Chief, we'll remember that."

Chapter Twenty-Four

DONOVAN returned to his office to find three piles of Photostat copies on his desk. He put his head out of the door and Leonora assured him that they had made three sets of the last six month's entries and that the originals were undamaged. Donovan told her to type the letter to accompany the volumes the next morning and then to look for the barber and when Luigi might be expected to visit him.

He settled down to see what he could make of the entries for September 23rd. He found the one that he expected at once. At 12.25p.m. on September 23rd, Mr Bessani had telephoned Luigi Coroneli from a public call-box. Donovan consulted his own desk diary and saw that his interview with Guiseppi Maranti and Silvestro Bessani had finished at 11.40 that morning. There was a small dot beside the entry in Maria's log of telephone calls.

Donovan searched the entries, a lot of them had the small dot and he gradually realised that all the callers or the people who Coroneli called who merited the dot, had Italian sounding names. It was not a long stretch to suppose that they spoke Italian. Reference to the day diary seemed to confirm this, as a general rule, there was usually a brief word about the subject of the call where the names weren't Italian sounding.

It looked as if Bessani had called from a public call box and spoken Italian. The chain of events was convincing to Donovan, That morning Bessani had learnt that the police were looking for Coroneli's son-in-law, he phoned Coroneli at lunch time and the son-in-law was killed in an 'accident' that evening. He would make use of that.

He called Sergeant Tyler and Constable Houston in.

"How did you get on with the Chief?" asked the former.

"Alright," grinned Donovan. "Bessani had been on to him. I told him that we will return the documents to Bessani tomorrow morning at ten and warn him that he is now responsible for their safe keeping."

"You don't miss a trick, do you?" said the sergeant.

"Good job that we took copies," said the policewoman.

"Yes," said Donovan, laughing, "I told him of our plan to get hold of some hair cuttings and he came up with two suggestions."

Tyler started to grin. "He didn't?"

"Yes he did, he suggested that one of us could get a job at the barbers sweeping the floor or we should be a tramp because everyone knows that tramps pick things up."

"I know that he was pulling your leg, Gov." said Leonora, "but we may have to do something like that. What I had in mind was sitting behind his chair and dropping something that will roll over the floor, like a bag of apples. Whoever does it should be able to scoop up a bit of hair in the process."

Donovan looked at her in admiration, smiling and saying,

"You know, that's a darned good idea, I'm a good mind to send you up to the Chief Super so that two inventive minds can work on it."

"I'm still trying to work out if there is any pattern in his routine that would suggest that he's going to have his hair cut," said Leonora.

"Like he always has it done two days before an important dinner engagement?"

"Yes, that sort of thing," she replied. "The only trouble is that he doesn't seem to go out to important dinners or things and, as far as I can see he doesn't have his hair cut, but I'm working on it."

Sergeant Tyler accompanied Donovan to the solicitor's offices the next morning. Mr Bessani's secretary told them that he was busy and couldn't see them. Donovan didn't know whether he was pleased or sorry. The secretary signed the receipt and was warned with due solemnity that it was now her responsibility to ensure that no harm came to the items.

Donovan wondered if she would be required to make copies before they were returned to Luigi Coroneli.

When they got back to the Yard they found a small woman sitting in Donovan's office with Leonora watching over her and endeavouring to make her less scared than she obviously was, sitting straight up in the chair with both arms clasping her handbag firmly to her bosom and an untouched cup of coffee on the desk.

Leonora saw them coming and came out to meet them, saying,

"Maria's mother wants to see you. She refuses to say why but insists that it has to be you. The desk didn't know what to do about her, she was obviously harmless, wouldn't say why she wanted to see you and simply refused to leave until she had. They phoned and I said that I'd come down and bring her up. She's in a bit of a state."

Donovan went into his room and told Mrs Harkness that he was Inspector Donovan.

"I don't want to be a nuisance, Sir, but Maria said that it had to be you. No disrespect to the young lady, she's been very kind but I have to give it to you."

"Take your time Mrs Harkness," smiled Donovan, "you're among friends. This is Sergeant Tyler and you've already met Constable Houston. Now what is it that you have to give me?"

She continued to hold her bag against her boson and said,

"She was always a good girl. Her father and I went without things to send her to the convent school and she did well. She should never have gone to work for that dreadful man. If I'd known what sort of man he was and what he was doing to…" she tapered off then recovered. " She put up with it so as not to worry me, you see. Telling her that he'd slash her face and things."

Sergeant Tyler made as if to speak and Leonora shook her head.

"It's all there, how he made her, er, become a woman, his woman to take when he pleased, him with a wife and all. Did he ever go to confession? I doubt it. If he did I expect that he told the priest a pack of lies. You'd be surprised at what people say." She thought about that and went on, "No, I suppose you wouldn't, being the police."

"I found it when I was going through her drawers, tucked right at the back under her, er, well, among her things." She turned towards Leonora and said in a motherly way, "It was you made me do it dear, all that trouble lifting and climbing over those boxes, so I moved them out –well, most of them anyway – and, because the only place I had to put things was her drawers I thought that I'd better clean them out first. That's when I found it."

"What did you find, Mrs Harkness?" asked Leonora quietly.

"The envelope, the one with, 'To be given to Inspector Donovan at Scotland Yard in the event of my death' written on it. It wasn't stuck down so I thought she meant me to read it first. That's how I know what he made her do and all."

"Have you brought it with you?"

She bridled, did the girl think that she was stupid?

"Of course, that's what I came for, didn't I?"

"Of course you did," said Leonora. "I only wanted to make doubly sure that it was safe."

"What's in the envelope?" asked Inspector Donovan who thought that the humouring process had gone on long enough.

"Oh, it's dreadful, how he came and got into her bed and made her, er, be nice to him and how he said that she'd have her face slashed if she didn't.... Well, to think that all that was going on for the past five years."

"That's what she wanted to tell me?" asked Donovan, disappointed.

"Yes and all that stuff that Mr Coroneli and the others used to talk about in his room. They didn't think that she could understand them but she could. Now I understand why she made me teach her Italian when she visited me. To think that behind his honest business he was mafiosi. I blame myself, I should have known better than to let my Maria work for a Sicilian."

"You've brought the envelope for me?" asked Donovan.

"Yes, Sir, here in my bag, its all there, dates and all, of them plotting how to make people pay them money. She says that the one called Leonardo wasn't as wicked as the other two and the one called Salvatori was horrible, always wanting to hurt people." She lowered her voice and said, "He boasted of them killing people."

"Could we see the envelope please?" said Leonora, extending her hand.

Mrs Harkness clutched her bag even more tightly to her chest and said,

"Maria wrote that I was to give it to Inspector Donovan."

"That's right, then" said Donovan, briskly, "Give it here."

He leant forward and grasped the bag and lifted it out of her arms. The bag gaped open and he took out a foolscap sized envelop more than a quarter of an inch thick. It occurred to him that as it got thicker, Maria must have found it more and more difficult to conceal in her underwear drawer.

Printed across the front with a felt tipped pen Maria had written the words her mother had recited. Seeing them in the flesh as it were, Leonora felt a sudden chill, what her grandmother would have said was 'somebody walking over her grave'. What dreadful premonition had made Maria prepare the notes and why bequeath them to Inspector Donovan? The answer to the last part was obvious, he'd given her his card when he'd visited the Coroneli offices and he'd probably smiled at her. He was probably the only policeman she'd ever spoken to and him from Scotland Yard, you can't do better than that.

Donovan assured Mrs Harkness that she had done the right thing in taking her daughter's last wishes seriously and that the contents of the envelope might well help the police to bring these wicked men to justice. Constable Houston would give her a cup of tea and a receipt for the envelope and it's contents and she must tell no one that the envelope existed.

Eventually Leonora escorted her to the entrance hall and saw her on her way. By which time Donovan and Tyler were halfway through the pile of separate sheets The early notes were in general terms, clearly she had reconstructed the events with the aid of her desk diary and didn't understand the Italian The last few months were in considerable detail, who was speaking with Coroneli and what they discussed with the date and time of everything that Maria had overheard or thought worthy of noting.

Leonora came back and proceeded to read the sheets that the inspector and sergeant had finished with. She rightly discerned that to her would fall the task of indexing and collating them. When he had read through all the sheets, Donovan pushed back the shock of hair that had fallen forward on his forehead and said,

"Phew, it's all there, now we've got them. I'll just pop up and tell the chief. I'll have to give him a copy and doubtless the Chief Super will want one, so make half a dozen."

When he took two copies to his boss, the Chief Inspector took him to the Chief Super. They had hardly got in the door when the latter asked,

"Got that hair sample yet?"

"No Chief and we won't need to now," said the Chief Inspector, putting a copy of Maria's testament on the desk before him, saying, "this is a copy of the document that was found in a drawer at Coroneli's secretary's mother's house. The secretary kept a complete record of Coroneli's activities in an envelope marked to be given to Scotland Yard in the event of her death. Her mother found it and brought it in for Donovan. It gives us sufficient to bring him in for questioning for thirty six hours. "

"On what pretext?"

"Take your pick. Conspiracy, extortion, living off immoral earnings, attempted blackmail and a host of other things, including murder and manslaughter."

"We'll probably have difficulty making anything stick."

"But if we bring him in for a night it gives us the chance to get his DNA and to search his house and car," said Donovan. "We might not be able to pin his son-in-law's murder on him but I'm sure that he killed Maria and we may be able to nail him for that."

"A DNA match would only show us that he was with her that evening, not that he killed her," said the Chief Super, "and you can bet that he'll have smart lawyers by the dozen pointing that out."

"Well Chief, we have to try."

"You don't propose to tell him where our evidence comes from, do you?" asked the Chief Superintendent.

"Not at this stage, time enough for that when we formally charge him and the lawyers start the disclosure procedure."

The Chief Inspector had been quickly turning over the pages of his copy, he said,

"According to this the other two are in it as deeply as he is. Do you intend to bring all three in at the same time, Don?"

"That's what I had in mind Chief, to let each of them know that we have been questioning the other two, and in this way to put the gist of the secretary's allegations to the three of them over the same twenty four hours."

"OK," said the Chief Superintendent, "go ahead but be absolutely sure to play it according to the book, I don't want these blighters getting off on a technicality."

Three sets of uniformed officers brought Luigi Coroneli, Leonardo Bianci and Salvatori Donati to the police station the next morning. Each demanded the attendance of his solicitor, none more loudly than the capo himself. They were put in well-separated interview rooms to await the arrival of their lawyers. Donovan would lead in the interrogation, Sergeant Tyler and DC Houston would accompany the scientists from forensic in their search of the three houses and offices.

At each house the searchers obtained objects from which it might be possible to obtain DNA samples. These and documents and weapons were parcelled for further examination.

They hadn't long been at the Coroneli residence before Sophia arrived, having been told by Silvestro Bessani that her father was in custody. She was cautioned not to touch anything and followed Leonora around, looking sullen and making occasional complaints. Why she said it, she didn't know but Leonora said,

"Come on Sophia, I know that it's rotten but we're just doing our job."

"Fine job that is," muttered the girl, "you ought to get a proper job."

"Like what?" said Leonora. "What did you do before you were married?"

"I was a beauty consultant."

"I thought that you must be something like that, you've got a lovely complexion. I like your hair."

"I do it myself," said Sophia.

"Do you cut it?"

"Yes and I do Daddy's too, it pays to keep your hand in."

Leonora gave a little sigh, so that was why she could find no reference to a hairdresser in Maria's diaries."

The other find was to prove much more important. The scientist examining Luigi's car took Sergeant Tyler into the garage where the car boot was open. He pointed to a three pin electrical plug with a length of flex attached. Nothing was connected to the bare ends of the flex. The scientist said,

"I use a lead like that for testing equipment, there's not another electrical device in this house that's not a straight commercial product and I wonder why he kept this?"

"If you're thinking what I'm thinking," said the sergeant, "take good care of it."

The man put it in a plastic envelope.

The following morning the head of the forensic unit phoned Donovan in great excitement,

"Don, we've got it. Coroneli's DNA matches that found in the dead girl."

"Good," said the inspector.

"But that's not all. Did your people tell you about the three-pin plug with the wire attached?"

"Yes, what have you got?"

"There are minute traces of scorched human skin on the two bare wires and the skin matches the murdered girl."

"So he knocked her out and then stuck the wire on her hand?"

"That's what it looks like."

"Remind me to buy you a drink the next time we meet," said Donovan.

"That's what they all say," said the scientist, sadly.

The inquest in Bournemouth to enquire into the deaths of Raymond Farrell and Laura Wells might have passed without much national press interest had not the Chancellor and his wife been called to give evidence of recovering the body of Laura Wells. They spent the night at the Tolbrite Arms, where they had been staying in the summer when they found the body. Peggy had insisted that William should set an example by not pleading pressure of ministerial duties and had made his staff keep his red boxes until the following day. They had had a precious evening together with only his protection officer sitting discreetly in the corner of the bar to remind them of the real world. They gave their evidence, bowed to the coroner and left. William's official Jaguar, his PPS with two red boxes and his officer with Peggy's car, were waiting outside the court. He gave Peggy a quick kiss and a hug which were duly photographed by a waiting press photographer, told her that he loved her and got into the official car. His PPS had the first red despatch box open before they drove off. Peggy was left to drive back alone, a by no means seldom occurrence for a minister's wife.

The coroner returned a verdict of unlawful killing, adding that he understood that the person who had committed these dreadful crimes had himself since been killed.

The mafia trials occupied the Central Criminal Court in the Strand and filled the media for several months early in the following year. Seldom had they reported such a parade of vice and wrongdoing attributable to a few men.

The first trial was that of Carlo Johnson for the murder of Bruce Somers and the malicious wounding of Charles Parham, with Luigi Coroneli, Salvatori Donati and Leonardo Bianci also indicted as accessories for planning the crimes and for the attempted blackmail of Southampton and Wolverhampton Wanderers Football Clubs. Carlo was found guilty of manslaughter and the other three were found guilty of attempted blackmail. Sam Hawkins and Len Girling gave evidence but the star, as far as the tabloid press was concerned, was Samantha, the heroine who had fought to save her boyfriend's life in the icy river. In any case, sex sells papers and her picture was judged to have a wider appeal than those of the two managers, they only made the sports pages at the back but she was on the front page.

Next, the four soldiers responsible for the Mayfair fires and for demanding money with threats at the Four Oaks Club, were put on trial together with Alfredo Corleone who was indicted as the instigator in each case. In mitigation, his defence counsel attempted to use the South London fires and murders as reason for his client to take pre-emptive action against such a vicious man as Coroneli. Even the judge was seen to smile at the stupidity of this argument. It cut no ice and they were all sent down for over ten years.

Much of the same evidence was used in the next trial, of Coroneli, Bianci and Donati and their soldiers for arson and homicide plus additional evidence concerning their network of vice. After a bitterly contested trial, all three were sentenced to twenty years imprisonment.

The final trial was that of Luigi Coroneli alone. He stood in the box, no longer the scornful, arrogant capo of the North London mob, but a broken man, already destined to spend the rest of his life in jail. The crown paraded all the evidence that it had about the killing of Michael Bernoulli and the circumstantial evidence that Luigi Coroneli was responsible for his death. They made some play of the part that the lawyer Silvestro Bessani's played in the affair. They then alleged that he had killed his secretary, Maria Harkness, deploying all the forensic evidence and culminating in the mind-chilling discovery in his car of the bare electrical leads with traces of Maria's scorched skin on them. Her 'secret report' was the source of great interest. In his summing-up, the judge described Luigi Coroneli as one of the most evil, corrupt, cold blooded murderers ever to appear in the Central Criminal Court and sentenced him to life imprisonment.

A good number of the newspapers made much of Maria's testament and used headlines like 'an accusing hand from the grave'. The Times simply headed the next day's article, 'Nemesis'.

The Law Society issued a statement that Silvestro Bessani would be the subject of an investigation.

Maria's mother received a nice little nest-egg for allowing one of the more popular Sunday newspapers to serialise a ghost written version of Maria's secret report. That the articles seemed to dwell on things that Mrs Harkness wouldn't have wished to be known about her daughter's five years of sexual submission to a murderer was unfortunate. But they paid well.

Printed in the United Kingdom
by Lightning Source UK Ltd.
119240UK00001B/127-129

9 781846 853296